Paradox

In memory of Enrico Fermi (1901 − 1954)

The Fermi Paradox: the apparent contradiction between the high probability of extraterrestrial civilizations' existence and the lack of contact with such civilizations.

or

Where is everybody?

Paradox

Stories Inspired by the Fermi Paradox

Edited by Ian Whates

NewCon Press
England

First edition, published in the UK August 2014
by NewCon Press

NCP 075 (hardback)
NCP 076 (softback)

10 9 8 7 6 5 4 3 2 1

Cover art copyright © 2014 by Sarah Anne Langton
Cover layout by Storm Constantine
Text layout by Storm Constantine

Contents

Fermi Paradox:
An Introduction

Marek Kukula and Rob Edwards

Where is everybody? This was the question famously posed by physicist Enrico Fermi in 1950 over lunch with colleagues at Los Alamos National Laboratory. It's a simple question, but its implications are profound and more than half a century later we still don't have a satisfactory answer.

The 'everybody' in Fermi's question of course refers to intelligent extraterrestrial life – aliens with a technological civilisation, who leave evidence of their existence and with whom we might even hope to have some kind of conversation. Inspired by sensational media reports of UFO sightings, Fermi and his colleagues had been discussing the likelihood of discovering real signs of intelligence elsewhere in the cosmos. By 1950 the scale of the problem was well understood: the Universe is vast, it contains at the very least millions of galaxies, each of which consists of billions upon billions of stars. If just a small fraction of those stars have Earth-like planets circling around them then the sheer weight of numbers implies that there should be many places in the cosmos where life could begin. Given that this state of affairs has existed for billions of years, surely intelligent life must already have arisen many times over?

Being a scientist, Fermi attempted to add a degree of numerical rigour to the discussion with some back-of-the-envelope calculations. By combining educated guesses about the frequency of Earth-like planets and the possibility of life arising, he came to the conclusion that alien civilisations should be numerous – and yet we see no credible signs of their existence. This is the heart of what has become known as the Fermi Paradox; a conflict between an overwhelming probability and a total lack of evidence.

Fermi's ideas have since been expanded and refined by a host of scientists and philosophers. Perhaps the most famous of these is the radio astronomer Frank Drake, who in 1961 codified the method of estimating how many civilisations might exist in our galaxy into an equation, combining numbers and probabilities whose values – in principle at least – we might hope to pin down with some degree of plausibility.

The first four terms in the Drake Equation are the rate at which new stars are formed in our galaxy, the fraction of stars that have planets, the number of these which are potential habitats for life and the fraction of planets on which life actually develops. Astrophysicists already have a good grasp of our galaxy's star formation rate and in the two decades since extrasolar planets were first detected it has become clear that the vast majority of stars have planetary systems orbiting around them. The vibrant new field of astrobiology is actively engaged in characterising what a habitable world might look like and it's exciting to think that in the next few decades we may even know how common planets with biospheres really are.

Astronomers have therefore made good progress in constraining the first half of the equation, but from here on things get much more difficult to quantify. The remaining terms consist of the fraction of life-bearing planets on which intelligence evolves, the fraction of these where a detectable technological civilisation emerges, and the length of time over which a typical civilisation remains visible before being destroyed or otherwise removing itself from view. These factors are the province of biologists, anthropologists, historians and sociologists and to date their values remain wide open to interpretation.

Even without the equation we know that right now there is definitely one civilisation in the Milky Way capable of signalling its presence across interstellar space. But, depending on the degree of optimism of the person performing the calculation, the Drake Equation gives wildly differing answers to the question of how many other civilisations there might be, ranging from 'a few' to 'millions'. And, whatever the final number, the fact remains that we have yet to see any sign of them. Drake himself has commented that his equation is really just a way of defining our ignorance: more of a prompt for discussion than a practical way of resolving Fermi's question.

The 'argument from probability' which lies at the root of the paradox is really just a mathematical way of framing the instinctive feeling that we all have when we look up at a night sky crowded with stars. There are so many planets out there, we tell ourselves, that surely somewhere in the Universe there must be other beings like us. This conviction is nothing new, and in fact for centuries the default assumption of everyone from astronomers to theologians has been that the cosmos is indeed teeming with aliens, some of them perhaps technically, intellectually and morally more advanced than us.

In 1543, when the Polish astronomer Nikolaus Copernicus published his revolutionary idea that the Earth, rather than being the fixed centre of the cosmos, was in fact a planet in orbit around the Sun, he inadvertently set in motion another intellectual revolution. For if the Earth is a planet then surely the other planets must also be Earths, each with their own landscapes, climates and even people? This concept was profoundly different from earlier ideas of supernatural gods and angels inhabiting the sky – instead these would be natural beings like us, living in environments similar to ours and subject to the same physical laws that govern human lives.

Later in the sixteenth century the Dominican friar, philosopher and mathematician Giordano Bruno took the argument further: if the Sun is a star, then the stars should also be suns, each with their own planets orbiting around them. With characteristic boldness he wrote in 1584 "This space we declare to be infinite, since neither reason, convenience, possibility, sense-perception nor nature assign to it a limit. In it are an infinity of worlds of the same kind as our own". Bruno was tried by the Roman Inquisition and in 1600 was burnt at the stake for a variety of heretical opinions beside which his assertions about the habitability of the cosmos were really rather tame.

A decade later, Galileo's telescopic observations of lunar mountains and the satellites of Jupiter lent empirical weight to the idea that celestial bodies were indeed worlds like the Earth, complete with their own landscapes and moons, and by 1692 Edmond Halley was able to state without controversy that "It is now taken for granted that the Earth is one of the Planets, and they all are with reason supposed Habitable". Halley's colleague Sir Isaac Newton was more cautious in public but his unpublished notes make plain where he stood on the issue: "For if all places to which we have access are filled with living

9

creatures, why should all these immense spaces of the heavens above the clouds be incapable of inhabitants?" Newton's position was probably based as much on theology as science: would a rational God really create such a vast cosmos only to leave the majority of it entirely empty of minds able to appreciate it?

Meanwhile, in his "Cosmotheoros" of 1694, Dutch astronomer Christiaan Huygens made the shocking suggestion that the inhabitants of other worlds need not look exactly like us. Anticipating the bug-eyed monsters that would become a staple of twentieth century science fiction, Huygens gave voice to a very human disquiet about the possibility of life which is not as we know it: "For when I do but represent to my Imagination a Creature like a Man in every thing else, but that has a Neck four times as long, and great round sawcer Eyes five or six times as big I cannot look upon't without the utmost aversion, altho at the same time I can give no account of my Dislike". The politically correct crew of the USS Enterprise would not have approved.

As improvements in telescope technology revealed the worlds of the Solar System in ever-increasing detail, the advance of science did little to dent the conviction that they must be the abode of intelligent beings. In 1780, in a letter to Astronomer Royal Nevil Maskelyne, the great Sir William Herschel, discoverer of Uranus and mapper of the Milky Way, wrote "Who can say that it is not extremely probable, nay beyond doubt, that there must be inhabitants on the Moon of some kind or another?" Four years later Herschel's groundbreaking paper on the icecaps, atmosphere and polar axis of Mars concluded with the throwaway remark that "its inhabitants probably enjoy a situation in many respects similar to ours". Somewhat bizarrely, at least for modern readers, he also speculated about the likelihood of life on the Sun.

The early nineteenth century saw no let-up in the feverish speculation about extraterrestrial life. In what became known as the Great Moon Hoax of 1835, the New York Sun published a series of sensational articles allegedly describing the flora and fauna of the Moon as observed by John Herschel, the son of William and himself one of the most famous astronomers of the day. The pieces were lavishly illustrated with lithographs of exotic landscapes and creatures, including winged, bare-breasted Moon maidens, and readers flocked to the newspaper. Clearly the public were just as eager as the scientists to believe in life elsewhere in the Solar System, especially if it was scantily clad. Needless to say, John Herschel had nothing to do with the whole affair but although the newspaper never issued a retraction he responded with (mostly) good humour, quipping that his actual research could never hope to be as exciting.

The polymath William Whewell in his 1853 essay "On the Plurality of Worlds" sounded a more cautionary note. Like Newton, Whewell had a religious as well as a scientific interest in the subject of extraterrestrial intelligence, although in this case it led him to the opposite conviction. The existence of myriad inhabited planets, he argued, would make a mockery of the idea that God could take a special interest in the people of this particular one, thereby contradicting Christian scripture. But Whewell was no religious fanatic and his reasoning was based on solid contemporary science. Foreshadowing the modern concept of the Habitable Zone – the 'Goldilocks' region around a star in which temperatures are just right for water to exist in a liquid state – he wrote "The earth is really the domestic hearth of the Solar System; adjusted between the hot and fiery haze on one side and the cold and watery vapour on the other." Moreover, by this stage it had become clear that the other stars exhibited a wide range of properties – not all of them particularly sun-like – so conceivably any planets they possessed might not be hospitable to life after all.

But the expectation of a Solar System rife with intelligent beings refused to die away. Later in the nineteenth century the Italian astronomer Giovanni Schiaparelli reported seeing strange linear features on the face of Mars and when the Italian word 'canali' was translated into English as "canals" rather than the more neutral 'channels' it provoked feverish speculation that these were indeed artificial structures, the product of sophisticated Martian engineering. One very prominent champion of this idea was Percival Lowell, a wealthy American businessman who founded his own observatory in the Arizona desert and published popular books setting out his vision of a civilisation that constructed vast irrigation canals to bring water from the polar ice caps to the equatorial deserts of a dying world.

Lowell's ideas were widely circulated and proved particularly popular with writers of science fiction stories. Classic tales by H.G. Wells, Edgar Rice Burroughs and Ray Bradbury can all trace their roots back to Lowell's exotic vision of ancient Martian civilisations and these romantic views of the Red Planet still colour our imaginations today. When Wells wrote of "intellects vast and cool and unsympathetic" regarding our world "with envious eyes" he was also referencing the Nebular Hypothesis of Pierre-Simon Laplace (translated into English by Astronomer Royal John Pond), which proposed that the planets further from the Sun were increasingly older and more evolved – setting a template in science fiction for crumbling Martian ruins and Venusian swamps teeming with prehistoric reptiles.

But by the early twentieth century scientific support for an inhabited Mars was already fading. An ingenious experiment carried out in 1903 by E. Walter Maunder of the Royal Greenwich Observatory demonstrated that the linear 'canals' were most likely an optical illusion, conjured up as the human brain joined the dots between natural, irregular features on the Martian surface. Meanwhile, as more powerful observing techniques became available, a very different picture of Mars began to emerge. Even at the equator, ambient temperatures were well below freezing, and the atmosphere was little more than a wispy halo of carbon dioxide. Apart from the polar icecaps, there was little sign of water on the surface or in the atmosphere and without a magnetic field the planet's surface was exposed to cosmic rays and harsh radiation from the Sun. Lowell was billions of years too late: Mars was not a slowly dying world. As far as the possibility of complex life was concerned, the planet was already long dead.

By 1950, when Fermi and his colleagues were wondering where the aliens might be, it was quite clear that they would not be found on any of the other worlds of our Solar System. The advent of the Space Age a decade later confirmed what scientists already suspected. As a succession of robotic probes revealed the planets in intimate detail it became clear that each world was complex and highly individual, but also very different from the Earth: Mercury was an airless cinder, Venus a searing, toxic hell, and the four giant outer planets were churning maelstroms of gas and cloud, lacking solid surfaces.

Although today there is renewed hope of finding simple microbial life in sheltered corners of the Solar System – in aquifers beneath the Martian sands, under the icy crust of moons such as Europa or Enceladus, or even in the methane lakes of Titan - the search for Earth-like conditions where intelligence might have a chance to evolve has long since shifted its focus to the stars.

Out beyond the Solar System the prospects are undoubtedly exciting. We are living in a golden age of planetary discovery, one that is redefining the way we think about planets and the possibility of life in the Universe. For most of human history the number of stars that were known to have planets orbiting around them remained stubbornly at one – the Sun – but in the last decade of the twentieth century that changed forever with the discovery of the first extrasolar planets, around the Sun-like star 51-Pegasi and the pulsar PSR 1257+12. Now the tally of confirmed planets is in the hundreds, with thousands more candidates currently under investigation and new discoveries being made almost every week. By extrapolating these results beyond the tiny fraction of the sky so far surveyed we can be confident that planets easily outnumber the billions of stars in our galaxy.

The hunt is now on for planets that closely resemble the Earth, and current indications are that worlds of the right size and at the right distance from their star may indeed be numerous. Less expected has been the discovery that many of the planets found so far look nothing like the familiar worlds of our own Solar System. Instead, a bizarre menagerie of Hot Jupiters, super-Earths, carbon planets, water worlds, gas dwarfs and even Tatooine-like worlds orbiting binary stars has replaced the neat division between small, rocky planets and frigid gas giants into which we had previously divided our planetary catalogue. If there's a lesson to be learned it is surely that the Universe is still full of surprises.

Despite the abundance of these brave new worlds we are still in thrall to Fermi's question. If the Universe is indeed full of planets, why do we see no signs of intelligent life?

Our galaxy is vast – more than 100,000 light years across – but the Universe is 13.8 billion years old. Even travelling at speeds well below that of light, it would not take more than a few million years to send self-replicating probes to visit every star in the Milky Way – and yet we see no credible signs of them visiting our Solar System. If the aliens were disinclined to embark on such a venture, they could stay at home and still notify the entire galaxy of their existence in just a few tens of thousands of years using radio signals – and yet, after decades of scanning the skies, SETI, the Search for Extraterrestrial Intelligence, has so far drawn a blank. Even if they have no desire to communicate at all we might still expect the aliens' technology to leave its mark in other ways, modifying their planetary atmosphere with carbon dioxide emissions or changing the spectrum and brightness or their parent star through energy harvesting schemes – and yet as far as we can tell, the rest of the Universe appears resolutely natural.

Over the years many suggestions have been put forward to try to resolve Fermi's conundrum. Broadly they fall into three categories: we really are alone – or the civilisations that do exist are so widely separated in space or time that we may as well be; the aliens are there but we're not looking hard enough; they are there but we can't see them because they are hidden from us or because the Universe is somehow stranger than we think.

Perhaps life is rare, either because the precise conditions necessary for it to occur are uncommon or because the chances of it arising are so vanishingly improbable that the Universe just hasn't been around for long enough. Some scientists argue that the Earth may be a rather exceptional planet after all, with its large, stabilising moon and uncommonly well-behaved sun. We may even lie in a peculiarly habitable part of the galaxy, central enough to benefit from the chemical enrichment of previous generations of stars but safely distant from the harsh radiation of the galactic core. In this case we might not be the only life forms in the Universe, but we could be among the first.

Even if life is common, perhaps intelligence evolves only rarely and, when technological civilisations do arise, they only last for a few centuries – the blink of a cosmic eye – before disappearing. Our own planet has been around for about 4.5 billion years and the fossil record appears to show that simple microbial life established itself almost as soon as the Earth's initial hellish conditions had settled into something more hospitable. Extrapolating from this single example it seems that life might get started quite easily – wherever the right environments exist. But it took another 3 billion years before complex plants and animals evolved, and intelligence like our own, capable of complex language and symbolic thought, has arguably only been around for a few hundred thousand years. Being smart has served homo sapiens well, enabling us to colonise the Earth and even sprinkle our technology lightly across the Solar System, but beetles, crocodiles, and horseshoe crabs have enjoyed much longer success, and all without feeling the need to build nuclear weapons or pump the atmosphere full of greenhouse gas. Intelligence may be useful to have but it comes with a self-destructive downside and it certainly isn't the only way to dominate a planetary biosphere.

Perhaps aliens are everywhere but we're not looking hard enough or in the right way? Since the 1950s we have had the ability to probe the skies for radio transmissions and, more recently, to look for other forms of artificially generated electromagnetic radiation such as directed laser pulses. But it is impossible for us to continuously monitor every likely star in every possible waveband – and these are only the signalling methods that we humans have thought of. Of course, since the early twentieth century we have been pouring our own signals into space in the form of radio and television transmissions and these now fill a spherical region about 100 light years in radius, encompassing hundreds of planetary systems. But the emissions become rapidly fainter with distance and even our most powerful radio telescopes would struggle to detect them from just a few light years away. In any case, as our broadcast technology shifts from analogue to more efficient digital systems, the strength of the signals we emit will dwindle and the Earth will fall silent once more. Our enduring contribution to the shared cultural heritage of the Milky Way could amount to little more than a brief pulse of twentieth century TV and radio.

Perhaps, biased by our own narrow perspective, we are looking in all the wrong places? A truly advanced species might shift its base of operations away from Earth-like worlds and Sun-like stars to regions where energy is in more abundant supply. The brutal environment beside an ultra-luminous star or the event horizon of a black hole could be an attractive proposition for such a civilisation. And, as we ourselves inch closer to creating artificial intelligence here on Earth, it raises the prospect that biological entities might be just a short phase in the lifetime of most civilisations, before they are superseded or uploaded into their own mechanical creations. Who knows where such machine minds might decide to live or how they might choose to communicate?

Perhaps they just don't want to talk to us? There may be good reasons why aliens wish to actively conceal their presence: if just one civilisation in the galaxy possesses genocidal tendencies alongside the technology to put them into practice it could make sense for everyone else to keep their heads down. Most terrifying of all, although we are naturally convinced of our own intrinsic fascination, advanced alien minds might simply find us too primitive, too violent or too boring to bother with. At the end of the day, aliens could just be incomprehensibly alien.

After centuries of speculation, debate and methodical searching we still don't know if we're alone in the cosmos. A message from the stars could arrive tomorrow, answering Fermi's question once and for all, but even if conclusive evidence continues to elude us it seems unlikely that we will ever completely give up the search.

For now, we have an unsolved scientific mystery with profound implications for the human race – what better starting point for a science fiction anthology? Science might have to wait a little longer for a definitive resolution to the Fermi Paradox but who knows, one of the stories in this volume may already have the answer.

Marek Kukula & Rob Edwards
Royal Observatory Greenwich,
June 2014

Catching Rays

David L Clements

Sarah shuffled in her seat, conscious that the Director was hovering nearby, waiting for the interview to finish.

"When do you expect to announce your results?" asked Horst. Sarah thought he looked relieved, sitting across the table from her in the canteen, nursing a bulb of fresh coffee. He was due to head back to Earth on the next lunar shuttle.

"It will take some time," she replied. "The collector's finished, but we need to install the traps before running a final test. Then we have to ramp up the power before we can collect the highest energy cosmic rays."

"A few months?"

Sarah smiled. "Longer than *that*. Even when we have things fully running it'll take a while to collect and analyse the data. A year at least, maybe longer."

"Thank you for your time," said Horst, closing his tablet. "That was great, and a fine way to end my visit. And if you find anything interesting, please contact me." He stood, rising too quickly and briefly leaving the floor. "Damn," he muttered as he flailed in mid-air. "How do you cope with this?"

Sarah laughed. "Practice, which visitors like you never have time for." She steadied him as he drifted back to the floor. "Have a good trip home, and we'll see you back on Moonbase Three in, what, eighteen months?"

Horst sighed, and nodded. "I guess so."

"I'm sure you'll do better next time."

The Director chose that moment to force his way into the conversation. "All done here I see," he said, smiling at both of them. "I hope you had a good chat with our latest brilliant researcher?"

"Oh yes," said Horst, while Sarah squirmed. "Very informative."

"Excellent. Let me walk you to the shuttle, there are a couple of things I'd like to discuss." Horst picked up his bag, and the two men left the canteen.

"Enjoy it while it lasts," said Petra. She was sitting at one of the other tables, behind a partition, listening to the whole interview.

"What do you mean?" asked Sarah.

"Being Moonbase Three's latest poster child."

Sarah didn't know what to say. Petra had been on the base for a while, doing development work on nanotechnology. "Happens to us all at the start. But it will soon change if you don't deliver successes, or they take too long to come. When your funding is cut nobody will want to know you."

Sarah's project had got most of the funding in the current round, beating the nanotechnologist's bid and several others. Petra stood with the gentle, smooth movements of an experienced lunar resident. "You'd better get your results before you're out of the spotlight, otherwise you'll end up on your own, far from home, making do with leftover equipment that isn't even appropriate."

"What about your postdoc?" Sarah asked, sure she had seen him only a few days ago.

"Gone. On the same shuttle as Horst. And our great Director has made it clear I will be joining him if I don't make a breakthrough soon."

Petra turned her back and walked out of the canteen.

Sarah exhaled slowly and left in the opposite direction, heading along one of the narrow white corridors to the small office she shared with Max, her postdoc.

"How are the final checks?" she asked as she slid open the door.

"Looking good. We can install the traps and start low field, end-to-end tests as soon as the Sun sets."

Their tiny office's only saving grace was the broad picture window dominating one wall. Outside, across the dark grey landscape, the infinitely slow lunar sunset was under way. The Sun hung on the horizon, slipping with glacial slowness behind black basalt mountains casting long, unnaturally sharp shadows across the regolith.

"Another eight hours. Then a few more for passive cooling to kick in," said Sarah. She checked her watch for the time back home in the Eurozone. "I'm off to bed. See you in the morning."

Black, airless lunar night surrounded them. Each suited figure had headlamps, one on each side of their helmet. Navigation lights and indicators blinked on shoulders, helmets and backpacks. Scattered construction floodlights brought further light and the semblance of warmth wherever they stood, but they only served to remind Sarah, Max and the rest of the crew they were working in one of the most hostile environments known to man. A coronal mass ejection, or other harsh space weather event, could catch them in a hail of lethal radiation, while the smallest micrometeorite could pierce a suit and deliver a high velocity bullet's worth of damage.

There were warning systems, but they were never perfect. Physically roaming the lunar surface was a calculated risk, but the final stages of construction and calibration could not be done with drones or remotes.

After four hours on the surface Sarah hoped everything was finally done. At least the cold trap in front of her was fully operational. "How are we doing?" she called on the group radio net.

"A few minutes more for me, but basically done," replied Max.

The rest of the crew needed more time.

Sarah joined Max and gazed at the sky until he had finished. She brought her gloves to her helmet, shading her eyes from light scattered from her headlamps, trying to see the pin-sharp stars that filled the sky.

"It's so empty," Sarah said over their private radio link to Max. "We're so alone." She shivered, despite her suit heating system. This was a recurring train of thought for Sarah while on the surface, looking away from the blue jewel of Earth at the vast black emptiness of the rest of the sky. "A sky full of stars, but empty of minds – as far as we can tell."

"That's not our job, boss," replied Max. "Leave that to the guys with the big radio ears and optical eyes down on Earth."

"Maybe," said Sarah. "But it doesn't seem right. We're spreading out into space, but there's no sign anybody else has done that. Ever. In the whole history of the universe."

"We'll find them," said Max. "They have to be out there, we're just not looking the right way."

Sarah was ready to argue the point, to deliver the kind of authoritative philosophical argument expected of a senior academic.

The head contractor's voice interrupted on the communal band. "We're all done, I think."

Sarah switched channels, a little relieved she wasn't going to dent Max's naive enthusiasm today. "Great!" She said. "Time to head back to the barn."

Bright lights, white nanofibre walls, a crowded room filled by a hot and humid yet breathable atmosphere. They stood inside the small habitat dedicated to running Sarah's cosmic ray experiment. It was a huge contrast to the surface. Sarah always felt a twinge of claustrophobia when she came back inside, but this time she ignored that in the excitement of, at last, having an experiment to run.

As soon as she was out of her suit, she headed to the control console. While she began the startup procedure, the rest of the crew gathered around.

"All traps running nicely," she announced. "Great work people." There were nods of appreciation and handshakes.

She typed more commands, checked more indicators. "E-mag scoops initialising."

High above the surface of the Moon, the other part of the system started up, a series of superconducting cables forming a network of fields filtering charged particles to the surface and Sarah's cold traps. "Looking good," reported Sarah. "A few minutes and we should have the first low energy captures!" There was scattered applause across the room, and one of the engineering contractors moved towards the fridge.

Sarah spotted the movement. "Hey," she shouted. "No champagne until we know it's working." Max and Sarah's closest colleagues laughed nervously, but the contractors looked disappointed.

Tension filled the room. Scattered attempts at conversation died away as they waited for the first crucial results.

At her console, Sarah watched the displays, monitoring instrument health and performance, awaiting the first chime that would announce the successful collection of low energy cosmic rays.

She made some calculations in her head, factoring in event rates, efficiencies, collecting volumes, once again checking calculations she had done years ago and knew by heart. "Yes," she nodded to herself, "if we don't have anything in a few minutes then we have a..."

A loud ping broke her train of thought. She smiled, and rose from her chair.

"Friends, colleagues, the cosmic rays have landed!"

Then came cheers, applause, and popping corks, as they celebrated success after years of effort.

Speeches followed, and an even greater throng of Moonbase Three personnel came down the long tunnel to Sarah's control centre. The Director welcomed a project that was certain to be a new, great success for Moonbase Three, and congratulated Sarah on getting it started on time and slightly under budget. She even caught a glimpse of Petra at one point, standing quietly by one of the consoles and looking out onto the lunar surface, a glass of wine untouched in her hand. She wondered what the other woman was looking at, and suppressed the urge to smile when she saw it was one of the cold traps. They were Sarah's invention, a unique technology that made the array possible. *I guess Petra has a right to be envious*, she thought.

Hours later, when the celebrations had ended, Sarah was the last person left in the control room as usual; clearing up glasses, collecting half-finished plates of food for recycling. Quickly deciding to leave the last of the debris to the operations crew to clear up, she went to the main console for a first look at her results.

She frowned. "No. That can't be right."

"I agree," said Max. "This doesn't make any sense at all."

The collector had been running for several days. They were in Sarah's office, hunched over a work station screen, looking at telemetry from the cold traps. The results she'd seen that first evening had not gone away, despite her hope they were a technical artefact.

"You agree the mass is too high, and the charge too low?" she asked. She should know more than Max about the experiment, and everything else, but wanted him to find a hole in her thinking.

He frowned. "High mass could mean a multiple hit, but that wouldn't explain the charge."

Sarah nodded. "More like a few thousand hits for that mass. So, something has gone seriously wrong." She sat back and shook her head. "We'll have to purge the collectors, do a total restart and hope this goes away."

"That would take weeks!"

"Quite. But this makes no sense. The Director isn't going to like it – his great new project taking a giant leap backwards."

Max turned from the screen and sat on the corner of Sarah's tiny desk. "Maybe it's just that single trap. The others are working fine. We could bring it back inside, strip it down, run tests..."

"We'd have to empty the liquid helium and warm it up before we could bring the trap inside. You know the rules. And we'd still have to do a full purge and restart afterwards."

Max turned back to the workstation, calling up the schematics and test history of the offending device, looking through screen after screen of results. Sarah sat, gazing out of the office window, staring at the bleak, lifeless lunar surface, pondering what to do next. The last person she'd seen doing this had been Petra at the startup party. Maybe Petra's interest in the detectors had been something more than envy at Sarah's success.

"I can't see anything wrong," said Max. "The test results on this trap are as good as the others, if not better. And instrument health monitoring says everything's just fine."

"Something must have broken!"

"What if the results are right?" asked Max.

Sarah rubbed her close-cropped hair. For a few moments she took Max's suggestion seriously, but then shook her head. "That's impossible. It would mean we have a tiny chunk of neutron star in the trap, a few hundred thousand nucleons in size. Something that small with so many neutrons wouldn't be stable."

"How would we tell?" asked Max.

Sarah thought for a few moments. "We couldn't with the trap's on board instruments, but there's stuff here, inside Moonbase, that could do the tests."

"Pity we can't bring any active traps inside thanks to safety regs."

Sarah looked at Max, still perched on the edge of her desk. "That's it for tonight," she said.

"What?" Max consulted his watch. "It's an hour until the canteen opens."

"You need to get some rest. Sit somewhere visible."

Max's mouth opened in surprise. "What?"

The only sound was her breathing, and occasional gurgles from the suit's cooling system. Sarah was breaking every rule in the book by going onto the lunar surface on her own. There would be a severe reprimand if she were caught, but she'd taken the necessary precautions. Her suit radio was off, its transponders silenced, and she had glitched the airlock and suit locker logs with a piece of software that was trivially easy to acquire.

If her suspicions weren't confirmed, what she was planning to do was worse than a solo trip on the surface; she would be breaking many more rules before the end of the night.

Slowly and carefully Sarah made her way from the control room's airlock, across the soft regolith, towards the scattered array of cold traps. To allay her suspicions, she had to examine every single cold trap in the array. Moonbase Three was well into lunar night, but the Earth hung in the sky, far brighter than a full moon, providing most of the light she needed.

She was halfway through her tour of the array when she spotted an odd shadow by one of the traps, a hint of light and movement where there should be none. Sarah hoped it was a gas leak, a blown compressor or some other technical failure. She didn't want to have to think that someone was actively working against her.

But, as she got closer, her suspicions were confirmed. A figure, wearing a suit identical to her own, was bending over the trap. She couldn't see exactly what they were doing, but she was sure it was an act of sabotage. And she had a pretty good idea who it was.

She turned her helmet lights off and worked her way closer, hidden in the shadows of the lunar night and the silence of vacuum. Then, just a few paces away, she activated the suit's recorder, opened a hailing channel, and set her lights to full power.

"Just what do you think you're doing?"

The stranger jerked in surprise, rising half a metre in the low lunar gravity, and losing their balance as they drifted back to the ground. Sarah would have laughed if she hadn't been so angry.

The figure flailed uncontrollably and landed on their back, revealing the ID tag on the front of the suit.

Petra.

"Jesus," said Sarah. "I know you're desperate, but sabotaging my experiment to get your funding back? That's low."

"What?" Petra was panting with the effort of standing up. The suits were awkward in the low gravity. "Aren't you going to help me?"

"Why, when you're the bitch screwing up my work?"

"Screw... You think I am sabotaging?" Petra's panicked flailing subsided. She rolled to one side, getting her left arm and leg beneath her.

"Why else would you be out here, on your own, in the middle of my array?"

Petra pushed herself partially upright, gloves sinking slightly into the regolith. Her suit was now covered by smears of the dark lunar soil. "It is your cold traps."

"I know what they are."

"They are brilliant. I wanted to copy the design."

"What?" Sarah wanted to believe it wasn't sabotage, that there was still some honour among her colleagues, but she had to be sure. "Stand away from the trap."

Petra moved back a pace.

"Further," said Sarah, "and stay where I can see you."

Petra complied.

Sarah bent down, keeping Petra visible in the corner of her eye, and inspected the trap.

Its surface was intact. The hard yellow casing unblemished, inspection hatches still sealed. On the ground lay a standard scanning device that Petra had dropped. Sarah picked it up and checked the readouts. It showed Petra had been scanning the trap to examine its internal structure. A non-invasive probe, nothing that would cause any damage.

Sarah tossed the scanner to Petra.

"I might believe you, if you explain *why*."

Petra caught the scanner. "Applications. Your traps have a larger, more stable cold space than anything used in nanotech. They could solve many of my problems, but I need the design."

"You could have asked."

"What? Here, where everything is commercial? You signed over the design the moment they accepted your proposal. There is no way I can afford what the lunar authorities would charge."

Sarah shook her head, though Petra couldn't see inside her helmet. "I have spares. You could have used one."

"But we are in competition. If I get a breakthrough they will cut your funding. Why help me?"

Sarah sighed. "Gods, you must have been here too long. Has it ever occurred to you that working together, sharing results and technology, is the right thing to do, no matter what the Director and management say?"

"But that's forbidden. I couldn't pay..."

"Do I look as if I care about the Director's rules?"

"Oh scheisse," said Petra. "I've been an idiot. And now you won't lend me anything. I'll probably have to pack my bags." She looked around. "Who else did our dear Director send with you?"

Sarah shook her head.

"You're on your own?"

"Yes. You heard what I said about rules. And it's worse than that. I want to bring one of these traps inside."

It took them an hour of hard work to prepare the offending trap for its illicit trip back inside Moonbase. Sarah was also careful to replace it with one of the spare traps so that a cursory inspection would find the array unchanged. Once that was done, and she was sure everything was running properly, they took a few moments rest.

"It's good to be outside," said Petra, looking at the sky. She brought her gloves to her helmet, shading her eyes from her helmet lamps so she could see the stars. "A glorious sky but nobody to share it with."

Sarah shivered, hearing Petra echo her own thoughts the last time she was on the surface.

"Are we unique?" Petra persisted. "And what would that mean?"

"We might just be lucky – a series of double sixes in the casino of life."

"Doesn't seem likely."

"If we weren't lucky, we wouldn't be here to have this conversation."

"You're an anthropic?" Petra was referring to the old idea that, for some reason, the universe needed at least one form of intelligent life in it.

"Nah," said Sarah. "It's a philosophy, not a science, and not a very helpful one. There are plenty of other possibilities. Perhaps there's a cosmic weed-whacker that gets rid of potential competition. Or maybe intelligent life doesn't last – we could still wipe ourselves out after all. Or maybe everyone uploads to supercomputers and disappears from the real world."

"Singularitarianism? I can't say that looks likely given my own work."

"So you've not invented computronium yet?"

Petra chuckled. "No, not yet."

"Okay," said Sarah. "Time to get this trap back inside."

The yellow box sat in the centre of the lab, challenging them to solve its mystery.

Sarah stared at the trap and tapped her finger on the desk. "Your neutral and electron beams are our best bet."

"About time I found a use for that stuff; they're just hand-me-downs from cancelled projects."

They started working together, connecting beamlines to various ports, attaching cables and fibres to provide control signals and readouts.

"You are sure this is not some kind of instrumental glitch?" asked Petra.

"I've spent ages ruling that out. Whatever's inside is way heavier than a uranium nucleus, moderately charged and..." She shrugged. She suspected more, but it would sound crazy. "That's most of what I know, apart from the fact that it's real, and entered the cold trap from the scoops."

"You're sure it's just one particle?"

"That's what Max asked, but the charge-to-mass ratio is all wrong."

Petra looked around. "Where is Max?"

"Given all the rules we're breaking, I wanted to keep him well away. The less he knows about this the less harm it'll do him if the Director finds out."

Petra nodded, and continued to align the first set of electron beams as the feed lines were pumped down to vacuum. "This should give us a better idea of the structure of whatever is in there." She nodded at the experimental rig they'd hacked together in just half an hour. There, that should do it." The machine fired a beam of high energy electrons into the cold trap, to bounce off whatever lurked inside.

"Wow," said Petra as she looked at the results. "Even the most complex nucleus is not *that* complex." She leaned forward to make some adjustments. "This is not a simple shell structure or liquid drop."

"Somehow, I'm not surprised," said Sarah.

"Something you're not telling me?"

"No! At least nothing concrete."

Petra stared at Sarah for a moment, then ran another scan. "Odd," she said, looking at the results. The old and new scans were radically different. "Could it be spinning? Something spinning and asymmetric could explain this."

Sarah shook her head. "No. The temperature inside is too low to excite any spinning modes."

"The electron beam?"

"Not enough momentum for that to do anything."

Petra nodded. "So either we have excited a substructure, or whatever this is too big to be an atomic nucleus! This – thing – maybe it's changing structure on its own!"

Sarah sighed with relief. "At least it's not just me."

Petra tilted her head querulously.

"Some of the internal tests in the trap produced something similar, but the results weren't good enough to be sure."

Petra nodded. "I'll do a time series at higher energy. Maybe that will give us enough resolution to see what's going on."

She set up the experiment and they moved to the kitchenette on the far side of the lab to await the results. "Tell me what you suspect," said Petra as she passed Sarah a bulb of coffee.

Sarah took a long, slow swig, giving herself time to think. She didn't want to sound like a lunatic, but she owed Petra an explanation given their collusion. She put down the bulb and, refusing to meet Petra's eyes, said, "This is going to sound mad."

"What you've got in that trap *is* mad!"

Sarah nodded. "I know." She looked up. "You were talking about extraterrestrial intelligence before we brought it inside."

"What's that got to do with anything?"

Sarah played with her coffee bulb. "I think it's a message."

"What?"

It was out. Now she had to give Petra the whole story. "If

intelligence is out there, it'll want to communicate. But we've found nothing in the radio, optical, any wavelength we've looked at. And nothing in gravity waves or neutrinos. But what about messages in bottles? Something more physical, like a tiny, tiny hard drive filled with data."

"Accelerated to nearly the speed of light and fired at the recipient?" said Petra, her eyes narrowing in thought.

Sarah nodded. "And sometimes they go astray, caught up in magnetic turbulence, say, thrown off course."

"And eventually into your cold traps." Petra sat back and sucked her own bulb of coffee. "Quite an idea. You'd have to be very lucky to catch one."

"Unless there are a hell of a lot of them."

Petra drank some more coffee. "If this were a storage device it would explain the complexity. But why does it keep changing?"

Sarah shook her head. "No idea. Maybe it's more active than a message, like a hard drive needing constant refreshing."

Petra frowned. "There's another possibility." She stood, strode to the experiment and switched the electron beams off.

"Is it done?"

Petra shook her head. "Where could you make something like this?"

"A big nuclear collider?"

"No. It would need precision construction. We can't manage that even at an atomic level. I know. I have been trying. But this thing is on much smaller scales, down at the nuclear level. There's only one place that would be the natural scale for such work."

Sarah thought for a moment. "A neutron star?"

Petra nodded. "Have you heard of strangelets?"

Sarah shook her head.

"There was a panic about them in the late twentieth century. The idea there might be a lower energy state for nuclear material than the nuclei we're familiar with, involving strange quarks. If a bit of it came into contact with normal matter it would be converted. You'd get more strange matter which would convert more normal matter – and hard radiation of course."

"Producing a runaway reaction killing everything."

Petra nodded.

"Couldn't happen," said Sarah. "High energy cosmic rays hit the Earth all the time. If your strangelets existed, we'd have been hit by one billions of years ago. Everything would already be over."

"Yes," said Petra, "if the strangelets were natural. Out there you mentioned the cosmic weed whacker. Maybe that's what this is, nuclear scale grey goo, sent by neutron star life to wipe out any competition."

Sarah sat with her mouth open for a few moments, then she laughed. "Okay – you win. You're madder than I am!"

Petra nodded and smiled. "Makes you think though."

The radiation alarm caught them halfway through dinner.

Everyone knew what to do – head to the storm shelter, the deepest part of Moonbase Three, dug metres into the regolith and surrounded by the base water reservoir. With that much shielding they could survive the worst solar storm. It was also where the base had its hydroponic garden, so even if the surface facilities were damaged or dangerously irradiated, the crew could hide underground, with food, water and oxygen made by the plants, to await rescue.

As the shelter door sealed behind them, Sarah and Petra looked at each other, sharing the unspoken question: *Was that us?*

"If it was," muttered Sarah as they moved through a crowd of their colleagues, "we should be back in the lab, fixing it before it gets worse."

"But if it is a flare we'd be dead," countered Petra. She had already sat out some bad solar storms.

Max came up to Sarah, looking dishevelled. "I was asleep," he said. "What's going on?"

"No idea," said Sarah. "Let's find the Director."

When they found him, he was surrounded by several engineers. "How bad is it?" asked Petra.

He looked up from the tablet he was studying. "Odd. Solar wind is up, but below dangerous levels, yet we're getting radiation alerts. From your lab. What are you up to?"

"Shit," said Sarah.

"We were in the canteen," said Petra, treading on Sarah's foot to keep her silent.

The Director turned to Sarah in exasperation. "What's your involvement?"

29

His interrogation was cut short by an engineer. "Radiation's dropping. Nearly back to normal." He looked at Petra. "Even in her lab."

"Right," said Pierre curtly. "Time for you to sort out whatever you've cooked up in there." He turned to the engineer. "Go with them. Once that's done we're going to have a serious conversation."

He turned to the rest of the assembled crew and announced the all clear.

Max burst through the door of Petra's lab a few moments after the Director and two other members of the safety team arrived. The engineer had called them.

Max saw stony faces all round, the room filled by a hostile silence. Everyone turned to look at him.

"The last conspirator," said the Director.

"What?" said Max.

"He's got nothing to do with this," said Sarah. She turned to Max. "This is down to me. Go back to your room and I'll talk to you when everything is sorted out."

The Director turned to him. "Leave this lab, young man, and you'll be on the next shuttle back to Earth, sitting next to these two."

Max was confused. "What?" He turned to Sarah, then caught sight of the cold trap sitting in the middle of the lab. "Hey, what's one of our spares doing here?"

"It's not a spare, Max," said Sarah. "I brought the trap here for further analysis."

"But that's..."

"Against all safety rules," interrupted the Director, "and for good reason as that radiation alert demonstrated. We have to make safe the results of this gross misconduct, and then you all wait for the next shuttle home."

Sarah's shoulders slumped. Not only had she failed to solve the mystery of what lay in the trap, she had failed to protect Max from her own mistakes. "He's done nothing wrong!"

"He chose you as a supervisor," said the Director. "That was enough. Now, get rid of whatever's inside that machine."

Petra and Sarah looked blankly at each other. "Get rid of it?"

"Out of this base, off the Moon, and as far away as possible. If you don't have any better ideas I'll happily launch it on a transfer rocket programmed to self-destruct beyond the orbit of Mars. And I'll take the cost out of your unemployment pay for the next decade, because you'll both be unemployable by the time I finish with you."

Sarah and Petra looked at each other. They'd focused on studying the particle and hadn't thought what might happen next. Petra moved towards the equipment. "We should do a last scan then."

"No," ordered the Director. "Neither of you get to operate any equipment. My engineers do that, and vet your instructions first."

One of the engineers stepped up to the console. "What are these scans, and how will they help get rid of this thing?"

Sarah looked at Petra, then explained. "We've been using high energy electron beams. The object in the trap is an exotic cosmic ray particle. We're not sure what it might be and were looking at its structure."

"And how will these scans help remove it?" asked the Director.

"Knowledge always helps," said Sarah, knowing how unconvincing she sounded.

Petra came to the rescue. "We need to know if it has changed so we can tune whatever action we take to its current state, rather than what we had previously measured."

The engineer nodded. "That makes sense."

With evident reluctance, the Director gave his permission.

Soon the results arrived. The mysterious chunk of nuclear matter in the trap was more massive than before and had a slightly larger electric charge.

"What does the growth mean?" said Sarah. "Is it a strangelet after all?" She was glad only Petra seemed to know what such a particle was.

"It is not runaway growth. Your weed-whacker scenario is not appropriate," said Petra.

Sarah relaxed a little – at least she hadn't caused the end of the world. "How do we get rid of it?"

Petra shrugged.

"That should be straight forward enough," said Max, as he looked at the results.

"Explain," said the Director.

"It's charged. It's easily accelerated if you drop it through an electric field." He thought for a few moments. "Getting it to lunar

31

escape velocity should be trivial. Solar System escape should also be easy." He jotted a few numbers on a tablet and passed it to Sarah, only to have the Director intercept it and pass the device to his engineer.

"Will that work?" he asked.

After a few moments the engineer nodded. "The difficulty will be getting it out of the trap, but even that shouldn't be too much of a problem."

"Do you need them here for that?" The Director indicated Petra and Sarah. The engineer shook his head. The Director turned to them. "Leave. You're confined to the common areas. Your access to all experimental facilities rescinded. The cosmic ray collector will have to be safely turned off as well, but that can come later." Sarah opened her mouth to protest, but closed it again, knowing she didn't have a leg to stand on.

She stood and turned to leave the room. Max and Petra followed her example.

"Not you, young man. You can assist here, then help us shut down the collector." The Director then turned to Sarah and Petra. "The two of you have until the next shuttle in three weeks to persuade me I shouldn't have you fired and charged with gross negligence."

It didn't take Max and the safety team long to set up an electromagnetic launcher for the tiny particle. Their main difficulty had been plumbing the beamline of the small accelerator to one of the external vents in the lab, so that the particle could leave the vacuum of the cold trap for the vacuum of space. The long, straight metal tube that facilitated this looked incongruous, like a smoke stack on a jet engine.

"Is it ready yet?" demanded the Director, who had hovered nearby throughout the construction process.

"All ready," said Max. The engineer standing next to him nodded in confirmation.

"So what are we waiting for?"

"Is the gun charged up?" asked Max.

"Ten megavolts and holding steady," said the engineer.

Max's finger hovered above the large red button that would release the trap's vent, and nudge the particle into the accelerator.

"Are you sure we want to do this? Sarah must have thought it was important."

"Your loyalty to your supervisor does you credit, son," said the Director, "but delaying any longer will only demonstrate you're a dangerous, head in the clouds fool like her."

Max thought for a moment, then pressed the button.

There was no climax, no noise, no lights.

"Is it gone?"

"Yes, Director," said Max. "It's gone."

"Where to?"

Max gestured helplessly upwards. "Out there," he said. "Where it came from, well away from any solid bodies in the Solar System, as you instructed."

The Director nodded to himself. "Good riddance."

"Was it one of these 'weed-whacking' strangelets?" asked the Director.

Three weeks had passed. The shuttle would leave in a day, and Petra and Sarah were delivering their report. They had spent the intervening time working on the data, and developing computer models of what Sarah had found. Given what they now knew, they were confident they could turn this disaster into a massive success.

"No," said Petra. "At least, not directed at us."

The Director frowned. "Explain."

"Have you actually read our report?" asked Sarah.

The Director shrugged, just a little twitch of his shoulders. "I'm sure it will just be an attempt at justifying the unjustifiable."

"Then why bother with this meeting?"

"For the record. In cases like this there has to be a review, and that's what we're having. I mostly want to know exactly how much of a risk you took with all our lives. Now, will you answer my question?"

Petra continued. "The thing in the cold trap took no notice of anything we did, just cycled through a series of structural transformations."

"A maintenance cycle," added Sarah.

"A ticking time bomb?" said the Director.

"No. We eliminated that possibility," said Sarah. "That's on page four of the report."

He ignored Sarah's dig. "What triggered the radiation?"

"The arrival of a weak solar storm," said Petra.

"The collectors recorded a burst of moderate energy protons and higher mass nuclei coming from the Sun," said Sarah.

"A small coronal mass ejection, as predicted," said Petra.

"Some of those particles, possibly carbon or nitrogen nuclei, hit our sample. They were transformed."

"Eaten," said the Director. He looked pleased at this possibility.

"No," said Petra.

"Nothing like that," added Sarah.

"Then what?"

"Using the data collected before you ejected it, we modelled the... device," said Petra. "It is amazing. If hit by a heavy nucleus, or protons above a certain energy, they become part of it. Gamma rays, pions, radioactive secondaries result. They triggered the alarm."

"In other words, dangerous," said the Director.

"But, and this is where it gets clever, it absorbs only a few nucleons at a time," said Petra.

"However," said Sarah, "given a huge supply of nucleons – which would only happen if it hit a neutron star – something very different happens."

"A phase change takes place," said Petra. "To something much more complex, and much more useful."

"It turns out," said Sarah, "this thing is a terraforming device for neutron stars."

"What?" The Director clearly hadn't been expecting that.

"It takes neutron star matter," said Petra, "and turns it into computational substrate, something hugely powerful, ready to run any code you want."

The Director looked at the two women in confusion, not sure if they were mad, tricking him, or somehow had turned the tables. Sarah was surprised he had been so careless and overconfident to not read the report. If he had, he would have been ready for this, had a response planned.

"You're saying this thing is a machine?"

They nodded.

"Made by some kind of intelligence – extraterrestrial intelligence?"

They nodded again.

"It's a colonisation tool." He looked a little panicked. "We're being invaded and you brought it into my Moonbase?" His face was getting redder, his voice louder.

"It was never a hazard to us," said Petra. "It's for a kind of life we didn't think possible, an environment utterly alien. They do not care, or realise, we exist."

"It came from a neutron star," said Sarah, "designed to affect other neutron stars. The intelligences responsible operate at densities millions of times greater than us. Everything in the Solar System, except maybe the very centre of the Sun, would just be overdense vacuum to them. But they're turning entire collapsed stars into computronium – neutronic computronium."

"The singularity happened," said Petra, "a long time ago, and a long way away."

"We have a lot of catching up to do," said Sarah.

The Director looked away from them for a moment, tapping his finger on his desk. "You're sure of this, certain these results will stand up to the harshest scrutiny?" They nodded. "You think that will protect you from the consequences of your actions?"

"This is the discovery of the century, Director," said Sarah. "The millennium."

"Where's the proof? This particle of yours is gone, the data only on our servers, which can fail. Without that, the two of you will sound like embittered cranks, making things up to get your jobs back."

"Until someone else finds one," said Sarah. "They must be pretty common. We caught ours in the first hours of collector operation."

"In which case it's someone else's discovery. Science moves on, you get left behind."

"Frankly, I don't care," said Sarah. "It would be nice to get the credit, I'll admit, so we have backups and we've sent an encrypted dataset to Horst and other press contacts. But if all that fails, the science will happen, even if I have to drop a few hints to the Americans in Moonbase Five. The science is the thing. And when the result gets out, you'll look an utter fool."

The Director leaned forward, resting his elbows on the desk, and looked directly into Sarah's eyes. "You took unacceptable risks."

"Yes, we – I – did. But it was the right thing to do."

"You didn't know that. There have to be consequences."

Sarah paused for a moment, sensing something had changed. "Are we negotiating?" she asked.

The Director nodded. "Yes. You've made a valuable discovery, but used unacceptable methods. There's no place for you on the Moon anymore, but we might still salvage something. You want the science out. I want full credit for Moonbase Three and don't want either of you going to the Americans or elsewhere. So, what do we do?"

"I publish the paper, this place gets the credit," said Sarah.

The Director shook his head. "That would encourage everyone else to take stupid risks, disregard the rules and ignore procedure. I have a counter proposal."

Sarah sighed. "I've had enough. This is no way to do science." She rose in her chair, but Petra reached out, laying a hand on her wrist.

"Wait – hear him out."

Something in Petra's expression caused her to pause, to doubt her position was as strong as she thought. A man like this didn't get to be a Moonbase Director without influence in many high places. Perhaps it would be better to have him on her side.

"Go on," she muttered.

"Given what you did, neither of you can get full credit. Some, perhaps, is due. It is an amazing and fundamental result. But too many people know what you did, and that cannot be forgiven. You can't just stay here and carry on. Let me propose this. Max leads the paper, gets credit for the result and gets the science out. Moonbase Three, and yourselves, bask in reflected glory. Max takes over the experiment, the two of you head home, a black mark on your lunar records, but your status secure as collaborators on this fine result."

"But..." muttered Sarah.

"Nobody wins," concluded the Director, "but nobody loses. And if you still think the encrypted archive you sent Horst will help," he waved a datachip at them, "he sent it back to me, and deleted his copy without distributing it. Who exactly do you think he works for?"

Sarah and Petra nodded, defeated.

But this isn't science, thought Sarah. *This is someone who left science long ago playing a game.* He played it well, but it meant nothing. The result, whoever got the credit, was the thing. It made a difference. It would change the world, change what people knew and thought about the world and the universe at large. That was the important thing. In the future, this result would be remembered. Long after all their names were forgotten, along with all the petty squabbles over who had found what and where, the result would remain.

They might be unknowably distant, and incomprehensibly alien, but humanity was no longer alone in the universe.

The Big Next

Pat Cadigan

"I am not going to tell you my name, not yet... [said Treebeard]... it would take a very long while: my name is growing all the time, and I've lived a very long, long time, so my name is like a story... in the Old Entish... it is a lovely language but it takes a long time to say anything in it, because we do not say anything... unless it is worth taking a long time to say, and to listen to."

"My Aunt Loretta and I used to walk around the lake here when I was your age," I told Cora, who was hopping along beside me on one leg, her braids flailing in time with the arms of the sweater tied around her waist. On this partly-cloudy Saturday morning, my seven-year-old was conducting an experiment to see which leg could go the greater distance. So far, the right leg had held out from the edge of the parking area, past the picnic tables, and onto the lakeside path. Quite a respectable distance; the left leg was going to have its work cut out. Now I put myself between her and the water so that, in the event of the right leg's sudden catastrophic failure, she wouldn't tumble in.

"Mom, you're blocking my view," she complained breathlessly. "I can't see the lake."

"Sorry about that." I paused on the dirt path; Cora stopped with me, had trouble balancing, and tried to hop up and down in place but her hopping leg was approaching the limit of its endurance. I put a hand on her shoulder to steady her. "How about you suspend the experiment for the time being and just walk? Then you can be on the side nearest the water and I won't worry about you accidentally launching yourself into the bullrushes."

Cora frowned for a moment. "Oh, you mean the cattails. Okay." She winced as she straightened her left leg, which she'd been holding tightly folded. "Can I have my pad and pen?"

Obediently I produced both items from my jacket pocket and

waited while she went down on one knee, using the other as a desk. The memo-book was new – she had filled two others with various observations and conclusions, using her treasured Souvenir of Lake Winnipesaukee ballpoint, a gift from her grandmother last summer. Since then Cora had mounted a campaign for us to go there ourselves so that she could return the favour. It was very light at first, a few mentions casually worked into conversation – *Do you think there'll be ice skating at Coggshall Park this winter? Hey, does Lake Winnipesaukee ever freeze over?* She stepped it up as the snow melted and the weather grew warmer: *Did you know that Lake Winnipesaukee is seventy-two square miles? Are there any lakes that big in Massachusetts? Have you ever rented a boat? Did you know you can rent one at Lake Winnipesaukee?*

Finally she pulled out the big guns: *I have to do a report on a historical place and I chose Lake Winnipesaukee. Did you know that a Native American tribe called the Winnepiseogees lived there?* As it turned out, she was supposed to have chosen a Massachusetts location; instead of giving her an F, the teacher had sent her to the library to complete a make-up report by the end of the day. The resulting C+ had been my brilliant daughter's first C ever. I didn't berate her – my own record was full of Cs and worse – but the shock of not being an A-lister, so to speak, was enough to shut down the Winnipesaukee campaign for a week.

"All done," she said, standing up and holding out the memo-book with the pen clipped to the cover.

"May I look?" I asked.

"Sure." She found the right page for me. "There."

My eyebrows went up at the figure. "That many exactly?"

She nodded. "It's a lot, huh?"

"And you're sure it was –" I checked the page. "*Exactly* one hundred and thirty-eight hops?" Cora nodded again. "You were able to keep track even while we were talking?"

"Well, yeah." Cora looked surprised at the question. "It's not hard."

"I don't think I could do it," I said, and then wondered how wise it was for a parent to admit something like that, especially to a seven-year-old.

Cora, however, wasn't convinced of my deficit. "Have you ever tried? Why not?"

"It never occurred to me." I showed her my watch. "I use this instead."

Cora made a face. "It's not the same thing."

I chuckled. "If you ever take a philosophy class in college, you're going to make the professor cry."

My brilliant daughter frowned. "If she gives me a C, *I'll* cry." Pause. "Or he."

"I doubt you'll do much crying over grades by then." A breeze came across the water at us and I motioned for her to put on her sweater. She obeyed but left it unbuttoned.

"Tell me something," she said; not a conversation opener but a request for information, any kind of information, as long as she'd never heard it before. This was something she had come up with on her own, although I wasn't sure how. I had the vague notion it had grown out of watching her cousins play endless rounds of *Jeopardy* and *Trivial Pursuit*. At the time, she'd still been in diapers, not even talking, but the kids swore she was paying attention. They were all big game-players, her cousins – board games, card games, and inevitably videogames; not so my brilliant daughter, not to the same extent. I once referred to this thing we shared as the Tell-Me-Something Game and was quite pointedly corrected.

Now I said. "My Aunt Loretta told me once, when we were walking here, that the last time the galaxy had revolved to this point in space, the dinosaurs were just starting to emerge on Earth. That's how long it takes the galaxy to make one complete revolution."

"How about now?" Cora asked. "What was happening?"

"We haven't moved enough since then for there to be any difference. Dinosaurs were still emerging. The times and distances involved are far beyond human experience."

"Oh. We move with the galaxy?"

"We do."

"I thought you meant that the galaxy passed by, like when you stand and watch a merry-go-round."

"That couldn't happen, honey."

I could practically hear the little wheels and gears work as she stuck a pin in that statement for later. "Okay, so how many years is it since the dinosaurs started to appear?"

"About 225 million." I smiled. "Have I told you something?"

She smiled back at me. "Yeah. It's a good one, too."

"I'm glad you like it."

"How old were you when your Aunt Loretta told you that?"

"I'm not sure. Nine or ten, maybe."

I could feel her satisfaction at being younger than I'd been. *Not a game, my ass*, I thought, amused. I expected her to ask me something else about Loretta but she surprised me. "Tell me something."

"Again? All right. According to fossil evidence, *Homo sapiens* – people like us – appeared about 200,000 years ago."

My brilliant daughter frowned. "Wait, I thought – how many years for the dinosaurs?"

"225 million. People were only 200,000." I watched her sorting the two numbers in her mind.

"I thought people were around for millions of years."

"Human ancestors – *Homo sapiens'* ancestors. *Homo erectus*, *Homo habilis*. And before that, *Australopithecus*. Do you remember the program we watched about Lucy?"

She nodded but her frown intensified. "It's not fair."

"What isn't?"

"That we don't last longer. We never get to see what happens. Like, if you and I were born in the Stone Age? When we died, it would have still been the Stone Age. We'd never know about Columbus discovering America or George Washington being the first president or when the men walked on the moon. Nobody gets to see what happens next. The *Big* Next, I mean." She gestured at the sky. "Like stars that are so far away, it takes the light thousands of years to reach us. The light wasn't here when we were born and when we die, it *still* won't be here. The stars'll never look any different as long as we live. It's just not fair."

For a moment, I thought she was actually going to stamp her foot; I wasn't sure whether to be laugh or cry. "The unchanging stars are what allowed people to navigate before compasses were invented," I said. "I'm sorry, I can't tell you how just off the top of my head but if you're curious, we can look it up when we get home."

My brilliant daughter wrinkled her nose. "Why are we so tiny when the universe is so big? We should be gigantic so that traveling around the galaxy would be like traveling around America."

"You're *definitely* going to reduce some poor philosophy professor to a quivering, tearful wreck," I said.

She shrugged noncommittally. We walked all the way around the lake and then I suggested ice cream. "Friendly's, not Dairy Queen, right?" Cora said seriously. Her cousins were all fiends for soft-serve dipped in chocolate; my brilliant daughter insisted that real ice cream was scooped from tubs, not poured out in *gooey ropes* (unquote), and nothing and nobody would ever change her mind about that (also unquote). While I was pleased, and occasionally even in awe of her confidence, sometimes I worried that my pride and joy might have a tendency to be too inflexible. Right now the world didn't give her much trouble about the way she thought things should be. It wouldn't be long before the gloves came off and there wouldn't be any make-ups or do-overs.

But then, according to my brilliant daughter, it wouldn't be long before it was all over. And the light from the stars *still* wouldn't have arrived.

I didn't think about it again until a few days later when I found her glued to the desktop in the living room, looking at web-pages about bristle-cone pines and other long-lived trees.

"Did you know they found the oldest tree in the world?" she said without taking her eyes from the screen as I pulled a chair up beside her. "It's in Sweden and it's over nine thousand years old." A moment later, her shoulders slumped. "Actually, it isn't the tree that's nine thousand years old, it's the root system."

"A nine-thousand-year-old root system is still pretty respectable, don't you think?" I said. "Look, it says there that the roots took hold right after the end of the last Ice Age. That's really something."

"It's not a tree," Cora insisted. "In California, there's a bristle-cone pine – a real tree – that's five thousand years old. That's like three thousand years before Jesus."

"Who only lived thirty-three years but has exerted an influence that has lasted for two thousand," I reminded her.

My little agnostic wasn't having any. "Jesus is like a root system. The tree is *there*. It was a tree five thousand years ago and it's a tree *now*. If that were a person, it would have seen a whole bunch of Big Nexts."

"How long has this been on your mind?"

"Since *The Day The Earth Stood Still*."

I couldn't help laughing. We'd watched the original movie with

Michael Rennie a few weeks earlier and then had a discussion about the possibility of extraterrestrial life. I'd expected my little agnostic to be equally sceptical about aliens and was surprised when she asked me, in all seriousness, what we were doing about making contact with people from other worlds. It had been a difficult conversation, even with a child as gifted as my darling daughter. Not because it was especially hard to explain the basics of radio astronomy and Goldilocks planets in sufficiently simple terms but because Cora seemed to want me to answer for what she perceived as a failure of progress.

Now she said, "If we don't find aliens pretty soon, then by the time they come here, they won't even find a root system."

"Then we'd best keep the root system and everything else as healthy as possible," I said lightly.

She tilted her head and frowned and I could practically see the little wheels turning again. A deep yearning for my aunt swept through me; I needed her guidance so much right then but she had died the year before my brilliant daughter had come along. There'd been no help for it – a root system, even a very old one, can support only so much new growth. I'd been eleven at initiation and I know kids grow up so much faster these days but seven, even a gifted seven, seemed too young. Still, the instincts were obviously making themselves felt, whether I thought it was time or not, whether I liked it or not.

I put my hand on the back of my brilliant daughter's neck; the skin shifted immediately and I could tell that the organ was fully formed. This was not even slightly premature.

Cora's face went blank for a minute and by that I mean a full sixty seconds. Colour crept into her face; a drop a sweat trickled down from her temple, travelled along the still-babyish curve of her cheek and disappeared under her chin.

Then it was done and I withdrew my hand. There was a new line on my palm, a scar that ran from the base of my middle finger to my wrist. Cora's neck was smooth, unchanged; our kind are marked not by what we know but by what we tell. That's just how it is.

"You know," Cora said in a startlingly old-sounding voice, "I kinda suspected something."

I nodded, although this wasn't necessarily significant. All kids, at some point in their young lives, wonder about who they really are – if they're adopted, if they're descended from royalty, perhaps in exile, if their parents are keeping some immense secret from them. I went through a phase where I was practically convinced that Loretta was really my mother and she had given me to her sister and brother-in-law because she felt I'd be better off in a two-parent family. Not so; Loretta had been unable to bear children. I was entirely my parent's biological offspring, theirs in every way except one.

Cora would have a million questions, just as I had, back in the day. Judging by the expression on her little face right then, I figured she was trying to decide what to ask first. I had always been honest with her, whether it had to do with where babies came from or where her father had gone. This, however, was going to be more difficult.

Nine-thousand-year-old root systems don't have this kind of problem with their saplings. They don't want to know why the root system's been dug in for all this time, why they're growing here, now, or what's the Big Next. But that's what happens when you put a brain in a lighthouse. Or a buoy, or a beacon. Or hell, I don't know, a highway marker. *Mile 80,771,390,434; last food & gas for 300,549,653,212 light-years, so plan ahead!*

I wonder if they really had no idea the single-celled organisms they left their markers in would evolve or if they're so long-lived they underestimated how long evolution would take. Or if something happened to the original visitors before they had a chance to tell anyone else what they'd left behind. Or if they simply lost track of time – God knows, *I* often do.

And then again, it's possible that everything is exactly as they intended it to be, that we two – my brilliant daughter and me, now – are not ladies-in-waiting, as it were, but records. That when we awaken in each new embodiment and contemplate whatever we can access of the previous lives, it's like another ring on a five-thousand-year-old bristle-cone pine. Although we are actually much older.

The first thing my brilliant daughter will ask me, I expect, is if there are any others. And I'll have to tell her that if there ever were, there aren't any more and I don't know why. Perhaps for the same reason there aren't any more dinosaurs. Those who left us here had no idea they'd be gone in only a single turn of the galaxy – no, less than that.

Cora folded her arms the way she always did when she was about to take serious issue with the world and I had a sudden, intense surge of hope that we'd be around for the Big Next of their return in this lifetime. My brilliant daughter is going to make them answer for the last five billion years and I really, really, *really* want to watch.

Baedeker's Fermi

Adam Roberts

12th April 1900; a bright sunny day. Sky so flawless a blue it looked as though it had been enamelled and polished from horizon to horizon by some celestial jeweller. From Cologne to Mayence we were travelling aboard the saloon-steamer *Deutscher Kaiser*. The journey upstream took us twelve hours, although the guidebook assured us the return voyage downstream takes as little as seven and a half. No man may doubt the muscular implacability of the Rhenish flow here, close as it is to the North Sea. Albert and I sat on deck all morning smoking cigars and watching the green landscape slide beautifully past, green as emerald, green the ideal ocean of the fairy tales. Albert particularly admired (he said) the view of distant hills, and behind them the spectral white of faraway mountain tops. I preferred the nearby vineyards. By seven we disembarked into Mayence.

We took adjoining rooms – with, of course, a connecting door – in the Hof Von Holland, located upon the Rheinstrasse. Both rooms had fine views of the river. It was a simple matter to obtain the services of a valet-de-place for five Marks the day – one German Mark has the monetary worth of a good English shilling, so this was not cheap. But he agreed to serve the both of us for the money, and these being the early days of our Rhine odyssey, we preferred not to haggle or pinch out pennies – our pfennigs, I should say

That evening we dined well, and strolled along the gaslit Rheinpromenade as far as the Schloss. Later, Albert joined me in my room and together we consulted the Baedeker. Mayence, in German Mainz, is a strongly fortified town with 72,300 inhab. (23,000 Prot, 4000 Jews), including a garrison of 8,000 soldiers. It is pleasantly situated on the left hand of the Rhine, opposite and below the influx of the Main.

"It says," I observed "that the Romanic-Germanic Central

Museum contains the most varied and interesting collection of ante-Christian antiquities in the whole of Germany."

"Ante-anti," repeated Albie, chuckling. "It is too painfully clear these guides are not written by native English speakers."

"The Library and the Collection of Coins occupy the second and third floors of the west wing, to which is appended a remarkable assembly of typographical curiosities, manuscripts and incunabula, A complete set of coinage from the court of Charlemagne is the collection's pride."

"I am more interested in the two valuable coins that comprise *this* collection," said Albie, slipping his hand into my breeches. There then occurred the event which, naturally, modesty prevents me from detailing. Afterwards we slept. I wanted us to share the bed in my room, which was certainly ample enough for two; but Albert, wisely I suppose, considered the possibility that a chambermaid, or hotelier, or even young Hans our valet-de-place, might chance upon us together and raise the alarm. So he returned to his room.

We rose late and broke our fast in the Weiner Café on Gymanasiumstrasse. The date was the 13th April – a Friday. Sharply drawn white clouds, perfect as puffs of white, mobbed the sky. A strong spring breeze had awoken itself, making the big trees lining the strasse move with an underwater slowness. But as I drank my wine-and-water and picked the last flakes of pasty from my plate, I bethought me how very comely was the pink and white stonework of the buildings of Mayence; how courteous and handsome the natives – even the Jews, of whom there were many in their funereal black. I reminded myself of how fortunate I was to be able to enjoy so much of the world's beauty with Albert. I was, I told myself, happy. I insisted upon it. If I insisted strongly enough, the feeling of chewing apprehension in my stomach would recede.

After breakfast we visited the Cathedral: an imposing block-shaped edifice of rose-coloured stone, with one superbly tall slate-clad spire at the northern end. Ingress was achieved via two marvellous and mighty brazen doors that opened onto the north aisle, and in silent admiration we walked the length of the building – 122 yards long, the Baedeker informed us, and supported by fifty-six hefty pillars. Albert translated some of the funerary inscriptions for my benefit, and I sketched a few of the statues into my notebook. There is a particularly well-rendered head of Saturn on an eighteenth-century monument dedicated to a certain Canon von Breidenbach-Bürresheim. The cloisters are tranquil, built in the Gothic style, and Albert and I sat side by side and smoked for an hour, as the shadows slowly swung about the great axis of the turning world. The Baedeker recommended visiting the Crypt, but by now it was lunchtime and the verger could not be found to unlock the door for us.

We strolled out into the breezy sunlight, north to the Platz Gutenberg, where a fine statue commemorates Mayence's most famous son, John Gutenberg, inventor of the printing press. We heard the start of the commotion here. It was Albert who first saw the changes in the sky. At the far end of Ludwigsstrasse a considerable crowd of people were in motion, and their shrieks and yells of terror carried cleanly to us on the clear spring air. A tram, rolling along its grooves down the street, stopped suddenly. I saw its driver scramble from the cab and abandon it.

"Clouds!" Albert yelled, suddenly – such uncharacteristic behaviour for this reserved, immaculately-mannered individual! "Clouds!" He was pointing upwards. For a moment I saw clouds, visible masses of water droplets suspended in the air according to the logic of their relative density. But then the ghastly reality struck me, a modern-day Saul on the road to a ghastly Tarsus – for water must always be heavier than mere air, and no structure of such size and evident solidity could support itself overhead. What we had thought to be clouds were not. They were something else. They were gigantic amoeboid *beings*, creatures of monstrous otherness. A Venus-shell of silver mist, animated by some incomprehensible will or mechanism, swooped low over Mayence's crenulations and spired-roofs. It was a *device*, a machine constructed on principles quite different to steam engines or electrical capacitors; a chariot for cleaving the high sky, a throne set about with rods and lights. Weapons? And seated in its heart, wraithed about by the very device it piloted, was a creature unlike any I have seen – resembling the meat at the centre of a cockle, but the size of a bullock; orange and quivering with life. I looked about me, my heart galloping, an hideous anticipation of perdition in my whole body. Every cloud was a chariot, and in every one monsters of various sizes were enthroned – from cattle-big to whale-big. They thronged the sky. "O strange!" I howled. "Strange strange strange!" The creatures I had first seen had brought its mist-chariot down almost to touch the ground. Now it began advancing towards me over the cobbles of the square. Its tangle of nude-muscle-fibre body jittered, and weird black tentacles, like tadpole tails, sprung up upon its torso. Thorns made of flesh. Beckoning cilia. I am not ashamed to say that I hurled myself down upon the ground – that I pressed my face against the stones, and wrapped my arms about my head, whimpering.

That evening we dined at a restaurant named Hanaczik, at the very top of Jacobsbergergasse. The main course was of middling quality, but dessert – apple torte and fine-whipped cream – was delicious, and the claret belonged in the first class. We strolled side by side along to Gutenbergplatz where the Theatre is situated, half-thinking of seeing a play. But we had not planned ahead and by the time we got there the performance had already started. It was, moreover, a Germanic translation of a Dion Boucicault play, and Albert was of the opinion that we could see Boucicault any day of the week at home. "We're in Rhineland!" he told me. "We ought to immerse ourselves in *Germanic* culture!"

"Oh that we could walk, arm in arm, through these streets," I declared.

He hushed me at once. "You wouldn't enjoy being arrested, Harold."

"These people?" I said, gesturing. The Platz was thronged. "Ordinary Germans going about their business – they pay us no mind. It's as if they don't see us. We are merely two foreigners, babbling in a barbarian tongue!"

"They'd see us pretty quick if we started behaving as spoony young lovers," Albert retorted, in a quiet voice. "And you'd see *them* too, if you looked properly –" So I looked again; and saw that the crowd of people possessed a markworthy homogeneity. Black-clad people, moving without timidity and yet with unobtrusive haste across the square. Jews. For the Friday evening commences their Sabbath, and I suppose they were returning from their temple to their homes. "These Hebrew gentlemen will be even less disposed to notice us," I said. "Keeping themselves to themselves."

We returned to the hotel, and sat in the lounge smoking and reading. Albert made his slow way, brow furrowed so deeply it was as though the book were a plough, carving up the soil of his head, through a work of German philosophy – that same Freddie Nietzsche upon whom the clever set in London is so keen at the moment. I read for the second time my copy of Herbert Wells' *War of the Worlds*.

The following day we caught the train to Frankfort.

On the train I completed my re-read of the Wellsian story. There was something about it that snagged meaningfully upon my imagination, though I couldn't decide for myself what this *something* was. As storytelling it made no absurd pretence to great art; Wells himself, a man I knew distantly – the acquaintance of an acquaintance – was no Goethe, or Shakespeare, or Homer. He was, in point of fact, a servant's son, bred in the honest humbleness of the Kent countryside. To meet him in the flesh was to be struck by his ingenious cleverness and his bouncy earnestness – both characteristics as clear markers as you could hope to see of his *lack* of gentility. True breeding cannot be counterfeited. This same fellow was now making a name for himself in the literary world with nothing more than a Penny Dreadful sensibility and a few handfuls of journalistic glitter cast upon the page. Nonetheless, his was the book that refused to leave my mind! Having read it twice, I was now certain I would read it a third time. What *was* it that so fascinated me? I asked Albert's opinion on the matter, but he was dismissive. "That trash," he said. "To call it a penny dreadful overvalues the work. Farthing dreadful, let us say. Lights on Mars? Strange creatures descending from the sky to wreak havoc in..."

He stopped speaking. For a moment we looked at one another. Indigestion clawed at my guts. "Sausage is supposed to be," I said, looking out of the window. "I mean, the people of Germany are *alleged* to be masters of the making of sausage! And yet my poor old guts are rumbling on that breakfast meal."

"Mine too," said Albert, returning to his philosophical treatise. "Intestines having a fearful job chewing over this stuff. It's unaccountable, I must say."

"You usually have the most enviable digestive constitution," I observed.

"Indeed!"

After a while the sensation passed out of my midriff, and I felt more at ease. For a while I attempted to peruse a local newspaper, by way of improving my German; but Albert grew cross-tempered with my continual interruptions to *his* reading, asking after the meaning of this word, or that word. So I threw that project over, and instead stared out of the window of our compartment. The train line passed for many miles through woodland; but then it broke free of the trees and ran alongside the Rhine. I stared at the waterway, which returned a muddy-silver version of the wide sky back to the heavens. The trees on the distant far bank were small as grass blades. The motion of the train, and the pacifying fullness and inexhaustible flow of the river, soothed me. Then, but then, oh but then fleetingly I saw something reflected in the body of the water – a mile-long snake in the sky, with fanning blue feather-like protuberances on its tail, and lights gleaming as portholes along its length. I cried out, and looked up, and there were tears in my eyes: I was weeping with a kind of terror of recognition, a strange throat-closing emotion combining horror and delight. Why delight?

The Central Railway Station of Frankfort is the largest and handsomest structure of its type I have encountered upon my travels in Germany (I hear the Berlin Banhof is larger, but I have yet to go to Berlin). The station overlooks its own spacious Bahnhofsplatz, from which wide and tree-lined streets radiate – Kronprinzenstrasse, Kaiserstrasse, Taunusstrasse. Inconveniently, however, the station is located a distance west of the centre of the city, and the hotels of Frankfort do not send omnibuses to meet the trains. We were obliged therefore to hire a private cab, and some foolish delay in loading our luggage was the occasion for Albert to lose his temper. It is not like his normal character to rage so, but *something* had agitated his balance of mind, and he railed at the blank-faced driver in fluent German for five full minutes. Eventually we clambered aboard and rode bumpily to the hotel *Schwan*, on the Goethe Platz. According to my Baedeker, it was at this luxurious establishment that the peace of 10th May 1871 was concluded, the defeated remnants of once-mighty Martial France forced to capitulate to the resurgence of German might. And what opulence there was inside! A large gilded reception hallway, and blood-red carpets soft as silk up the two arching stairways. The *Schwan* also operates a mechanical elevator, in which, with some small apprehension at its prison-like sliding grill and confined space, the two of us ascended to our room.

I'm sorry to say we quarrelled like children as soon as the porter left us to ourselves. I rebuked Albert for his ill-tempered words to the cabriolet-driver, and he retaliated with hot words about me *sticking my nose in* when I 'couldn't even get my mouth around the simplest deutscher terms'. We parted badly, and I tried to cool my fury by wandering through the streets of this strange city with only my guidebook to direct me. I stood beneath Schwanthaler's Monument of Goethe, erected in 1844, twelve years after the poet's death. The reliefs on the front of the pedestal are allegorical, and on the ones on the sides are figures from Goethe's poems. I strolled to the Römer, the townhall of the former free imperial city, and the most interesting edifice in Frankfort from a historical point of view. The façade presented three lofty gables to the Römerberg, or market-place, opposite. I passed the Cathedral without going inside, and instead wasted an idle hour in the Städel Art-Institute, a handsome building of grey sandstone which contains collections of pictures, engravings and drawings by all the great European masters, as well as numerous casts and busts. The main picture gallery is especially rich in specimens of the early Flemish and German schools of the 15th and 16th centuries, as well as many pretty Dutch interiors from the 17th century and even a few from Italy. The names of the artists appear on the picture frames.

I took a solitary luncheon, feeling gloomy indeed, and watched the passers-by. Frankfort has a population of some 179,800 inhabitants, including 18,000 Jews and a military garrison of 1800 soldiers. The city lies in a spacious plain bounded by mountains, on the right bank of the navigable Main. Wherefore did I comprehend such dread, in my very guts? Of what was I scared? That Albert did not love me? No, for I knew he loved me, and I said so, to myself, aloud, quietly and in English. Saying the words, like a charm, helped reduce the sensation of intestine agony a little. But then a new fear leapt up in my heart – did he doubt my love *for him*? Such a supposition was not to be endured. I left a banknote on my table and ran straight off, not even finishing my pitcher of Rhenish, all the way back to the Schwan, and up the stairs – for I could not abide the thought of locking myself in that elevator cage – to our room. Albert was there, sitting with his feet up on the rail of the balcony, smoking and reading. The little emotion I could read on his face, that beautiful, reserved, manly face, was enough to reassure me that he knew. We had no need of words of apology. Instead I drew the shutters, and wedged a chaise-longue against the door to prevent the ingress of unwanted servants or maids, and took him to the large bed, where we lay together as Achilles and Patroclus had once lain, millennia ago.

Into the Trojan lands, astride a horse larger than a palace. How could Ilium not see the danger, in that vast equine structure? *They* believed they had won, and saw everything – even their own defeat – in those terms. And so it was that they were fooled by the horse.

In the comfortable shadow afterwards, with the slats of the shutter laying parallel strips of sunlight over his naked flanks, we two talked for a long time. I confessed to him of my own often roiling stomach, and of my bafflement as to the cause. Albert confided in me that he too had been feeling a sense of dread ever since Mayence. He couldn't understand it, any more than I. Though he had toured through Germany many times, yet never before had he felt so apprehensive – of what? He knew not. "It may be this accursed stuff I'm reading," he growled. "This Nietzsche is a devil – self-confessedly a devil. His job, as he conceives it, is to make his readers doubt everything they have hitherto taken for granted! It is, I do vouchsafe it, a most uncomfortable proceeding."

"What of truth, though?"

"Oh, *truth* is mutable, saith the sage. Truth is power, not science; or rather, it is *science*, but science is power too. The strong legislate what is true, and after a while we forget from whence it came. Our habits of thought are stronger than strait-waistcoats. We walk about with habit-coloured spectacles before our eyes, and see everything as we are accustomed to see them." He shuddered, and I embraced him to warm him, and this in turn led to a manlier embrace.

We dined at the hotel, and the wine helped ease our mutual sense of existential dissatisfaction – or our sense of saturated satisfactions, as a man who has eaten too much rich food moans about his stomach.

The next day we spent the morning at the Zoological Gardens, admission 1 Mark, built upon the grounds of an old estate, in the sink of the ruins of which is a remarkable salt-water aquarium. Afterwards we walked upon the Old Bridge, and stood in its centre, looking out upon the Main. The bridge is fashioned from red sandstone, and dates from 1342. The middle is embellished with a statue of Charlemagne, by Wendelstadt and Zwerger, and nearby is an antique cross of iron, with, in Catholic style, an iron-fashioned Christ upon it. A small figure of a cockerel surmounts this, memorial to an old story that the architect completed his bridge by means of a treaty with the devil, in which he agreed to sacrifice to the antichrist the first person to cross it. But the canny builder held back the crowds, and sent a hen over the span before anything else.

Passing along the Schöne Aussicht Obermainstrasse, I noticed a street cleaner leaning on a wide broom. He was brushing the road in long, slow strokes. Curious as to what he was clearing away, I stepped over to him. My eyes stung. My stomach was abruptly burning with an inner blaze. I felt deeply, unconscionably afraid – but of what? Of what? The sweeper was moving piles of – I know not *what* they were. Dozens of them. A multitude of tadpole-like beings, each head the size of a bowling-ball and the colour of myrrh, the tails double-bladed and freaked with silver and blue. A semi-transparent jelly coated the heads. And though some of these weird monsters were clearly dead, many writhed sluggishly, and strained to move themselves in the heavy and unfamiliar gravity of our Earth. I knew, looking upon them, that they possessed powers of thought and will and even of spirit at least the equal of ours. Yet here they lay, heaped and discarded, in great banks of shuddering alien flesh.

The sweeper stopped. The sweeper had stopped long minutes before, and was staring at me in frank alarm.

"What are you doing?" Albert called to me. "Why are you gawping at that fellow? You're spooking him, my dear boy." He added something in rapid German, and the street-sweeper looked over at him, nodding slowly.

"What's he –?" I asked. "What's he *doing?*"

"Sweeping the streets, you goose."

"Sweeping *what?*"

Albert was at my side, and slipped his arm through mine. "Rubbish, of course. What else? Come along." And he led me off.

After luncheon, Albert returned to the hotel for a sleep, but I did not feel sleepy. Instead I walked the streets, my mind pleasantly idle. I passed the old Leinwandhaus, which in English is *Draper's Hall*, a structure dating originally from the first half of the 14th century, and provided with a splendid array of turrets and pinnacles, recently restored. There was nothing about which to be alarmed. I was in a civilised city, with a purse full of gold, and a head full of learning. I had my guide book in my hand. God was in his heaven and all was as right with the world as I wanted it to be.

I took a seat outside a café on Hotzgarten and drank a glass of German beer in the sunlight. I brought out the Wells novel, and laid it on the table in front of me. Something about its oatmeal-coloured binding filled with me a sort of revulsion, and yet I felt the compulsion to begin re-reading it for a third time. I resisted this. No good would come of it. Instead I brought out the Baedeker, and read up about Darmstadt, attempting to determine whether it was worth detouring south of the river to visit that place.

My glass contained nothing but suds and air. The waiter removed it. He brought me another.

"You are a believer, I see, in the efficacy of Baedeker," declared a fellow from a nearby table.

I conceded that I was, and introduced myself. The stranger told me his name, and got up to reach across so that we could shake hands. He sat back in his seat. "It is always a pleasure to meet a fellow countryman when abroad," he said. He moved his chair round to face me better and wished me health with a sup from his glass. He was a pleasant-faced elderly fellow, with a grey-white beard trimmed to cover only his chin, and a broad pink forehead reaching, under some strands of brown hair, all the way up to the top of his crown.

"You do not use a guidebook yourself?" I asked.

"I find," replied my new friend, "that to tour a town with a guidebook in hand is to see only what the guidebook permits."

"There's no law that it must tyrannise us so," I countered. "One may stroll where one wishes! Only in *that* case, one will not know where one is, or what one is seeing."

"I fear I have expressed myself badly," said the man, with a queer little smile. "I do not mean that the Baedeker forces us to walk this street or that. I mean that we do not see Frankfort – we see only Baedeker's Frankfort. I mean, we tick off the things the book lists, and see them only as the book describes them. And when we leave, and think back, we find ourselves remembering not the city, but the pages of a book."

"There may be something in what you say," I admitted, laughing. "Is the choice so stark, though? Slavery of the mind – or ignorance?"

"Is that other book *The War of the Worlds*?" he asked.

"Do you know it?"

"Indeed I do. And think highly of it, I must say."

"It fills me with a strange dread," I blurted, and as soon as I said it I realised the truth of it. Dread clung to the book like a smell. I nudged it away from me with my knuckles.

"Do you mean," the man asked, "that you fear Mr Wells' predictions might come true, and Martians lay waste to Woking? I know Woking, sir, and figure the possibilities for post-bellum architectural improvement would outweigh the inconvenience!"

"You are from there?"

"Ascot," he said. "You?"

"Chelsea. But, no, no, you are right to mock."

"I beg your pardon indeed if I have done anything so ill-mannered!"

"Not in the least. Most kindly, rather, you have pointed out how small my nonsense is," I nodded. "Still: it is not as prophecy that the book upsets me. There is an... uncanniness to the narrative. Or not even the story: just to the material *fact* of the book. I am," I added, moved obscurely to confess myself to this stranger, "touring the Rhine cities with a friend of mine. There is much for us to enjoy, and many fine sights. And yet sight increasingly fills me with –" I stopped speaking.

"Dread?" he prompted.

"Such that I almost wish – Providence forgive me – to be blind, that I might never again have to worry about what *can be seen*."

The man was silent for a while, and drained his glass of hock and soda water. The waiter, hovering behind, approached; and the fellow ordered a new drink – in French. "I speak no German at all," he confessed to me.

"My Deutsch is rudimentary, I fear. Though I have enough to order a drink, thank God."

"Fortunately for me they all speak French hereabouts. I understand," he continued, looking directly at me, "why you are fearful."

The acidic bubbling sensation sparked-up in my gut. My heart began to beat faster. "You do?"

"I have seen what you see. Books like *that*," and he tipped his chin at *The War of the Worlds*, "are something of a favourite of mine. Scientific romances."

"You have not seen what I have seen," I said, in a trembling voice, "because I have not seen anything."

"And neither have I. And no more have all the hundred-thousands who live in this city. And still we see. They," he added, looking upwards. I actually (it makes me ashamed to say it) scrunked both my eyes tight shut, rather than follow his gaze. "They – are not hostile, I think."

"I might hope you are correct," I said, in a small voice, "I must fear you are not."

"Mr Wells has clearly seen them clearer than most," the stranger agreed. "And he thinks they come to wage war. But I wonder if – if they mean only to greet us. To say hello. And in their incomprehensible implacability they continue trying to greet us, as a fly butts his hairy head over and over upon the pane the glass. Or do they comprehend how difficult it is for *us* to meet *them*? Is that why they persevere so – could it be from kindness?"

The waiter returned with a new glass of hock-and-soda, gave us a stiff little bow, and retreated inside again.

"Perhaps it is as difficult for them," I said.

My new companion nodded once, twice, long deep nods, as if this were a new thought, and he was pondering it. "What if Mr Wells stands at the head of a new form of storytelling?" he said.

This provoked me to a sharp speech close to rudeness. "That trash? Never – never! Sir, forgive me, but I consider myself something of a *literatus*, and Mr Wells has no posthumous reputation to which he can look. Read the novels of Henry James, or of George Meredith, or Gissing, and then read this novel, and then tell me which is truer to life!" I was growing heated, and took a sip of beer. The stranger was looking intently at me.

"Truer to life is the point, of course," he said, in a distant voice. "True as a straight line is said to be true. True as a portrait is said to be true. Unless the cosmos itself is so constituted that the portrait precedes the sitter? Schopenhauer believed Will the structuring principle of the universe; and what is Will if not the idiom of mind? Well, then, it might not surprise us if the physical sitter, on his stool, in his artist's studio, finds his nose changing length, or his eyes moving further apart, or his hair-colour darkening, as the portrait dictates." I must have looked aghast at such a suggestion, and the fellow laughed.

"Of course, it's nonsense!"

My heart lightened. Of course it *was*! God was in his heaven, and all right with the world. I was touring, in the grand manner. The man I loved was asleep in the hotel, and soon I would return to him. I had seen nothing untoward.

"To repeat myself, though," the other fellow said, musingly. "What if Mr Wells *does* stand at the head of a new form of storytelling? If he does, I'd wager many more people will… see. I'd wager the newspapers would fill *up* with accounts of strange beings, and lights in the sky, and tentacles and I know not *what*. But I daresay you are correct, sire. I daresay the twentieth century belongs to Mr James."

We parted on good terms. On the way back to the hotel I went to the Opernhaus, and purchased two tickets for the evening's performance.

Zeta Reticuli

Paul Cornell

On September 19-20th, 1961, on a road in New Hampshire, Barney and Betty Hill were the first people to experience the modern version of what would later come to be known as 'alien abduction'. They recalled many details of their experience, including Betty's detailed image of a 'star map', only under hypnosis. In 1968, an amateur astronomer called Marjorie Fish constructed a three dimensional map of nearby stars and claimed that a match for Betty's map could be found from the point of view of the multiple star system Zeta Reticuli.

Nn is watching for where it knows the faint star will rise. It hasn't lost its knowledge of the stars, despite the degradation. This star is special, of course. To Nn, if to nobody else. It's a puzzle to Nn that so many have become so obsessed with what was done near that star, with what they allege has come from that star, and yet they don't connect that to the star in the sky itself. They don't point at it and say there, that's where this fear is from. They don't know where it can be found.

Nn likes this time in main morning, before the pollution from the manufacturing burrows closes down the sky. On minor mornings, when only the small sun is up, Nn sometimes can't make itself leave its tiny gifted pod. It just stands there, thinking about finality. It does not have to work. Opting for gifted consensual degradation gave it that, at least, and a handful of plant at meal time. Nn remembers when there were three plants. They had three even on the expedition. It remembers itself and the rest of the crew eating the other two plants offhandedly, unaware that this would become a luxury. But of course the instruments with which they navigated were already a luxury, even the walls they were contained within. So much so that the pod had been taken apart and melted down soon after they'd returned, metal being much more important than history. History is now the rarest luxury of all. Instead, there is myth. It is Nn's fate to stand on the border between those two things.

Nn hopes that today, as it makes its way, as usual, in the day-long walk it takes for recreation and in the hope of finding plant leftovers, nobody will recognise it. Nn has sometimes been stopped by those with mental degradation, who want to hiss loudly in its face, but they are not the worst. The worst are the drones with theories about Nn's mission, usually that the grand burrow are hiding something about what happened, or, worse, that Nn must know all about the Barney and Betty, and what they are here to do, and is keeping a secret that Nn for some reason will suddenly reveal to them.

Nn is continually amazed that they are concerned about these things but not about the degradation all around them. The lifetime of a new drone is set shorter each year. Their worries about the expedition are artificial, have been constructed. Nn's own fears about it are grown inside it. Nn has come to think that the constructed fear is there to immunise these drones against real fear. Nn wakes from the first state of reality almost every night to find itself in the second, still in those memories. It then has to will itself into the third state, before it really wants to, to get on with the day before the day has come. Memories live in Nn like a parasite.

They were lost, that was the most terrible thing. They were the first of their kind to go out there, and they made their tunnels between the stars, and they placed beacons, as their people had always done when going on expeditions on the surface, of the world or of the universe, but they had lost the last beacon, and were despairing of ever getting home.

They had taken the pod in and out of the second state of reality, putting their heads into the soil and out again, as the metaphor went, afraid to be seen by the creatures of the world they had found, amazed and scared that those creatures were so like themselves: two arms; two legs; and the eyes –! Nn still felt that fear every time it thought of them: those small, inscrutable eyes with tunnels in the centre of them, like the thing was looking right into you, with a flap of skin so they could withdraw their attention, so that they were in control of who they admitted into their third state of reality. Nn had heard in the clickings along the tunnels, from experts, that it was now thought that biological material from that world where life was so ancient might have had time to drift as far as their own suns, might have seeded or bonded with the earliest life in the burrows. The creatures of that world they had visited, the only life the expedition had found, were the ancients, the creators. Nn thought the myth that had grown around them was about the feeling that the expedition had disturbed them, as a newly hatched drone disturbs the hatcher. Nn feared for the young picking out those clicks from the hiss of the nightly sharing. No wonder this myth preyed on so many of them, seemed to make them mad. There was the feeling in the air of the tunnels that they were being punished. Nn could remember from his own earliest days when that hadn't been so. Or at least when it hadn't felt as overwhelming. Or perhaps that was just how the newly hatched always felt. Perhaps the sense that reality was punishing the conscious was a universal thing.

The leader of the expedition – it was dead now, they were all dead but Nn and perhaps Ghh, Nn hadn't asked after it in the clicking – had decided they should set down in the third reality and interact with the creatures of the world they had found themselves falling into the burrow slope of. They might find out where they were, and how to get home. They had put on their uniforms, their luxurious caps and suits, all in the black of the night, the same they had been seen off in with glorious hisses and clicking that had vibrated around the whole world. Nn wondered if they had hoped to impress these huge beings, that this sign of their importance at home was meant to translate. As if one could ever impress that which hatched you.

The crew had waited by their pod, the lights on it wastefully full on, for one of the pods they had observed to approach along an artificial trail. Nn remembers those lights, white in the strange air of that world, that to their amazement they could breathe, unlike that of any other world they had found. The thought of the lights reminds Nn now of how quickly light information is degraded as it leaves a world, how what had been clickings sent on the electromagnetic spectrum became noise, almost before the final edge of the burrow slope of any drone worlds around a hatcher star. What their lights had been trying to say was that they were important, that their visit to that world was meaningful. Who knows if the Barney and Betty had got that message, or if they had heard something else? Who knows what their world had made of it? Every now and then, Nn wonders if the myth can somehow be true, if the Barney and Betty are really –? But then it stops that seed thought inside itself, feeling that there is the path to final degradation.

They had spaced themselves out across the trail, like young drones aiming to catch a beast, when there had been beasts. Nn remembers the taste of the air, so full of water and plant. There was too much of everything here. The head of the expedition had joked that they might annex this world, if they could only work out where it was, because it had so much that was needed back home. But none of them had thought that was possible. The thirteen of them were the most their world could manage to put out into the dark. They had found ways to many stars, but no matter what the plant at the end of the tunnel, they could not see how it would be possible to make more pods like this to follow them. Even then, they had known that. The expedition had been a way for the grand burrow to say they were big, and now here were Nn and his comrades, doing the same against the gods.

They had waited, across the track, trying to muster their authority. They had waited for something to arrive that they knew would be terrifying. But then they had not known just how terrifying it would be for their world.

Then there had been answering lights in the distance. Nn had waited, breathing only a little, trying to get information from those lights. The pod had appeared, and slowed, coming to a halt as the creatures inside it saw the lights that said something was across the track in front of them. Nn had joined with the others in clicking from his brain, making the electromagnetic messages that encouraged its own people to move from the third state into the first. The pod stopped, its lights went off. Nn and its comrades paused, clicked to each other to be brave, to approach. Nn remembers that it was the first to move, but that might be just the signal degradation of time. Nn got to the pod, and looked in through the transparent part of it... and saw them.

They were enormous, at least twice as tall as the tallest of Nn's comrades, and they were full citizens then, fed on three plants, who had eaten beast. The creatures wore luxuriously varied clothes, many different colours and textures. Their faces were big as beasts, their mouths and noses enormous, to eat all this world had, to breathe this big wet air. Their skin colours were both opposed to the beautiful varieties of grey that Nn's people were hatched in for their lives in tunnels, another startling luxury: one was much lighter, one much darker. Their bodies were different to each other too, varied in shape in multiple ways.

That was the first time, as they turned to look at Nn, with expressions that Nn could interpret, to some degree, as that of stunned beasts, and so it knew the clickings had been effective... that was the first time Nn had seen those eyes. They bored into it. They sought to make a connection, to impose their meaning on Nn, who couldn't close its own. It was as if they threw meaning imperiously around them, wasting it, splashing it. They seemed startled not to have done so in this moment, having done so all their lives. Nn forced down its fear and clicked to them to get out. They did, their shadows impossibly huge on the track. Nn reached up a hand, its own fingers so thin, and took the enormous hand of one of them in its own, and led her, because they were about to find, as with some of the extinct beasts, that this was a her, towards Nn's own pod.

They had taken the pod and their visitors and their pod out of the third state as soon as possible, in case another pod came along, and brought too many creatures to deal with. The creatures slowly asked questions, in their loud voices. Their language was expansive, so many sounds. The leader of the expedition clicked into them again, found that language, and then they at least had the sense of what was said. The leader spoke to them in their own tongue, its voice quiet and sibilant in comparison to how they said the same words, and it had to avoid some sounds it couldn't stretch its mouth to say. It asked questions about what they knew of astronomy, about whether a number of specific multiple star burrows could be seen from this world, about where the biggest electromagnetic source in the sky was. The creatures could hardly answer, had the same limited knowledge of what they did not need to know as any drone did. Nn remembers feeling angry at them: these were not all wise hatchers; they would be no help in getting home. That feeling has been lost as the myth was made into artifice by repetition. The crafters wanted to examine the creatures for their records, as was their duty, so what they would find out to be the male, what would later become known as the Barney, was led away by them, while the leader showed the female the map of burrows that the expedition had built up during their wanderings. It showed the eleven worlds they had burrowed to. She looked at it for a long time, but seemed bemused, her huge finger wandering just as lost across it, taking no message from it. Nn remembers wondering at the time if these two were degraded by their world, were, to whatever extent, victims of it, if the expedition had the bad luck to pick such as that. But it had put the thought from its mind quickly: they brought such luxury with them, would any who were hatched into such excess ever be degraded? This one was the Betty, or rather she was not the Betty yet, she was just Betty, as she had called herself, Betty Hill. Dee dee dee. Nn can still recall the leader's voice buzzing strangely as it repeated the expansive and formal name. The huge name of a god.

Nn took Betty into the other part of the pod, where the crafters were examining Barney. They had inserted a needle into his strange sexual organs. He was protesting, weakly, which had put the crafters on edge. They were worried that he might move back into the third state, and attack them, and then all would be lost. They drew out the needle, and projected what they had found onto the wall. Nn saw the horrid, scuttling shapes of how these creatures reproduced. The males threw this stuff out, and it could infect any female that got it inside them. The crafters told Nn that only one of these millions of cells would successfully mate with an egg. They had that from Barney's knowledge. It was, again, frighteningly expansive, an obscene waste. The crafters told Barney to lie face down on the table, and inserted a rectal probe. They sampled what he'd eaten. The screen revealed such variety, so many sources, so many flavours that seemed to have no point except pleasure.

Betty was looking on, with a huge expression on her face, her feelings so obvious, as if she was projecting herself on the wall. It was actually a little hard to look at her. She seemed to occupy so much more space than her physical body did. The crafters told Barney to get up, and started to soothe Betty into getting onto the examination bench. They did this carefully, fearfully, and finally, her expression changing into something between emotions that was a shout and yet at the same time nebulous, she did so. They examined her womb with the needle, and, to Nn's relief, she wasn't carrying a child inside her. Nn squirmed at the idea of these creatures doing that. It was so unsafe. As if they felt able to waste their children as well.

Now, Nn sees the star appearing over the mound of a burrow to the east. It should feel a chill because of it, but over the years the fear has become Nn's touchstone, its only certainty. This world, running down, its people and history draining away, hasn't got much mythology left. What it does comes from that place. Nn is pleased, almost, for a moment, that it found that for its people. But no, it's a burden, something that mocks them as they die. Nn wonders if the creatures near that star remember them. The expedition tried to click into Barney and Betty that they shouldn't. But how certain could they have been that such big brains would obey? Perhaps they should have treated them more gently. Would things be different if they had? Nn keeps trying to find reasons for the myth. But perhaps myths are built because of different processes than reason. Perhaps myths are from the second state of reality.

Nn watches its star rise for a while, until the light of great dawn is in the sky, then begins its usual round. Things are as they always are to the extent that, as usual, Nn finds itself spending much of the time in the second state, its body just doing what it usually does, head popping out of the burrow only when something unusual is sighted on the daytime trail. It is towards the end of the day when it sees something surprising ahead, and it takes a moment to realise what it is seeing.

Here is Ghh, another member of the expedition. It is alive after all. Ghh is from a distant burrow, but Nn has often thought that it could go and see it if it really wanted to. Not wanting to is from the first reality and wanting to from the third, and that border is also one Nn stands on. Still, here Ghh is. Nn raises a hand and Ghh looks surprised to see Nn, not displeased on the surface, but certainly shaken inside.

They talk, initially, about their lives now, but there isn't much to say. They talk about the expedition. Nn realises, with horror, that Ghh believes the myth. "We disturbed something," says Ghh. "Strength like that, has to be a beast, following what hurt it back to its home. What a waste of what it has otherwise. Think about it."

Nn argues that the creatures would have come in force. That there is no reason for them to behave as Ghh thinks they are doing. They have so little. Surely if they came, they would come to save. Or, if not, to conquer.

"That wouldn't punish us. They'd have to look after us then, to actually be hatchers. They punish and run."

By the end of the conversation, Nn is very tired. It asks Ghh how its degradation is going. Ghh says not long now. Nn wishes it well, leaves it knowing they will never see each other again. Nn leaves Ghh with no means of finding it, which makes sure of that, really. Nn returns to its burrow alone as the light is fading.

Nn fastens its burrow and stands in the darkness, listening to the clicks and the hiss from down the tunnels. It stays in the third state a long time. It wonders if there is a sort of signal that can also be a creature, that can take a culture repeatedly, continually, across the universe, that is so proud that it does not have to hide and burrow. If they are coming here, it thinks, it's good, in a way, because that means they must be striving to understand this place.

The seed has been planted. Nn lets itself drift off into the second state, and finds itself again back at that night. It moves into the first state and sees the universe, consciousness inside it, spreading out, thinning, being wasted, maintaining coherence only through the stupid will of those who can close their eyes.

Nn knows what's coming. It shifts back into the second state, then quickly into the first, at unexpected light.

They have entered through the wall. They stand there, imperious expressions filling the room, unknowable and yet insisting that they will be known. Here are Barney and Betty Hill. Nn doesn't try to run. It wants to know what they bring. It only hopes they bring something, even if only meaning.

They step forward and lay hands on Nn and lead it quickly over the border.

The Ambulance Chaser

Tricia Sullivan

Faugh, the smell! I've only been here a few seconds and already I want to make my excuses and go. Your car has one of those petrol-station air-fresheners in the shape of a tree. It interacts foully with the scent of your chocolate-digestive-biscuit farts. That your intestines are hot and disturbed I notice immediately, but you don't notice me. You are as blissfully unaware of my arrival as you are of the looming danger that I've been summoned to handle.

I begin evaluating your physical thresholds, since in all likelihood I will be required to violate them in some way. I can trick any human body into high performance in an emergency.

There must have been some dreadful mistake. Your body must be eighty of your Earth years old. And what have you been doing all that time? Smoking cigars and drinking scrumpy? Your arteries are a mess. Osteoporosis has compromised your spine, so that you can just about peer over the steering wheel as you wobble through the village at 20mph. At least you're wise enough to drive slowly; you have the reflexes of a drunken warthog.

Well. What a brave new world this is. For me.

You leave the village speed barriers behind, finally accelerating to what seems to be your top speed of 40 mph on the rural A-road. That's when the pocket of intestinal gas starts to swell your rectum. You try to lift your bottom off the seat to let the gas out, but it's not quite. . . ready. Sometimes these farts need to be coaxed. You need a bit more leverage, don't you? You take your left foot away from the clutch (where you have the appalling habit of resting it lightly – my sympathies to your mechanic) with the intention of bracing that foot on the floor so you can straighten your left leg and hold yourself off the seat while you bear down with your anal sphincter.

There's a lorry in your rear-view mirror. Much too close. You see it.

"Bloody lorries –"

You initiate what is surely a familiar torrent of invective as you press down with your left foot in an effort to get that wind out.

I think it's time to make myself useful. Now or never. I flow into your tendons and brainstem and the surfaces of your skin. Not a moment too soon, because your left foot has stepped on the brake by accident. Out comes the fart. The lorry sounds its horn, an immense bellowing that overwhelms even your dull senses and makes you startle. Now you're all confused. You try to correct your mistake, but you can't remember which foot is which. The lorry makes contact with your rear bumper even as you step on the accelerator to get away.

You step on it hard, but the bump from the lorry has sent you across the middle of the road. You're up to 70 mph when you come round a sharp bend. As luck would have it, a pair of cyclists are riding abreast coming the other way, and a Land Rover is gearing up to pass them, and –

Fortunately I have already got into your brainstem. Hello, that's me. *waves* Your sense of timing is atrocious and you are afraid of your own shadow, but I know what I'm doing. Getting out of this alive requires precision steering, a tightly locked feedback system between your eyes and hands, and judicious use of the brake. None of which you can do. There is no guard rail on the left. Just a thread of dirt and a lot of trees that you really wouldn't want to hit.

"Oh Mary mother of shit!" you're shouting, eyes wide. I'm working the parking brake. Your Astra goes up on two wheels and then lands in a series of bounces. The Land Rover brakes and pulls in behind the cyclists, tyres squealing as its driver fights the wheel. In your rear view mirror it can be seen sliding off the road and into a hedge. Your hands are letting go of the wheel and seizing it again in a series of jerks so rapid that they seem digitized. You are now completely on the other side of the road, facing incoming traffic. I pump the brakes, I steady the wheel, and I get us back on the left. I slow the car and put on the indicator.

Then I leave you to it. You manage to have a small crash trying to get yourself into the layby. This is a sort of afterthought; you're not hurt, but you do take out a bit of hedge. The lorry piles past you as though nothing's happened, but your pine tree air freshener has flipped up and is wedged between the rear view mirror and the ceiling of the car.

After this there is a lot of standing around by the roadside, officials in hi-vis attire, you dazed and curiously exhilarated. No one has been hurt. Everyone is astonished at your performance. You blame the lorry driver for everything. Of the fart you mention nothing.

Well, it's time for me to leave. Your body is exhausted. You are shaking and sick. My work is done.

And then. . . and then. . . but this can't be right.

I can't get out.

I can't get out.

Your nightmare is over but it would seem that mine's just begun.

The police drop you off at Rose Cottage, a semi-detached stucco residence beside the village post office. They offer to call someone to come and stay with you but you brush them off. The moment the door shuts you're pouring... what is that? Tell me it's not Pimm's.

"Why do you have to be such a piss-taker?" You say this aloud, and then you suck down a fairish slug.

Piss-taker? I'm afraid you're too thick to realize that the manner in which I present myself is limited by your inboard parameters of what constitutes a being, and yours are defined by some queer mixture of ITV and the Queen's Christmas Message. If I'm a piss-taker it's because you've made me that way.

You shudder as the drink goes down. "Don't blame me. Mind your manners."

You pour another one and reach for... oh, not the chocolate biscuits. You wouldn't.

You would. You run a bath and take the bottle and biscuits with you. You start ringing everyone you know and telling them all about your exploits.

I'm feeling a little panicky myself by now. I've never, ever got stuck inside a human. I didn't even know it was possible. You lower yourself into the bath, aching all over.

"I don't care," you say to the phone. "It was worth it. Never knew I had it in me."

You don't have it in you. I overrode your thresholds. Your body isn't meant to do any of that.

You put the phone down.

"What do you want with me, anyway? I'm not religious, you know. If you think you're going to control me you can just bugger right off."

I'm not interested in controlling you. I'm not good with fine motor skills, anyway. I couldn't, for example, make you type or speak. It's not in my remit.

"Your remit. And what would that be?"

Not allowed to say.

"What is this, Star Trek? My love, we're stuck with each other now. Might as well come clean. I know you're an alien, so what gives? I assume you're not here to knock me up!"

At this point you emit a cackle so piercing that it hurts your own ears.

What makes you think I'm an alien?

You laugh and laugh and laugh. It's unsettling, actually.

Days pass. We lie on your settee watching *Escape to the Country* and *Fat Families*. When the teenager next door practices drums, you turn your volume up past the distortion tolerances of the equipment. You beat on the wall with your shoe.

It seems the cyclists have been talking. The local paper phones to ask if they can do a piece on your remarkable piece of stunt driving.

This is a very, very bad idea. Drawing attention to us this way.

"Us?" you say, interested. "I didn't realize we were an *us*."

Then you tell the reporter to bugger off. She rings back the next day. Then she comes to the door.

You stagger outside, still aching and a bit bruised, and show the reporter the bit of pavement where the traffic tends to mount because the road is so narrow. You tell her she should be writing about this in the paper and not about you. But she's not interested.

"Do you think postmenopausal women are underestimated?" she asks you, earnestly.

You shut the door in her face.

"Where do you hail from, mate?"

You did not just call me mate.

"You heard me. Where do you come from?"

I come from inside your consciousness.

"You saying I'm delusional?"

I'm a mathematical being. Mathematical intelligence permeates everything around you. It's in the leaves and the ocean and the magnetosphere; you just don't have a way to sense us directly. In time your descendants may evolve the ability to perceive beings like me. Mind you, at the rate we're going I wouldn't wager money on it.

"Rubbish. You're an alien. What planet. What star? My niece had a star named after her son when he was born. Do you come from the star David Mcgillicutty?"

How long is this going to go on? I have to find a way out.

"No, I suppose you'd call it something else in your language. Grvtthhzzng."

You wipe spittle from your lips.

"Anyway, I've been thinking. These powers I've got now. I could use them. Get a few things done."

You start by dying your hair black. I watch you do it in the mirror. You make a terrifying sight.

Then you get out a pad of paper and a red biro.

To-Do List
1. Install spy camera to catch Grant McKenna letting his dog poo on the football pitch at night
2. Sort out those awful drums
3. Get tattoo
4. Get Piercings
5. Mount campaign to slow down lorries near bus stop
6. Buy those boots what the punks used to wear
7. Put comfort insoles in boots
8. Storm Parliament

First you order a spy camera on the internet. That's easy. You feel well warmed-up after that so you decide to take on a more physical challenge.

You march next door to the house where the drummer lives. You pound on the door but no one answers. You're weighing options.

1. Purchase one of those ghetto-blaster radios. Are those still around?
2. Forget the idiot teenager. Drive into town and hit the tattoo parlour.
3. Wait a moment. No car. So both of those are out.
4. &%!* Aha! An idea.

You return to your own property and change your outfit. You go out through the back door and march down the garden to where your shed meets the garden fence. You push the wheelbarrow against the fence and stand wobbling inside it, peering over into the garden next door.

"I'll need some help with this," you say to me.

I have no intention of helping you break into your neighbours' house.

"Well, won't it be fun for both of us to spend the next two weeks in hospital if I fall and hurt myself," you say as you don a pair of gardening gloves to protect your hands from splinters.

Fine. With a growing sense of disbelief (and perhaps shame), I boost your neural activity. It's a bit like trying to get the Millennium Falcon into hyperspace: you feel like you're held together by sticky tape and wishful thinking. With my help you heave your hips over the fence, flinging yourself into the flower bed on the other side. You land on your feet (I'm that good).

Breathing hard, you approach the back door. No, that's out of the question.

"Do it, Alien. Do it or I'll do it myself, and I'll probably fall and get hurt."

I'm not actually sure I can do it. You're not a very large person, and it's a solid door, deadbolted because the neighbours are at work all day.

You start looking around for something to smash the window with. It occurs to me that I could calm you down, put you to sleep, if I were any good at that sort of thing. It's not my area. I usually work in war zones and natural disasters. Besides, if you were to fall asleep in the garden in the cold and the rain, well – oh, I'm losing my grip now. Nothing like this has *ever happened* to me. Not ever.

"Stop moaning and help me." You take a couple of steps back and address the door, head down like a bull pawing the sand. If a bull were wearing a lavender tracksuit.

Oh, all right then.

It's not that you're too old – your species is related to apes, and all of you have untold strength that lies untapped. No: it's that you don't have a strong enough impression of what your body needs to do. Given a clear impression and the right neurochemical juice, even your stringy unused body has the necessary resources.

I light you up. It's your rate coding that determines your physical capabilities, and I can make your body release the neurochemicals that characterise psychotic rage or the euphoria of PCP. I give your CNS the neural impression of you taking out the door, and it calculates force vectors and chains of joint angular alignment without conscious effort from you. Your brain takes care of business. Me, I'm there in your tissue, overriding the Golgi tendon reflex that prevents your muscles from over contracting lest they be ripped to shreds – a big enough electrical impulse coming down that muscle can tear it and even break a bone, but you claim you don't care and I know you're going to need every bit of power you can get. I give it to you. You push your upper body back and your hips shoot forward; your right leg hits the door and, at just the right moment, I throw the extra impulse into your muscles so that your foot accelerates through the plane of the door. You reel away, watching as the whole thing flies back with a *whoof!* Right off its hinges.

That was rather well done, though I say so myself.

Upstairs in the teenager's room, you have a good snoop around. You take a box cutter out of the pocket of your tracksuit. You eye the drums. Then a shadow falls across you from the doorway.

"Get out of my room or I'll call the police."

You laugh.

"Whose side will the police be on? Yours? Look at the state of you. I can't even tell if you're a boy or a girl. I seem to remember you were a girl."

And you actually poke at the teenage drummer's chest to try to prove it to yourself. She slaps you away and the movement jogs the computer mouse. A screen full of code comes up. Hmm. Someone's more than just a drummer.

"Mrs. Mcgillicutty, put the box cutter down."

You realise you're still holding the box cutter. It would have been so satisfying to slash those drums. Thwarted, you feel like crying and then remember that you're a superhero now.

The code is a phone app. It's a game. Not the addictive kind that makes people crack their screens with their fervent thumbs. A new kind. And there's a beauty to it. It's striking. I'm transfixed. I'm sure there's something to this. This young person is special.

The teenager is furious, though. She stands between us and the screen, blocking our view.

"How did you get in? The back door's been broken down. What's going on?"

"These bloody drums are a menace. I've had enough of them." You hold up a pair of noise-cancelling headphones. "It's all very well for you, isn't it? You put these on, but what about the rest of the neighbourhood? How about passing some of these out to all of us?"

"I thought you were hard of hearing. Sorry."

You *are* a bit hard of hearing. Remember the time you thought the councilwoman on your doorstep was an anti-pornography campaigner and gave her an earful?

"You –? You thought –? How bloody hard of hearing would I have to be? I'd have to be in Ecuador not to hear your godawful racket!"

Out comes the box cutter again. No, I'm not helping with this. I quite like a drum solo, myself. Besides, you can't win here.

"Mrs. Mcgillicutty!" shouts the drummer. "Put that box cutter down! Put it –"

Second time this week for you and the police. Luckily no one is hurt. They take your box cutter away. They look at your jet-black hair and murmur to one another. You get a phone call from your GP asking you to come in for a check. In case there was an undiscovered head injury after the collision. You refuse. You hitch a ride on a moped and get tattoos on Tuesday. On Wednesday you pierce your nose. This puts you at number five on the list, so you go out to the shed and get some old plywood and a can of black spray paint that's been there for years. You start working on your protest sign.

"See, I'm not long for it, Alien. You saving me like that was a wakeup call. I'm not going back to mouldering in front of the telly. I have a few things to do before I pop off, and I'm going to see them through."

I don't know what I'm doing here. Why did I save you? Was it the cyclists I was saving when I controlled your body? Was it the lorry driver? Was some other event in the causal chain affected by my actions? These things aren't given to me to know; they aren't, in fact, knowable. There are too many uncertainties. I just show up and do my best to boost physical performance.

"But *how* do you know to save us?"

I can't explain that because you can only think like a human. Our intelligence operates at levels you can't access; for that matter, I can't access it while I'm on this mission. I'm just a function.

"So you're like one of those accident solicitors that advertise on Sky. An ambulance chaser. Profiting by other people's misery."

Is that your idea of thanking me for saving your life?

"Should I thank you? You saved me for some reason but you don't even know what it is. Maybe I'm going to be the next Hitler."

I wouldn't rule that out entirely. In fact, I just want to leave. I feel somehow that this whole situation is an operational error. But I'm stuck.

And you think I'm an alien but I'm the opposite of that: I have been here all along. *We* have been here. (We aren't exactly 'we', of course – but if you lumber my identity with your grammar, it's all I've got). We aliens – as you imagine us – we don't come from another planet and we don't travel in ships. We are everywhere in the universe, even here on Earth – but we're also just out of your reach because you lack the necessary level of abstraction to perceive us.

To help you get to that place where you will eventually be able to interact with our reality, we sometimes have to take a nip-and-tuck in time. We sometimes have to tweak causality just a little. Saves a lot of unnecessary hassle. Nobody wants another Permian-Triassic extinction; so inefficient. So I'm afraid we don't follow this so-called Prime Directive at all. If we think we can help you, we help you. Just like you move a spider out of the bathtub. Don't tell me you don't do that. I've seen you.

Think of us in terms of a serial killer, or a child playing hide-and-seek – we want you to find us. We want to get together with your intelligence and make ever more complex systems; we want to raise your consciousness and our own and that of all things – because consciousness wants to be bigger. It's a basic thrust of the mathematical universe: order accelerating to maximize entropy. Higher order is the way the universe gets dragged screaming into its own heat death – we are the fun part.

That, my dear, is *our* game.

"Well, turning us all into robots may be your game but my game is to get the traffic in this village slowed down. So come along."

You heft your home-made placard. It reads: *SLOW THE FUCK DOWN*. You had a little thrill when you painted the expletive. You stand on the strip of pavement outside Rose Cottage, beside your neighbours' front door. Traffic does indeed slow down. Drivers laugh and wave, but you are stony-faced, dead serious. Your skirt stirs in the breeze of passing vehicles; their wing mirrors just miss you. It takes all your strength to hold the sign because I'm not helping you.

The door beside you opens and the drummer steps out, earbuds in place, dragging a backpack full of schoolbooks. You and she perform an odd dance as she tries to get round you without being clocked in the head by your sign. She glares at you, then at it, and you say, "Are you going to video us, then? On your phone? I want to trend on You Tube."

She has removed one ear bud. She says, "You can't trend on You Tube, Mrs. Mcgillicutty. You trend on Twitter."

"Right. I meant that. Go on, take a video of me. This is for you, you know, and the other young people. It's only a matter of time before somebody gets knocked down on this road."

"I can't. I'll miss the school bus."

And she steps into the road to avoid your sign. The ear buds are back in.

A car swerves to avoid hitting her from behind.

Here we go again.

Everything is a bit hectic at this point. Swerving car. Oblivious girl. Coming the other way into the narrow bit of the road is a cement lorry at some speed, bearing down on the post office and its attendant houses.

Everything is in slow motion because of the enhanced sense of time that I've imparted to you. Even so, it doesn't last long.

The cement lorry driver sounds his horn full blast. You drop the sign in the road and shove the girl up against the wall with all the force. I am in your throat and your skin; I am in your spinal engine.

But then you surprise me. The girl is out of the way but you turn. You believe yourself invincible now.

You actually go back for the sign. You step in front of the lorry. You hold your palm up like a lollipop lady and you start to yell, *"Slow down!"* But you only get as far as *"sl –!"*

I can't teach your body to stop a cement lorry at 42 mph. Nothing I can do. The only crumb of comfort is that at least I'll be out of this compromising situation once and for all.

This is it. The end. Goodbye, Mrs. Mcgillicutty, and fare well, wherever you go.

And I'm out! What a relief. On to bigger and better things.

So now I'm going to tell you what I really think. Now that I don't have to listen to *you*, you stupid alien, it all comes clear.

Things always come clear when you're dead.

You thought you'd been sent to save me because somewhere in the causal chain, my death would have destroyed the technological whatsit that will bring my species closer to your kind... whatever they are, the Kvppthanggrnt, I guess. Apparently these matters are often mysteries. It's all that blah-blah, what you told me about the connective tissue that binds my species in abstract terms being far from obvious and other gobshite that I didn't really listen to because I was enjoying my Pimms.

Which reminds me. I'm going to miss chocolate digestives.

If I'm honest, I thought it was all about the drummer. She writes code, doesn't she? You were so interested in her computer. I thought: the loud teenager I saved will grow up to write some important computer thingie, she will become a cryptographer or the discoverer of something. You had me convinced she would make some kind of bloody contribution to the great movement of humanity towards a higher level of something-or-other.

But now that *I'm* in *your* body (such as it is – or actually, isn't) I can see the causal traces. I can look on that business you call time's arrow. I see the young drummer's whole future laid out. I see the pathways and I see the range of her possible deaths. *It's all hopelessly difficult for you to understand, dear* – is that what you said? Well, not anymore. The bottom line is, it wasn't important to save the drummer. It wasn't important to save the cyclists. It wasn't the other driver. It wasn't anyone I met or talked to in subsequent days, nor the driver of the lorry that I stood up to – he'll have nightmares for *years*, there was so much blood. Hah!

And it wasn't an operational error, either.

So why? Why were you sent to me?

What was it for? Eh? What's it all about, Alfie?

It's about you needing me. Because however you may sneer at me, however I don't seem to fit the job description, deep down I have what it takes to be a superhero. So what if I found out too late in life? I'll be at my best now I'm dead, and I'll be looking out for the people you decide to invade.

It's true. I can help you do your 'job' (if we can call it that) *better*. Do you feel me lodged in you just as you used to be lodged in me, hanging around making snarky comments? Yes, love, there is an 'us'. I'll be right here commenting when you jump into people's neural circuitry just long enough to help them dodge a bullet. I'll be sure and let you know when you're doing it wrong. No need to thank me for that, my love.

You can think of me like a good-will ambassador from the human species. If you want to save people, you need me with my *Strictly Come Dancing* metaphors and my 'Keep Calm' tea towels.

Dreadful, isn't it? I feel just the same as you. But I'm dead anyway, and beggars can't be choosers.

So let's go save some people. No; don't say a word. You do the neurochemicals, I'll do the talking. Don't try anything dodgy, or I'll fart. Now that I'm dead, you really don't want to smell that.

Lost to Their Own Devices

Adrian Tchaikovsky

This is what drones are for. This is what robots are for. But he had sent out the drones and he had sent out the robots. He had hundreds of hours of recordings currently being analysed by the ship. He had watched his little army of cameras and instruments march out and then march back. But there were some things a human being needed to do. Not for the history books, not from some old notion of racial pride, but for himself. Beyond the airlock was an alien world. Beyond the airlock were the bones of an alien race.

Not literally their bones. Probably they hadn't had bones, and any organic remains were long gone, as was most of the atmosphere and the geological activity of the planet's core. Dead; a dead world, and it had been so before Sellig even left Earth, before Armstrong had stepped onto the moon, before Caesar and Solomon and the lost cities of Sumeria.

Except not quite dead. Of that long-ago race, that lost species, one live thing remained.

"Commander Sellig, the airlock is ready for you now," came the careful tones of the ship's computer.

Sellig checked the safety readouts on his helmet's display. The computer had talked him through the risks he was liable to encounter, although it had not tried too hard to dissuade him. Perhaps it had more of a human perspective on things than he gave it credit for.

Standing in the airlock, he sensed the change of pressure as the air was pumped out and the alien atmosphere was pumped in. Methane mostly. Certainly there was very little free oxygen, and the geology suggested that there never had been, that the nameless race that had peopled this orb had possessed a quite alien biochemistry. Perhaps not even a biochemistry at all, Sellig mused. Perhaps there were no organic remains because there had been nothing organic to start with. *They could be all around. We might not recognise them as life.* But he didn't believe that. They had built in materials enduring enough to have survived the long, slow death of their world, the shrinking collapse of its star into a sullen cool dwarf. They had been human enough to leave permanent relics that he could look upon and know, *this is a place with walls, there was an inside and an outside.* Even that small commonality brought with it a wealth of information about what – who – the extinct aliens had been.

Convergent evolution. It could make them closer to a human mindset than the majority of species that ever arose on Earth.

The outer door slid open, and there was nothing between him and the alien expanse that one small step would not banish.

It should have felt like a giant leap, that step, but the scale of the looming ruins was such that he was dwarfed, made miniscule. The architects had not thought small; his imagination made giants of them.

There were certain staples of human construction that the aliens had not been concerned with, it seemed: straight lines, roofs. Either that or what he was seeing was only the bare scaffolding of their civilization and the rest had evaporated or rotted or sublimed, or... When Sellig strode forwards, he walked an erratic path between structures that resembled many-sided gourds reaching up until they split into what might once have been dozens of delicate sky-touching fingers. The majority of these had been lost to time, lending the apex of each structure an exploded, jagged look. A count of the sides and struts and other features revealed numerical patterns revolving around odd prime numbers. The material was something siliceous, with a complex interaction of other elements, and the whole bound into a crystalline matrix that the ship was still trying to analyse. There was nothing like bricks, no division into smaller components. Best guess was that they had been laid down at the molecular level, as though the entire civilization had been set out by a colossal 3D printer.

There were no colours. The surface of the dead planet was as grey white as that dead moon Armstrong had planted his puffy, insulated boot on. The structures were pale in the star's fading light. The exteriors were smooth, almost frictionless. Inside, the drones had found some evidence of what could have been decoration or writing or... something, anyway. The designs were incised in great dense swathes seemingly at random over the walls, almost invisible to the human eye save as a blurry shadow. At 1000x magnification they were revealed as intricate knotworks of lines, crossing and recrossing, looping and spiralling. The computer was analysing the design for repeated patterns, but so far it was the most abstract of art. Sellig had spent a long time staring at the enlargements, trying to connect with what he saw, but whatever response those minutely detailed inscriptions were intended to evoke would need to come from a mind, a heart, a sensorium quite unlike his.

"Show me a live one," he instructed the computer.

"Follow the drones, Commander," replied his one companion on this cold and abandoned world. One man and his operating system, against the hazards of a hostile creation.

A many-legged drone scuttled ahead, drawing him closer and closer to one of the great pod-buildings until he was lost within its shadow. Another thing the aliens evidently had no truck with had been doors. Each structure was entered from below through looping tunnels up to thirty metres long, frequently with both ends within five metres of each other, separated only by the wall. It was a mad piece of inefficiency to a human mind, but to the aliens it seemed to have been the only way to go about things. No two tunnels had the same pattern of loops or curves, no two tunnels met up with each other. The cross section diameter of every tunnel fell between four and five metres. Walking into that great vacant mouth gave Sellig a curious double jolt of atavistic fear: he was descending into unknown depths, burying himself alive; he was surrounded, all at the same time, with a great, inhumanly proportioned space.

The gourd-buildings themselves were divided by a multitude of internal walls, each barely more than a metre or two long, each running the full soaring height of the structure, so that the whole became a house of doorways, openings giving on to other openings until the centre was reached. Above, the pale gleaming substance of the structure faded into the eternally crepuscular sky.

We know almost nothing about them. We cannot know what they looked like, even something as basic as the building blocks of their metabolism, or their hereditary material. His wonderings peopled the past of this planet with winged gods.

But one thing we think we know. Because there was a single thing they had left behind, aside from the picked-clean skeletons of their buildings. *We think we know what happened to them.*

And now the drone had led him to the centre of the maze, where the anomaly rested in its depression on the pale floor like God's own dark marble.

It was black as a hole; emitting no visible light, but then the aliens did not seem to have worked with anything so human as our spectrum. Viewed through the instruments of the drones, it gave off just enough radiation for us to come up with a hypothesis. Scans suggested the interior was packed with a fractal complexity extending down to the subatomic level, a dense snarl of organisation far beyond anything our technology could accomplish in a thousand years. And it was live. It emitted some little energy and had to be consuming far more. The ship had hypothesised that at its heart was a wormhole to the system's sun. The ship had gone so far as to posit that this was the reason star had become the sullen dwarf it now was; the drain from this device and the thousands of others. They had killed their own sun, frozen their own world, to achieve this.

It was where they had gone. Not a portal to another dimension, not a doorway to distant stars: this lightless sphere contained its own worlds, worlds no doubt sculpted like clay from the quantum foam. The builders, possessed of a technology that would have made them gods to any lesser race, had looked at their planet, their solar system, perhaps even their galaxy-spanning empire, and they had found it wanting. So they had made something better, we surmised, and they had retreated inside it and pulled up the ladder so that nobody could follow them. They were still in there, somehow, living lives of infinite virtual potential. This was what the ship and I believed.

And perhaps, after sufficient study, we might even be able to open up their stately pleasuredome, and unravel the missing half of their story. Perhaps these were the aliens that we would meet, out here in the vast dark beyond our world. But not now. More patient and more educated human beings than I would have to study and puzzle and scratch their heads.

I reached out, but stopped short of touching it. Mere superstition: the drones had clicked their manipulators against its hard surface without yielding a response. There was no reason to think that some mystic commonality would allow the relic to recognize me as something more significant than their mere mechanisms. And yet my gloves held off, a few centimetres from the surface. In the end, I did not dare.

If only I could have brought one back to the ship! But the science teams would have to travel, to bring their blades to bear on this knot. Tests by the drones showed that the sphere, small enough to fit in two cupped palms, must weigh more than my entire ship. Data suggested it weighed so much that there must be some force preventing it from simply sinking into the substrate and down towards the planet's cold core.

I stared into the dark of it, willing it to show me something fit for human eyes: a gleam, a glint, the sight of distant stars. But there was nothing. The minds that had conceived this wonder had never conceived of anything as mundane as I.

And then the ship was speaking urgently to me.

"Commander, you must return immediately."

I started and stared around me at the bone-pale interior of the alien structure. "What is it – is there movement, an energy signature-?"

"Not on the planet, Commander, but long range watch drones have detected another ship entering the system. I have identified it as Allardi's *Chrome Star*."

Pirates. There would always be those more interested in theft than study. Allardi and I had crossed paths more than once, but I decided that this must be the last time. Moments later I was scrambling out of the alien relic's presence, bounding back to my ship. We had spotted Allardi. Had Allardi spotted us? Almost certainly. We needed to meet him in space, not slow and cumbersome within the planet's gravity well.

I was aware of a new tension within me as I hit the acceleration couch and gave the ship my orders. This would be the real test. Now we would see how things played out.

"Ready all combat systems. Adopt attack plan B," I instructed. Mere human reflexes were not sufficient to execute the manoeuvres of space combat, but human ingenuity was still a tactical ace in the hole, and I had planned for this encounter long ago. "On my mark, commence."

I felt the end of the turbulence as we cleared the thin atmosphere with unseemly haste and then the ship the ship the ship the ship the ship the ship the ship the ship the ship the –

The interior of the spaceship shuddered and stopped moving and a string of errors scrolled down the inside of his eyeballs. Malcolm ripped the headset off and came close to throwing it across the apartment in a fit of pique.

"Goddamnit, Stuart!" he shouted at the room. "You were supposed to have fixed this."

The calm voice of his Home Wizard said, "Do you want me to message Stuart Cochrane?" It was the same voice that the ship's computer had used, the game borrowing from his home systems for a fuller virtual experience. That was one of the little touches that kept Malcolm working with Stuart, despite the bugs and problems.

"Yes, tell him I have user feedback." He pushed himself off the experience couch and stomped some feeling back into his feet, which were jabbing him with pins and needles now that he was back in reality. The sensation was unsatisfactory. The body currently housing Malcolm Sellig wasn't a patch on the virtual frame of *Commander* Sellig.

"Have the Kitchen Wizard prepare a snack as well," he added. The couch had kept his body healthy and hydrated, but he always came out of a game session with a terrible case of the munchies.

"Hey, Mal!" Stuart Cochrane's cheery voice came to him. Malcolm's Communications Wizard stimulated his visual cortex so that he saw an image of the thin, angular man before him, working with the information Cochrane's system was sending over.

"Hey, Stu. Look, I've been playtesting FerMMO again –"

"It's great, isn't it," Stuart chimed in with his trademark enthusiasm for his project du jour.

"Yeah, look, it really is, good work man, but it crashes when you fight the pirates still. I reported that last time, and it still isn't fixed."

"Ah, crap." Stuart's image rubbed the back of its neck. "Man, I fixed that. It was working fine. It's a really good sequence... Have you changed your system specs?"

"Nothing," Malcolm told him. "You sure you actually fixed it, and didn't, I don't know, *dream* doing that?"

"It's on the log as fixed," Stu said. "Means I must have looked at it. If you don't trust me, trust the system, right? But something hasn't taken, obviously. Look, man, I'll make this a priority, okay? Very next thing that gets looked at."

"Great." Sensing that his friend might take all this a bit hard, Malcolm added, "But it's good, the rest of it, really goodSuch a *real* experience."

"That's what we're about, man," Stu agreed, grinning.

"I'm really looking forward to when we crack the anomaly, find out what's inside. We get to meet the builders, right?"

Stuart's eyebrows went up. "Hell no, man. That's the mystery. It's *alien*. Humans can't process what's in there, right?"

"But... *You* know what's in there, yes?" Malcolm frowned. "There's a, what, a logic, right?"

"Man, it doesn't need one. It just needs to be weird and alien and make you wonder."

"But..." Malcolm thought back over the four or five planets he'd explored in the game. "When do we get to see the actual aliens? Any aliens?"

"Man, you know why it's called FerMMO, right? The whole paradox thing? Humanity gets out in the galaxy, but where are all the aliens, yeah?"

"Look, I understand that," Malcolm put in quickly. "But surely you've scotched that already with us finding ruins and, you know, any trace at all. There isn't a Fermi paradox, because there definitely *were* aliens even if there aren't now. So, look, if you have *that* in FerMMO, then surely you can let us actually meet some, maybe way later on, but still... or it's going to be a bit of a let down after a while."

Stuart steepled his fingers. "Are you submitting that as formal feedback?"

"Er..." Malcolm was slightly thrown by the phrasing. "Yeah, I guess I am."

"I think that falls outside my parameters. I'll submit that to Mr Cochrane and he will have to decide whether to change his instructions to the Game Design Wizard."

"..." Malcolm just stood there staring at him for a moment, making a noise in his throat that didn't quite resolve into words, until he blurted out, "I thought I was talking to Stuart."

"You are speaking to Mr Cochrane's Social Interaction Wizard," the image of Mr Cochrane informed him. "Mr Cochrane has been playtesting FerMMO for the last two weeks."

"Two weeks, ah..." Malcolm tried to remember how many times

he had spoken to Stuart recently: quite a few. In fact, now he thought about it, he had found the man considerably more congenial than usual.

"Ah, well, yes, let him know. Tell him he can call me to talk about it if he wants... I'll leave some opinions with my own system if I'm, you know, occupied."

"Of course," said Stuart Cochrane's Social Interaction Wizard. "Did you have any other feedback?"

"No, er," Malcolm felt weirdly thrown, as though real life had cast up a string of error reports itself. "Just tell him, er, good work, man. It's really good."

"Thank you." The image's answering smile was so spontaneous and genuine that Malcolm wondered how he could ever have mistaken it for the real man.

After the call had ended, he looked about his apartment. He wanted to go back to FerMMO, but Stuart's Games Designer Wizard would be a good few hours sorting out its current batch of bugs. Perhaps something old school, Dragonhack or Stealthrunner... The couch beckoned, with all its myriad possibilities.

But the conversation with Stuart – or *not* with Stuart – had unsettled him, as though the ground he was standing on had proved unexpectedly brittle, about to give at any time. He wondered idly when he had actually last spoken to the man, the real man. Or anyone, actually. The games were theoretically all multiplayer, but the technology had advanced sufficiently that telling a player from a computer-run character was essentially impossible.

Discomforted, he went over to the window and lifted the blinds for the first time in what felt like an age. In his mind was the dead alien world with its impenetrable mysteries – impenetrable precisely because there was no mystery, just a set of tantalizing clues without a centre, designed to inspire awe without ever explaining themselves. *Didn't there used to be real mysteries...?*

He peered out of the window at the night above, but the sky was hung with so many blinking, blazing adverts and messages and animated images that he could no longer see the moon, let alone the stars.

In The Beginning

Gerry Webb

The beautiful patio garden exploded as a hail of bullets stormed in. Alex dived and rolled towards the French windows. Far too late. What saved him was the active glassite sunscreen he had put up only yesterday to help him work in the middle of the day when the suns reached full intensity. Meanwhile, statues, potted rare plants, wall mosaics, the lunch plates and glasses being carefully laid out by his butler Chivers and (*bloody hell!*), Chivers himself, erupted and jerked under the merciless volley of lead. Alex rolled through the drapes into the lounge and kept down until he reached his desk. Then he cautiously stood and hit the alert to his security section. He needed a few minutes to think and to catch his breath before his personal security arrived – he was getting a bit old for this sort of thing. He could do without the local guards crashing into the apartment so he left the general alarm well alone. There was clearly nothing anyone could do for Chivers anyway.

Alex was tall, still in good condition, and his fortuitous gene mixture had served him well, but flecks of grey were creeping into his hair and moustache. He stood quietly by his desk, looking at the beams of sunlight which found their way in through gaps in the heavy curtains to the patio, ten metres away.

First consideration: the neighbours. None of them would panic, of course. The families were a tightknit group and everyone in the senior citizens' complex was, by definition, experienced in such matters. The real trouble was that this was the first breach of security the new space colony, the Shepherd, had experienced, and it came disturbingly early. The cylindrical hull of the habitat had not even been completely populated yet.

Hardly surprising considering the vastness of the Shepherd. It was one of the largest (*Cleaver*) class of space colony and at the very limit of 'sensible engineering', well in excess of the *Rama* class. The six metre thick 20km diameter maraging steel hull allowed a standard Earth gravity for just under a third of a revolution per minute. A hull length of 100km allowed very generous estates for the 250,000 population on the inside of the cylinder even after the specified lighting, landscaping and services had been installed complete with hills, valleys, rivers and trees. The 10m of regolith that the Albion families specified for their comfort had been laid ten year ago and some of the estates were beginning to look impressive, up to the usual standard.

Even so, Alex and the other pensioners liked to keep apartments at the 85% gravity level in the terraces on the hemispherical ends of the cylindrical habitat so that cascades of gardens, waterfalls and views along the cylinder could be arranged. The shots must have been well-silenced and must have come from one of the places on the hemisphere where engineering work was still going on. The idea that any of his neighbours would harbour an assassin, even accidentally, was unthinkable, but he knew his security would cover everything anyway.

Second, his partner and the family. Clearly, communication of any kind to anyone at all should be considered insecure until the situation was clarified. He simply had to wait until his team had swept the apartment for any bugs. Luckily, his beloved partner of more than sixty years was 20km away, establishing their estate. He missed her badly and hoped everything was okay. Security would be reaching her soon in any case. Similarly, his known mistresses past and present would be discreetly informed and protected.

But what about poor Chivers? His 'gentleman's gentleman' had been willed to him by his father as part of his estate some years ago now. He had become far more important than a simple body slave, and had become a companion, secretary and honest advisor. He looked around. The sound of the fountains on the patio only emphasised the quietness,. Empty shelves, niches and display cases stared back. Who was going to unpack and lay out his collections now? Over the years Chivers had become as great an aficionado, if not greater, of the collectables as Alex himself. The treasures fell into three very different groups.

For himself, Alex collected literature, technical works and objects from the pioneering era of the space age, over 400 years ago. The pride of his collection was a DeHavilland *Spectre* rocket engine, already in its display case nearby. From it, both he and Chivers had derived their ultimate satisfaction – the envy and chagrin of fellow collectors. What else was collecting for? He was negotiating on the ultimate prize, a Reaction Engine's *Sabre* MK 1, although he couldn't imagine where they were going to put it. Perhaps he should found a museum? No. Perhaps in his will. This collection was definitely for himself.

For his partner there were the objects of fine art, enabling her to extract similar envy from friends and neighbours.

While he much appreciated the pleasure to be drawn from such popularly appreciated collectables, he was not drawn to them with any obsession and regarded them more as investments. He did, however, gain some satisfaction from the objects that originated on Earth even if they were comparatively dowdy compared with these from off-Earth artists.

These two collections, while interesting to those of similar tastes, were not definitive in any way. The third one was. With it, Alex could show off the reasons for the vast resources of the Albion Alliance: their mineral wealth. His mineral collection was second to none and his personal skill and management in directing the intelligent prospecting probes in their long trips around the outer solar system had established his seniority in the key councils and organisations of the colony. Foresight, skill, and choosing the correct business specialisations in the rush into the solar system in the early 22nd century had enabled the Albions to become, by the early 25th, one of the two dozen or so groups rich enough to afford the *Cleaver* class habitats. The gigantic hulls were built by Bond Engineering in their asteroid belt main complex, then moved anti-sunwards out of the belt to be fitted out to the bespoke orders of their wealthy owners. The Shepherd was the fourth for the Albion alliance and had begun its fitting out 10 years ago. As this neared completion, an order for the 5th, the *Gatland*, was already being placed. The Albions were, literally, astronomically rich.

Alex's collection was spread throughout the various boardrooms and meeting places of the alliance but he kept some of the most beautiful to decorate his personal quarters. Rare and exotic crystals, sectioned and polished rocks, unusual ores, the mineral wealth of the solar system in its uncountable variety waited in cases in the storerooms for him and Chivers to unpack. Chivers! *Pull yourself together and think. Behave as befits your patrician status.* He took a deep breath.

The big questions for security were: How? Who? And why?

Clearly, the patio had presented the only opportunity for a hit as all of the apartments in the complex had entrances which opened into a maze of corridors, buried in the inner hull, complete with all sorts of security devices. The private gardens, patios, balconies and windows of the complex faced down the length of the colony, to catch the view and the light. There were observation decks, bars, restaurants, libraries and other communal facilities under the stars on the outer hull, but entry there would be even more difficult than from the inward side. His thoughts were interrupted by the house intelligence in its contralto female voice. "There are personages outside entrance 3, sir. Considering their rudeness in advancing before being cleared, I can only assume they are your security team." Keeping well away from the drapes to the patio, he went through the second hull-side exit of the lounge, down 50m of hall and into a generously proportioned real-wood panelled entrance lobby. The viewers showed six personages outside – three of them human, two of whom were women. At his command, the door opened.

"Hi, Frank, why the fuck is one of your team wearing a dinner jacket? It's lunch time!"

"That's Jim. He's part of my personal team, but he was on temporary loan to the entertainment club on D deck. They were having trouble with some of the fitters and needed a good bouncer. I've brought him to look after you."

"Okay. I guess he can wear some of poor Chivers' gear. I'll show you where it is, Jim, as soon as I can move around my own bloody apartment."

While the two women with their specialised robot detectives moved briskly past to examine the scene, Jim bowed curtly, his artificial lines showing a little.

It was against Albion family law to build artificial beings that were undetectable. The words TIN! MAN! Across his knuckles helped. "Thank you, Sir. I am pleased to meet you."

Frank disappeared into the apartment with the rest of the team. Jim hovered, trying to look discrete while his sensors scanned for any anomalies.

A short while later Frank called them into the lounge, declaring it clear, and presented a summary of the situation. Despite looking like a younger version of Alex, he was not a clone (they were often used in security). He was, in fact, a grand-nephew: the Octavion to Alex's Julius Caesar. "We don't know who or why yet, but no other suspicious activity seems to have taken place over the whole of the Shepherd and none of the other counsellors or division heads have experienced any trouble. I would guess this may be personal or related specifically to our division's prospecting activities. You haven't annoyed any husbands lately? Don't worry though, the whole security division won't rest until we fully understand what went wrong and seal the gaps. We are at our most vulnerable right now, during fitting out. The assassins chose a very narrow window of opportunity to smuggle in whatever or whoever was needed.

"One thing we do know is that this wasn't a live shot but a rather elaborate booby-trap. We found traces of a remotely-triggered weapon at the edge of apartment complex, in a control room that's being readied for when the propulsion units are fitted. The weapon appears to have self-destructed immediately after the attack, presumably to cover the perpetrators' tracks. Our people are still trying to recover some identifiable bits.

"The trap was elaborate, tripped by that prize mutant gardenia you had delivered a couple of days ago. Its DNA is programmed to respond to *your* DNA when you sniffed it, triggering the remote gun to spray the dining area with bullets. You were set up by your own favourite flower."

"Bugger me," said Alex.

"Yes, they very nearly did. If you hadn't wandered off behind that screen, your bits would have been all over the patio with Chivers'."

Alex didn't need reminding.

"Whoever set this up," Frank continued, "they clearly didn't care who else was on the patio. It could have been your partner, kids, the CP even. Any ideas?"

"The chairperson is off colony, but point taken. As for who… If it's business, I think the most likely suspects would be the Lomonosov group. They're ruthless enough."

"Perhaps. But don't jump to conclusions. This looks like a one-off, a booby-trap that won't be tried again. But I'm still worried something else may be attempted. Can you stay put for a couple of days?"

"I have a council meeting in three days' time and my kids to teach tomorrow."

"Surely the kids can wait."

"No, they're important and I don't want to disappoint them. I like teaching and, above all, it's my duty."

"All righty, I'll try and fix it. We'll switch the class to a secure location. That should keep them safe. Even so, you will have to take Jim with you."

"Does he have to come into the class?"

"Yes. Why? Will he scare the kids?"

"No, not if he's out of that daft monkey suit. The kids are thirteen – they've got to get used to this stuff. It's going to be part of their life anyway. I just don't want to look wimpy."

Jim smiled and said in his bass voice, "Sorry sir."

Alex shrugged. At least his heavy had more brains than he did.

Frank said, "Three days from now we'll have a couple of drinks in the stellar bar and joke about this. In the meantime, you've plenty of space for the girls, detectives and Jim to stay here without even rubbing shoulders. They will tidy away the mess and take care of poor Chivers. Jim will stand in for him while the girls finish the investigation. Remember, even you have to conform to their requests at all times."

"I know, security before business before pleasure."

"What are you teaching, by the way?"

"We're halfway through a special course on the Fermi Paradox and its implications."

"Well, good luck with that. I'll let myself out and will be back the day after tomorrow. Just try to relax." Jim, in full butler mode, let him out.

The girls turned to him and one of them, Janet, said in a low but very feminine voice, "Councillor, please resume your usual routine. We shall try to be as unobtrusive as possible. If you have any special requirements, please let us know."

What an offer! But he managed a meek "thanks" and sat at the desk, desperately suppressing improper thoughts. Contacting a mistress was out, security-wise. It looked like an early night with cocoa.

At least in the morning he felt better for a good sleep. Jim brought him breakfast in bed and the news that, from an analysis of past comms, he had been the only target and, strangely, a break-in had been planned. Well, he knew how, but was not much closer to who and why. It was a puzzle. Burglary was four hundred years out of date. What the hell could they have wanted?

Jim, looking a bit more respectable, drove the car by his own route to the class, mostly down the body of the Shepherd. It was well before midday, the light from the three evenly spaced longitudinal strip suns yet to reach its maximum; even when it did, there was little danger of sunburn, the spectrum being carefully 'chopped' away from that of natural solar radiation to avoid general overheating of the habitat.

Jim sat discretely at the back of the class with the teacher, and after the kids' respectful 'Good morning, councillor', Alex asked, "Are all communications, robots, slaves, companions, outside?"

"Yes, councillor."

"Then you may sit."

He handed out the marked homework and then set a half-hour test on the last two lessons. All conducted with paper and pen.

A sense of pride filled Alex as he watched the children work. Since the space-age had reached its maturity around 300 years ago, with full human life cycles being lived away from Earth, 'space children' had become adept, first in those sciences and skills necessary for survival, and latterly in the philosophies, politics and cultures needed to prosper away from Earth. Therefore he was teaching to a far from naïve audience.

Signs of primitive life had been detected on extra-solar planets, so the lack of any evidence of intelligent life after centuries of search had increased the acuity of the Fermi Paradox. This was the third class in his series discussing the Paradox itself, after which the course went into the likely cultures, politics, or ideologies which would spring from either a positive or negative answer to Fermi's question 'where are they'? That's why only the elderly such as Alex were allowed to teach this subject – it was just too important. As the revered writer Arthur C Clarke had remarked over four centuries before, either a positive or negative answer to the question 'are there any intelligent aliens out there?' was philosophically shattering. He needed to get this part right. The fact that a third of the class were his great or great great grandchildren did not matter. He was a patrician, and godfather to them all.

He would steer the class towards a discussion of the intelligence-to-spacefaring terms of the Drake equation. If the answer to the Paradox was 'we are alone' the reasons for it would be somewhere there. It was a credible answer considering the wars and mayhem that had been endemic in all of human history and which had even intensified during the space-age. Perhaps, although humans had made it thus far, technical civilisation was still impossible in the long term. The weapons were just too powerful. Looking at the collapse at the start of the iron age (technical) the collapse of the classical world (ideological), the collapse of Islam (invasion), the world civil wars of the 20th century (socio/political), the collapse of solar civilisation only 200 years ago (the Resource Wars), it was easy to be pessimistic. The fact that each collapse had been more and more costly in human life and the degradation of ideals was not promising. The next collapse could be the last.

Still a few minutes of the test to run. He looked protectively at the kids. Sixteen girls, twelve boys. Patrician kids to be trained in the ideology and mission of the Albion founding families. And to be ready to die for them.

In the aftermath of the resource wars it had been decided to increase the male to female ratio, to allow some redundancy. The balance was approximately restored by the time they were forty. Males were somewhat expendable and usually assigned to the more risky functions of the colony while the females were doing the more important things such as government, security, and breeding. As with earlier tribal societies, when properly engineered this kept the ratio of dim or aggressive males acceptably low. In any case and in any generation, unfavourable gender ratios could be compensated for with slaves, lower clones, licensed human robots and so on. Gene enhancement had been banned 200 years ago. Nevertheless, it was clear that some colonial groups were cheating.

The test was finished, merits awarded and the planned discussion on the likelihood of technical, spacefaring aliens elsewhere in the galaxy began. He loved the beauty of the topic and the extreme demands of knowledge that it demanded, from physics to biology, intelligence, culture and politics. As always, the class discussed the vastness of space and what it would take for intelligent life to cross interstellar distances. In this century the kids had one big aid to concentration: robotic probes had already been launched towards half a dozen systems within twenty light years where lifesigns had been detected. None would be transmitting results until the kids were much older, towards the ends of their long lives. There were a few moments of silence as the implications of this sank in.

Then: "Sir, I will be old before I know if any interesting life exists outside the solar system."

"I'm afraid so, Richard."

"Why can't we live longer?"

"Actually, 140 is a pretty good span, half again what was thought possible before the space age and on the limit of what we can achieve."

"But the distances to the stars are so huge."

"Only if one is thinking on an individual human scale."

Lucy, one of his stars, took up the baton "But isn't that the only way we *can* think?"

"Again, only if we are dealing with things on our scale. To think outside that is difficult but not impossible, and with the disciplines of physics and maths to help us, we have discovered both the quantum and cosmic universes. The time scales are the real challenge. The impossibility of grasping minute quantum time-scales is clear, but most people fail to see how impossibly large cosmic time scales really are. In fact, these are a clincher for the Fermi Paradox."

He had their full attention now.

"As you know, standard propulsion bays with a nuclear engine and sufficient fuel can propel our colonies around the solar system. Mountings for such a unit are being fitted to the Shepherd at the moment. Now suppose that an extra-large engine is fitted, together with a container for the Helium 3 and Deuterium fuel as big as the Shepherd itself . Calculations show that with such an arrangement the Shepherd could be accelerated up to 1% of the velocity of light and so would be able to cross the entire galaxy in 10 million years."

"Now imagine that the Shepherd stops at the first opportunity and founds a colony, which then builds up wealth and sends out other ships, and so on. Oceania on Earth was colonised in this way. With quite reasonable assumptions, the galaxy could be completely colonised in 250 million years. I agree that the people who do this will evolve genetically, socially and ideologically and some will not want to go on, but galaxy-wide the diversification should be enough that some always will. Thus, even with the technology we now have, the galaxy could be colonised in only a fiftieth of its lifetime. So if starship building civilisations are at all possible, the Galaxy could have been colonised many times already! The problem is that we have never detected any signs of such intelligence in any way, either organic or machine. You can see how perceptive Fermi was to point this out in the 1940s."

Lucy showed her sharpness. "Does this mean that we're doomed because technical civilisation always fails for some reason and starships are never built?"

"Very good, and definitely something worth discussing in detail. However, this general solution to the Fermi Paradox is unlikely, as humans have lived and prospered in space for over 300 years, so many of the extinction threats are much lower than when we were confined to one planet. Both anthropogenic and cosmic threats are greatly reduced because we are now diversified into many different cultures throughout the solar system, although a galactic gamma-ray burst or black hole remain causes for concern. In fact, it is because of the latter that some of the absolutist religiously driven colonies are pushing for human seeding of the galaxy in some form."

"On the other hand, most of the less extremist groups such as ours reason that such cosmic threats are low enough to ignore until we can develop faster methods of interstellar transport. The data that we have seems to support us. If what you say is the answer, it would be more likely for a human rather than a cosmic factor to cause our downfall. If you consider the weapons used in the Resource Wars, just about everything that would have finished us if we had been confined to Earth, such as biological and nuclear weapons, were deployed. Not only that, but advanced machine intelligence subversion as well. Most of our security measures today are directed towards preventing our competitors or enemies (which is sometimes a fine line) from practicing similar subversion. However, the tendency for humans to fiddle with things just for the hell of it remains, even though hacking is one of the highest capital crimes. The last thing we want is any more kinds of robot revolution."

He glanced at Jim, who was doing his best to look harmless and smile benignly. The result was disturbing.

"Nevertheless, because we have survived all the types of self-derived threats that could have finished us on Earth, I am inclined to think that the human doom factor is probably overrated as the answer to the Fermi Paradox. It is, in my opinion, far more likely that the social civilisation, technical and other higher terms in the Drake equation are much smaller than most of the experts calculate."

Several hands shot up, but Lucy was first.

"Does this mean we are the chosen race?"

He waved the burst of hands down and brought the class to order.

"Let's not get messianic. I agree that some of the extremist groups are preaching this line and some are getting enough resources together to launch the robotic probes we discussed earlier. We calculate that it will not be long before one or two of them will be in a position to mount a human expedition, although whether these will be generational, hibernatory or simply seeding we cannot say. Our agents are working hard trying to find out. Not easy, as the most likely groups are pretty fanatical and suspicious of outsiders.

"No, the fact that we may be the first spacefaring civilisation in the galaxy does not necessarily mean that we are chosen. I think it simply means that we have been very lucky."

The lesson then veered into a discussion of various religious systems, proofs of God and so on. Just the sort of thing he enjoyed. Everyone over a hundred years of age was required to teach the history, cultural values and ideologies of the Albion families. He didn't know any of his friends who didn't just enjoy doing so but valued it. Nothing compares to learning from kids. In fact, Alex fully intended to accompany them on their educational trips to Earth, which were due soon. He would love the chance to visit a few museums of the early space age. His favourite had just acquired a fully restored *Skylon* and he would give a lot to see that.

At lunchtime he handed the kids back to the teacher. "See you in three days for history."

"Hope so. The kids always enjoy that."

On the way back, Jim carefully guided the car around and over some beautiful estates, all of which (as had been agreed and specified by the council) were distinctly Mediterranean, in keeping with the rest of the habitat. The last hull of the group, the *Cleator*, had been decked out as a 'green and pleasant land' as might be expected. The décor of the next, the *Gatland* was still being discussed, although a majority seemed in favour of a sub-tropical mid-oceanic climate like Madeira. When working as a fleet, this variation added to the interest of travel. Of course 'Mediterranean' still allowed room for stylistic variation. Roman villas and Byzantine Palaces were common, as were those in Greek, Arabic and Art Deco styles. Less common was modern terrestrial, both pre and post RW. The gardens were by no means fully established yet, but the effect was already Arcadian. They passed groves of cypresses, fig trees, olives and so on. Someone was breaking the rules with a beautiful magnolia.

Jim broke the silence. "I'm afraid you won't be able to use the patio yet, sir."

"Good job I've plenty to do indoors, then. We'll have a late lunch after which I'll get down to preparing for the council meeting the day after tomorrow."

"Very good, sir. I'll busy myself after lunch. I'm sorry I'm not Chivers."

"Not your fault, old chap. He was with me so long we had built up a vast amount of memories together. What really hurts is that he was my father's for many years, a link to my dad that's now lost."

"Didn't he do any memory downloads? I could try one."

"Of course. Thanks for the offer, but even if I let you do that it wouldn't be the same without his full personality interaction which, as you know, involves the whole body and a lifetime of wear and tear. Anyway, because of the distributed nature of memory, the recordings are never right. You just wouldn't be the same. No offence intended."

"None taken, sir."

Next morning, after Jim had brought him a light breakfast of smoked salmon, wholemeal bread lightly toasted, and a glass of Chablis, Alex was finishing the council work when the girls came in to let him know that, as far as they could tell, the entire complex of flats and their intelligences were now clean. They handed him a copy of their report and left.. He then kept himself occupied by walking around his flat to consider whether any modifications were needed before he and his partner held their first dinner party in a few weeks. The main and five guest bedrooms were completely ready but the lounges, library, art room and the spacious dining room were lacking some décor and fittings. Also, most of the spaces for the artwork and display cabinets for his minerals collection were empty. His collections were still in cases in the three store rooms. Quite apart from his collectables, Chivers had put three cases of the latest samples into his workroom/laboratory, ready for him to inspect, check and classify. He walked down to the lab. All the equipment seemed to be installed and the power supplies, drainage systems and ventilation were on. He checked a drawer and the tools all rested in their proper places. Good old Chivers, he'd made sure that this place would be ready, as soon as Alex was able to continue assaying the samples. Ah! There were the three new boxes, each around 25 kilos (in standard gravity), stacked near a small work-bench at the back. They were evidently very important; his prospecting department had classified them as 'secret' and for his eyes only, but he hadn't had the chance to investigate them yet.

He went to the safe and took out the log book. The samples had come from one of his farthest surveys, right out at the inner edge of the Oort Cloud.

The first of the exploration probes had been sent there many years ago. They were state of the art: the helium 3/deuterium motors were the best available (from Bond Martin engineering) and the intelligence highly specialised and incorruptible..

The probe that brought these samples was only the second to return. The first had been back for six months and the results were still being assessed. This one had been back only a couple of weeks and these samples rushed to him. Intriguing, to say the least. Communication with probes, even coded, was only sporadic and never attempted at all if the probe hit something valuable.

Jim walked in, interrupting his thoughts. "Frank is coming, he will be here in five minutes or so."

"Bring him to the lounge by the patio, there's a bar in there…" He looked at his watch. "And it's lunch time."

Frank came in smiling, which was encouraging. Alex pointed at the bar.

"Like a shot? I assume you'll stay for a bite."

"Can we skip lunch? I have to get my report ready for the council. There's a special summary for you." He tossed a folder onto the desk. "I'll have a quick one though. Whisky. I know you always have something decent, and the good news is that we can enjoy it on the patio."

"That *is* good, although I think I'd like to sit well behind the screen."

They went out with their glasses and sat amongst the flowers. The clean-up had been so thorough that only one or two scars and chips were visible to the expert eye. Alex privately thought that he would leave them as a cautionary reminder.

"Well?"

"We certainly know how, and now have a pretty good idea of who, but we have no idea yet as to why, except that the motive seems to have been burglary."

"Go on."

"A study of the residential complex's security recordings has shown that several attempts were made to break into this apartment over the last couple of weeks while you and Chivers were out. All efforts, and some were pretty damn clever, to subvert the intelligences of the complex were unsuccessful." Frank looked smug. "Our security's bloody good, actually.

"The assassination attempt was a last, desperate throw. The gun, triggered by the Gardenia, was supposed to take out both you and Chivers, leaving the way clear for a quick in-and-out burglary. Your survival buggered that up. We've managed to recover some organic clues amongst the wreckage of the gun, and it doesn't look as if the perpetrators are local. We're pretty sure that none of our competitors or even friends were behind the attack and your suspicions about the Lomonosov are definitely out, so keep them to yourself; we need their trade. We're not sure yet, but the closest technological and biological match we've found suggests *New Eden*, a group of colonies run by one of the religious groups, 'The Promised Ones', I think. Problem is that if it *is* them, I can't see why. We barely give each other the time of day. Any more scotch?"

"Yes, I need another myself."

A lot of things were bobbing around in Alex's mind as he went back to the bar.

So far he hadn't mentioned to anyone his growing suspicion that the three boxes sitting in the laboratory were connected to recent events; first, because he didn't *know* they were and second, the 'eyes only' notice.

If they *were* relevant he would get a bollocking from Frank for not telling him immediately and, if not, what the hell? He'd better go to the laboratory – and without Jim.

In the quiet of the lab he hefted the first box from the top of the stack and onto the bench, checking its description in the log book. It read: 'caution, metallic molybdenum alloy samples'.

Amazing. One of the sources of the wealth of the Albion group had been trade in molybdenum for the helium 3/deuterium propulsion units of colonies, interstellar probes, his own prospecting units and many others. But it was the last thing he expected from the Oort cloud – and it was *metallic*. Impossible. He didn't read any more, took the standard precaution of putting on a mask and gloves in case there was powder, and opened the lid. He could check the details of its origin in a minute.

It wasn't just metallic, it was components. He put some out on the bench. The eight pieces in the box were all about the same size, around 30-40cms. Some clean, some twisted, some stained and marked. He half-recognised what some of them might be without being able to place them exactly. He checked the composition in the log book. It was indeed a molybdenum alloy – and an alloy of no composition that he knew.

He checked the origin. This was part of a large quantity of pieces of similar material, some up to tens of meters in size, that the probe had dug out of an agglomeration of mostly methane ice on one of the rare small planetoids on the inner edge of the Oort cloud. It was hundreds of millions of years old.

Blood pumping in his head, he put the pieces on the bench back, re-stacked the boxes, returned the log to the safe, went out of the lab which he mechanically locked and hurried back to the lounge and bar. Frank would be getting curious.

Jim would clearly know something was wrong but would be too polite to ask.

"Is everything all right?" Frank asked from the patio.

"Yes, fine. Just needed a piss." Alex poured himself a truly stiff one and defied the gods by downing it in one. His hand still shook as he carefully put down the glass.

He was the first human ever to touch an alien starship.

The Trail of the Creator, The Trial of Creation

Paul Di Filippo

Aboard the *Final Theophany* I had assembled a small but efficient crew consisting of the meanest, deadliest, orneriest, smartest and most embittered set of intergalactic killers I could dredge up during ten years of cruising all the lanes of civilized space and quite a few of the more savage precincts. Out of sheer self-indulgence, I had given them all human names familiar to me so I wouldn't have to be bothered with trying to recall or pronounce their original exotic monikers. After all, I was Captain and footing all the bills.

Maxwell Silverhammer stood three meters tall in his bare green scaled feet and carried, as if it were a toothpick, a giant mallet whose head was fashioned of purest quark matter from the heart of a neutron star. The portion of his face not taken up by black fangs was filled by one enormous bloodshot eye.

Jagello appeared at first to be merely a sessile nest of whiplike, besuckered tentacles surrounding a sharp parrot beak of a mouth. But then he would reveal enormous snapping chelae that could propel him at lightning speed and which were capable of snipping a man in half.

Drumgoole manifested as a grey-complexioned wispy wraith with a mummy's face, all parchment skin and kite-stick bones, flimsy as a clothes rack. But when he enfolded his victim and began irresistibly tightening, all impressions of fragility vanished.

Corinthia, barely one meter tall, hailed from a heavy planet and resembled a troll or gnome from Terran legend, down to a complexion full of warts and scars, and a nose like a small cucumber. I had seen her stop a fusillade of shredder flechettes with her formidable chest, leaving her laminate armour like Swiss cheese but her bruised skin intact.

Myself, I go by the name of Moortgat, and although technically human – whatever that means these days—my kind is divergent from the baseline. I'm the result of inbreeding for survival on a deathworld where every element of the ecosphere was lethal to the human species. My skin exudes toxins, my eyelids are impenetrable, a braid of three of my hairs can serve as a garrotte, and my farts are explosive when voluntarily primed. Not a pinup boy.

Seeing this ugly, fantastical assemblage of beings – and I included myself of course – some ancient, pre-spacefaring Terran might have thought that we represented a good assortment of aliens from around the multifarious galaxy, a panorama of the myriad heterogeneous miracles produced by the ingenious Darwinian chemistry and physics of our different worlds.

But of course, nowadays everyone knew better.

'Aliens' did not exist. Nowhere in the galaxy could be found a sophont with an utterly exclusive genome.

Every sentient creature in the universe, no matter how oddball their physiognomy, was genetically related.

We were all one species, sharing up to ninety-nine percent of our genes, all of which used the universal DNA substrate. Same amino acids, same method of translation into proteins, all the same cellular processes right down the line.

Had any of us four males on board the *Final Theophany* wished to do so, and had it been physically possible in any particular mating to connect genitals, we could have inseminated Corinthia and produced a viable foetus. (Believe me, this was not a fantasy that any of us harboured.) Even without a carnal connection, such a thing could have been easily done artificially with nothing more elaborate than a syringe.

Just like Terran canines, which ranged from half a kilo in weight to well over one hundred kilos, and exhibited a huge range of appearances, the intelligent population of the galaxy hid cellular uniformity beneath their varying facades. We were a universe of mutts. Admittedly, the analogy was inexact, the situation more bizarre than with dogs, given the anatomical gap between, say, someone like Jagello and the rest of us bipeds. But even if scientists still had their questions about certain aspects of how we remained interfertile despite such large variations (they often rang in embryological morphic resonance), the basic fact was scientifically incontrovertible.

Every single sophont across a hundred billion star systems was related. Or so we surmised, based on an incomplete expansion across about one-third of that realm.

Of course, such a finding immediately raised the question of how such consanguinity came to be. Ours was the first interstellar age. No previous FTL empires had ever existed. The archaeological records had been plumbed on a half million inhabited worlds without producing one shred of evidence for any widespread civilization of forerunners. So the scenario where an empire of homogenous beings decayed and, over a few million years, sent its isolated populations down a variety of evolutionary paths proved untenable.

In the end, the best theoreticians in the whole galaxy were left with only one reasonable hypothesis.

All the races of the universe had been seeded separately by some individual or small band of individuals, leaving no archaeological traces and employing as root stock the same malleable germplasm.

In other words, there was a Creator, and He or She or It had populated the galaxy with His or Her or Its designs. (Let's call that bastard God Him from now on, for convenience.)

In many individuals, this scientific revelation inspired awe, reverence and bliss.

In myself and my crew, the notion of a God who had promiscuously fecundated our galaxy with a plethora of intelligent races of all body plans had instead engendered hatred, disdain and rage.

You see, each of us – Maxwell, Jagello, Drumgoole, Corinithia and yours truly, Captain Moortgat – had belonged to our own world's One True Religion which maintained that the Creator had fashioned the dominant species of our 'unique' world in His Own Likeness. It was a belief born of primitive planetary isolation, and maintained precariously in the early years after First Contact. But after a few centuries of discovery and correlation, the widespread broadcast about the reality of universal miscegenation had definitely killed the concept.

This irrefutable revelation – that all the galactic races issued from the hand of the same mad demiurge who had, in addition to crafting his 'chosen' race, spawned equally privileged 'monsters' left and right – had sparked suicides and apostasies galore.

But in us five it had bred only one overwhelming urge.

To find and assassinate the irresponsibly profligate God who had made us.

For a group of five sentients who hated each other's guts, we got along pretty well. The fact that each one of us was a living affront to the bedrock theology of the others – an affront each of us longed to bloodily erase – was subsumed in our quest to find and kill God. Of course, my appropriately heavy poison hand of discipline, employed only when necessary, also helped to maintain a surface calm.

So once we were underway along the navigable labyrinth of the Dark Matter Web that threaded the visible cosmos and provided galactic civilization with its FTL links, I had no hesitation about calling my crew out from their private cabins and assembling them in the refectory of the *Final Theophany* for a discussion of our plans. I expected them to behave even in those close quarters – or else.

No chair was big enough for Maxwell, so he just towered by the table's edge. Corinthia, on the other hand, had to perch atop several pillows on her seat to see over the rim. Resting on the floor, where he left a spreading trickle of scummy brine, Jagello simply extended an eye stalk up to the common level. Drumgoole seemed to float an inch or so off his seat, wafted back and forth by the room's gentle ventilation.

"All right, you mooks," I said, "listen up. Now that we are away from any chance of being overheard by busybodies who might try to stop us, I can reveal our first destination. We are going to make a raid on the Syntelligence Institute on Souring Nine. Our goal is to kidnap one of their boffins, a human named Ilario Mewborn."

Jagello's voice sounded like a toucan crunching an entire stalk of bananas. "What for we take this man?"

"Because he's discovered how to track God."

If I had closed my eyes, I could have imagined Corinthia's husky tones emanating from a sexy gal of my own planet, someone whose epidermal toxins would have blended with mine to make an aphrodisiac sweat paste. Of course, the gruesome reality of the dwarf was nowhere near as alluring.

"You signed us on with the promise that you already had a way to track the creator. What gives?"

"It's true, I do have a stochastic projection of His path. But I just learned that Mewborn's got something much better."

Determined from the fossil record and biological markers, the evolutionary age of every sentient race so far discovered had been precisely calculated and arrayed in a database, then sorted. The oldest race proved to be the Thumraits, aquatics who resembled a cross between a squid, a seahorse and a clam. Their fossil record extended back five million years. The youngest race so far encountered were the Quisqueya, a bunch of plump pancake-shaped things that lived by clinging to the rock faces on their world, absorbing sunlight and licking fermenting moss. Their existence stretched back a mere three-quarters of a million years, and they had not even achieved their full sentience yet. But their sampled 'human' genome was unmistakeable.

Now, playing connect-the-dots with the planets of the sentient races in order of their age produced a unidirectional path for the Creator's malignant life-spawning journey, a path which could be extended out beyond the Quisqueya into the unknown light years with a certain degree of accuracy, assuming, as we had to, that the Creator was still active some three-quarters of a million years after his last recorded abomination. My plan had been simply to follow the projection, stopping at every likely world.

I explained all this to my crew.

Maxwell rumble-lisped a response. (Large fangs did not an orator make.) "And thish Mewborn, what ish hish invention?"

"He's discovered that the Creator's method of travel leaves a distinct signature in the Dark Matter Web. The signature is almost eternal, but fades gradually with time. He's plotted the traces against the archaeological record and it fits perfectly. We can use Mewborn's gadget to home in on the Creator's current whereabouts much faster and with more certainty than by following the stochastics. We'll just ride His transportation gradient until we come upon His present location. Then – goodbye, God!"

Drumgoole's hypnotic voice, one of his tools for taking prey, resembled a ghoulish whisper from another dimension.

"I will guarantee this human's cooperation, have no fears."

"Fine. Then we're all in agreement. Souring Nine, here we come!"

The defences of the obscure and isolated Syntelligence Institute were laughably rudimentary. Nothing but a few robotic security guards patrolling the outside perimeter. They were brought to a juddering stop with the broadcast of a simple Universal Halting State Trojan. Confident that their lofty, pure researches held no allure for thieves or pirates, the Institute had never hardened up. A blow from Maxwell's weighty hammer took the front door of the Institute clean off its hinges and sent it rocketing across the empty reception area.

Expecting a mob of workers and panicked screams, we got only emptiness and silence.

"Where the hell is everybody?" Corinthia demanded.

"Don't know, don't care," I said. "We're just after Mewborn's tracking device. Let's move before the cops show up!"

After dashing down corridors where several doors led to labs and storerooms but no offices, it finally dawned on me that the staff of the Syntelligence Institute consisted of Ilario Mewbon alone.

We found the boffin cowering under his desk in a centrally located room. Jagello extended a claw and pulled him roughly out.

Ilario Mewborn presented as a puny baseline human, and not a particularly impressive specimen at that. Sparse strands of mouse-coloured hair failed to conceal his spotty scalp. He stood not much more than one-and-a-half times Corinthia's height. His drably wrapped limbs approximated Drumgoole's spidery structure. And for some reason he wore antique eyeglasses. (I learned later that he was allergic to contacts and scared of surgery or implants.)

Although not as loud or basso profundo as Maxwell, I had a respectable bellow. "Where's the Creator tracker? Quick!"

Mewborn's quavering voice sounded like a goat's bleating. "Oh-over th-there..."

I walked to where he pointed. A large plastic drum was the only possible item. I pried off the top. Inside quivered a translucent gelatinous mass threaded with glowing, sparkling organelles.

"What the hell is this!"

"It – it's the tracker. Honest, it truly is!"

Approaching sirens penetrated the building.

"Grab everything, Mewborn too, and let's roll!"

The *Final Theophany* showed Souring Nine her tail faster than you could say 'God is dead'. We were in the unpursuable depths of the Dark Matter Web while the planetary cops were still unlimbering their guns.

In the refectory the five of us crowded with a menacing

expectancy around a seated Mewborn. With sweat dotting his brow, the little scientist sipped delicately at a glass of restorative electrolytes and cyana-berry juice, his composure gradually returning. Finally he looked calm enough for questioning to be effective.

"Okay, pal, what's with the tub of pudding?"

Mewborn's voice exhibited a certain disdain at my ignorance and pride at his own accomplishments. "That, my loud and pockmarked thief, is urschleim, my own discovery and invention. It's taken decades, but I've done what everyone said was impossible. Employing every single genome of all the sentient races, I have reverse-engineered the mother plasm from which they all arose. In that barrel you behold the raw material employed by the Creator, the clay from which we were all initially fashioned."

I went to the barrel and peered in with more respect and curiosity than before. "Can you use this stuff to make new races then?"

Mewborn grew crestfallen. "No, that supreme accomplishment is, as yet, denied to me. But I intend to learn how from the Creator Himself."

"And this urschleim will lead you to him?"

"Indeed! It resonates superluminally to his presence, like an infinitely sensitive radar with only one target. I have learned how to interpret the patterns of the urschleim's twinklings, which mirror the traces of the Creator's passage through the Dark Matter Web." Mewborn got up and moved to examine the sparkling gelatin. "And right now, our course is taking us away from the Creator! You need to reverse at once!"

Before mindlessly following Mewborn's advice, I consulted the alternate stochastic analysis of the Creator's projected trail and found it agreed. "Okay," I said, "you call the course until we reach God. But I gotta warn you: you're gonna have to question Him real quick, because He's going down for a dirt nap as soon as we lay eyes on Him. Unless we decide on a little torture first."

Mewborn used a forefinger to slide his glasses further up his nose. "I expect God might have something to say about His disposition as well."

The five of us would-be Godkillers once more occupied the dining area. We had installed Mewborn and his vat of amalgamated jellyfish

111

guts in his own cabin. The door remained unlocked: there was no place he could run, nothing on board he could sabotage, no way he could communicate with any authorities.

I addressed my posse. "You dickheads can wipe those satisfied grins off your faces." I was stretching the facial complacency accusation a bit here in Jagello's case. "The easy part of this mission is over. Now starts the rough stuff. First off, we're going into uncharted territory. No telling what kind of weird astrophysics we'll run into. No one even knows if the Dark Matter Web remains navigable in the same way out here. Redmayne and Crispwell set out to chart it, and they never returned."

Jagello rasped out a question. "What for maybe we worry about other sentients? What trouble they bring?"

"Well, figure it out for yourself. The youngest race in our neck of the woods is the Quisqueya, and they haven't even conceived of the wheel yet. Every other Creator-endowed sophont we encounter is going to be even younger. Now, for sure, some races might have been created meaner and more on the ball initially than those pancakes. And local conditions might have forced them to evolve faster. But I'm still betting none of them have attained spaceflight yet. *And*, unlikely as it seems, we might even find some non-Creator-determined independently intelligent species. Don't hold your breath."

A senseless comment to make to Drumgoole, who performed his internal gas exchange through spiracles, like a bug.

"Nonetheless, we still gotta land from time to time to verify with some cell samples that we're on the right trail. Having Mewborn along, by the way, should speed up the testing, him being an expert on the universal germline and all. But when we're planetside, the odds are less in our favour. Even five mean bastards with a lot of deadly junk in their hands can be swamped by a horde of creepy-crawlies. So we've got to stay sharp and on our guard."

"Jush let me at anyone who tries to shtop us!" said Maxwell. Corinthia seconded him with one of her race's blood-clotting war whoops, while Drumgoole emitted a sibilant hiss and Jagello clacked his pincers. It made me feel good to see the crew so pumped.

We broke up the meeting and retreated to our private chambers, where we spent most of our time, lacking the spiritual empathy to mingle socially with our blasphemous counterparts. I had just fallen asleep under my armoured bedclothes (old habits from a deadly homeworld died hard) when a hammering on my door made me jump up. Corinthia was outside yelling.

"The human's strangling or having a fit or something! The noise is awful!"

I ran down the corridor to Mewborn's room and burst in, with the rest of the crew close behind.

Looking like a fish fit only for throwing back, the naked boffin was having sex with the tracking device, moaning and groaning fit to bust. He had decanted the person-sized mass of flickering gelatin onto the floor and was porking it vigorously, his pitiful boner insignificantly dimpling its mass. Oblivious to us, he began to holler sweet nothings into its non-existent ears.

"Galatea, my darling! The Creator will shape you, yes, He will! Form, sweet form, and you'll be mine, all mine!"

Mewborn climaxed with a howl and slid off the slick insensate bolster of glittery urschleim.

"That ish the most disgusting thing I have ever seen," Maxwell said, and I had to agree, if only with regard to the rampant sentimentalism.

I grabbed Mewborn by the loose skin at the back of his neck and hauled him to his feet, shaking him violently in the process.

"What the hell do you think you're doing, prof? We need that hunk of plasm in good working order."

Without his oldschool goggles, Mewborn squinted like a neonatal kitten at my face, even though his was only centimetres away from mine. He didn't even have the grace to be embarrassed about his actions, but instead assumed his usual savant's assuredness.

"Galatea will come to no harm by my tender ministrations. In fact, such frequent intercourse allows me to synch more closely with her internal display, and interpret it more accurately. So I fear you will all have to accustom yourselves to this ritual."

Maybe he was legit. The tracker's interior constellations seemed to be pulsing chromatically with fresh information. I threw Mewborn onto his bunk. "This is the living end. Guided through the interstellar unknown by a colloid-porking pervert."

"Please do not insult my woman. Galatea belongs just as much to our consensual lineage as does as any other race in the galaxy. In fact, she has more claim to primogeniture than even the Thumraits. So please, treat her with more respect."

I regarded the gently quivering elongated blob on the floor with barely controlled revulsion. The Creator had much to answer for.

"Okay, Adam, why don't you shovel Eve back into her bucket. We've got a long road ahead of us."

Emerging from the Dark Matter Web and taking stellar readings, we discovered ourselves to be some ten thousand light years from anything that could be called home. Pretty spooky and mind-blowing, even for me and my crew of badasses, who had embarked on this mad quest with half a notion that we'd never return. But I shrugged off any jitters and got on with the business of nailing the Creator wherever his latest lair might be.

The first planet where we stopped to take a biological fix on the Creator's trail of course had no name, being previously undiscovered. I decided to call the place Horseshit, after its dominant race, which resembled tiny Terran horses – if Terran horses had featured heads like four-eyed praying mantises.

We landed the *Final Theophany* in the middle of a herd of these scale-model critters, and I went out to bag one. They swarmed aggressively all over me, their nipping mouthparts failing to pierce my skin and their little hooves giving me a pleasant recreational scratching on my perpetually itchy epidermis. The horse-mantises began to die in droves as my epidermal poisons got to them. And while that was pretty good confirmation of our shared chemistry, I nonetheless took a few croaked ones back into the ship for analysis.

Mewborn looked up from his hologram readouts and said, "Mitochondrial drift and several other metrics indicate this race is approximately half-a-million years diverged from the urschleim. Born much more recently than the Quisqueya. So we are that much closer to the Creator's current whereabouts, just as I predicted."

I got everyone back into the ship – my crew had been out killing mantis-horses by the wheelbarrow-loads for practice – and we took off.

That 'evening' we had a little celebration of our first success. Maxwell, Corinthia and I could get loaded off the same kind of stimulant, so we passed around a bottle of Glassoon's Acritarchic that I had put aside for just such a moment. Pretty soon we were harmonizing raggedly on several pop tunes currently the rage back in the civilized portions of the galaxy. Drumgoole treated himself to the tasty radioisotope-enhanced blood contained in several small living animals, whom he suffocated, crushed and absorbed in delicious prolongation. As for Jagello, he went on a hyper-oxygenation binge, huffing the inebriating gas until all his tendrils danced in hypnotic rhythms and his claws spasmed in uncontrolled delight.

I felt a momentary kinship with these living, breathing affronts to all the tenets of my beloved religion, and regretted that, should any of us survive the encounter with the Creator, I would probably have to turn my weapons against them, if only to forestall my own extinction at their hands, stemming from me presenting the same intolerable infidel face to them.

As for Mewborn, he did not join us, but spent the party time sticking it to his mute colloidal floozy in an orgy of imaginary romance.

I won't bother detailing all the stops along our odyssey. Not very interesting, over all. But I will mention something odd. The newest races we encountered began to show a certain decadence or degeneracy. Back in the civilized realm of our galaxy, there existed approximately one-quarter-of-a-million races, each with a different body plan, even if just by some minor variation. Say what you will about the Creator, you had to admit He or She or It was truly inventive. And none of the races, however weird, were what you could call abominations. Their somatypes all exhibited a certain organic completeness or aesthetic utilitarianism. Admittedly, evolution had played a part in smoothing out any initial irregularities. But they had started from clever designs.

Not so these younger, newer races. Many of them seemed dysfunctional for their environments – for any environment. Useless limbs, badly distributed organs, mediocre sensory abilities, narrow bandwidth nervous systems – you name the deficiency, they exhibited it. Not all glitches were present in every race, of course, but enough separately in all of them to convince me of one thing.

The Creator was going senile. Since the birth of the Thumraits some five million years ago, He had been engaged in a continual orgy of invention. The wear and tear of that ceaseless genesis had to tell hard on any being, however capable and long-lived. The Creator was running on empty, but kept on going.

Instead of making me feel sad for the unknowable Being who had populated our otherwise non-sentient galaxy with intelligence and awareness, the revelation just made me worry that He would kick it – had already kicked it – before we could catch up with Him and administer the well-deserved and satisfying *coup de grâce* ourselves. And so I redoubled our speed and sampling activity, pushing my ship and crew harder than ever.

Which is probably how we lost Drumgoole. By rushing into an unknown situation too fast and overconfidently.

We ended up naming the planet where he died Drumgoole's Folly. Not that anyone would be adding it to their charts if we never returned, a prospect that seemed more and more likely.

The sophont species left behind on Drumgoole's Folly consisted of a spiky airfish resembling a floating porcupine mated with an avocado. Their defect was that they seemed unable to rise much more than a meter off the ground, leaving them easy prey to every nasty creepy-crawly native to the planet.

I had just netted one of the airfish for cellular analysis when Drumgoole, possibly feeling a bit peckish, decided that he could do with a little treat. So he wrapped himself around two at once and began to squeeze –

The explosion rocked me back on my feet, and even harmlessly juddered the ship where it sat. After quickly recovering– when you're used to missile-birds dive bombing you from youth, such blasts are taken in stride – I saw my surviving compatriots picking themselves up as well, and that there was nothing left of Drumgoole but a few tattered and scorched parchments flapping on the breeze.

Mewborn – luckily safe inside the ship during the accident – soon discovered that the airfish possessed a unique mating process. The males and females each secreted one half of a binary explosive compound. A pair self-destructed during their one-time sexual encounter, sending their indestructible fertilized eggs far and wide for best dispersal. Drumgoole had had the misfortune a) to corral one of each gender; and b) to pop their explosive bladders and cause the untimely non-horny mixing of their contents.

After that incident, we were all more cautious at planetfalls, but also more focused than ever on making speed to confront the Creator before suffering any more attrition that might stymie our righteously murderous goals.

One day in transit, far beyond any previous exploration, Mewborn came to me and said, "I believe I've worked out the pattern for the intervals between the Creator's jumps. Not as simple as it first seemed. Time spent building a new race out of urschleim is directly related to the complexity levels of the previous build, plus the ambient dark matter power sources the Creator theoretically feeds on, factored with..."

Losing all patience, I grabbed Mewborn by his shirt and shook him. "Just tell me the practical stuff, you jelly-humping sicko!"

The boffin adjusted his glasses calmly and said, "The planet after next should be the one where the Creator currently resides."

We named the world Omega. Not the most original name maybe, but fitting. Here was where the Creator would meet His end, and where all sentients would be forever more liberated from His endlessly insulting packaging of intelligence into more and more bizarre containers, as if He were a cookie factory stamping out a million differently shaped cookie slabs with the same dull invariant frosting sandwiched between.

Now, ideally, we would have hung in orbit and just dropped a couple of planet busters down on him. But this tactic was impossible for several reasons. First, planetbusting armaments were closely interdicted by all galactic authorities and cost umpty-ump billion SVUs apiece even if you could lay your mitts on one in a terrorist bazaar. Second, until we went down we had no certainty, despite Mewborn's insistence, that the Creator was even present on Omega. And third, most importantly, we all wanted to off the immortal bastard personally, face to face, to get our hands bloody and see Him grovel and beg and suffer for His sins. To that end I had stocked various portable instruments of extreme lethality which we now broke out from the formerly locked armoury and familiarised ourselves with.

"If only Drumgoole could have been with us on this glorious day," mused Corinthia.

"He ish here in spirit," said Maxwell.

"Creator dead, Drumgoole kick his ass in hell," contributed Jagello.

Mewborn made no comment, but just drummed his fingers nervously on the barrel containing his Galatea.

We had pinpointed what we believed to be the Creator's presence on a vast open plain so large as to be discernible from orbit.

"Hold on to your guts," I said, "we're gonna drop in fast."

At the controls, I sent the *Final Theophany* down like a missile-bird from Hell.

Grounded, the four of us barrelled out of the ship before our sound waves even caught up with us. We raced to preset strategic positions, but then came to inconclusive stops.

The Creator was so huge, we might as well have been trying to cordon off a mountain.

The best thing I could compare Him to was an alabaster Sphinx conjoined with a veined and marbled slug.

From his ground-level 'waist' up, the Creator looked vaguely 'human', with a skyward straining muscled torso and two arms. A neck broad as a four-lane highway supported a head whose like no one had ever seen. Multiple faces beyond count existed in a ring around the entire surface of the skull. These face were in constant flickering phase-change, flashing through split-second recognisable representations of all the races that populated our galaxy. But above the main head was a fractally smaller head, exhibiting the same flickering conformation. And above that another, and another, and another...

I was reminded of certain images from Terra, the gods of a land named Tibet.

So much for the half of the Creator that rose vertically from the dirt of the plain. The recumbent portion of His body was an unadorned fleshy tube tapering from the size of a major undersea transportation tunnel down to a tip as big as me.

And at this cloacal tip, the Creator gave birth.

As we watched, a billet of glistening urschleim identical to Galatea began to slide out. As it passed through the bodily aperture, it was massaged and palpitated by a number of hand-like manipulators ringing the opening, a kind of fringe of digits. These ministrations triggered fresh coruscations from the colourful organelles within the jelly log, no doubt prompting its future development into yet another sickly vehicle of sentience. The billet plopped down onto the dust and grit of the plain and wormed away to make room for the next.

As we watched, the Creator, all oblivious to us, began to speak to Himself in a voice that for all its celestial booming still held a note of weary whining. I suspected that each of us heard that voice in our own native language.

"Think it, shape it, drop it. Think it, shape it, drop it. Push it out, push it out. On and on and on. Never stop, can't stop, how stop? Tired and old, tired and old. Oh, how it hurts! Stop, stop, stop. Start, start, start. Think it, shape it, drop it...."

The insane maunderings of this diseased God acted to jar me and the others out of our first dismay and disbelief, and to recall us to our intended holy blasphemy. His guilt could not be more clear, and sentence must be passed.

"Kill it! Kill it now!"

And so we unleashed our weapons on the God. Particles and waves, explosives and blades, blunt force and ultrasonic shakings. I saw Maxwell bury his heavy hammer up to his wrists over and over, wrenching it back out along with great gobbets of Godflesh. Jagello carved himself a passage into the bulk of the Creator and began to chew and churn invisibly forward inside. Corinthia was a whirlwind of flashing vibra-swords, sending out a mist of pale lymphatic fluids as she hacked her way like a rock climber up the back of the God.

As for myself, I exuded poisons of a toxicity I had never before attained, embracing and melting the flesh of the Creator while at the same time ripping out meters of veins with my clawed hands, like pulling tree roots out of the soil.

But the Creator was big and tough and hard to kill. He had survived for millions of years under all kinds of unimaginable conditions, and was not going to succumb easily now. Our attacks seemed to be weakening Him, but at the same time we seemed incapable of inflicting a fatal blow. The one-sided battle surged on and on until even our frenzied determination and strength faded and demanded a pause.

All begored, we dropped back from the hulking God and onto the gravelled plain and sought to regain our energies.

That's when my attention fell on Mewborn.

The puny professor had trundled his Galatea in her barrel over to the butt end of the Creator, and was now trying to position his girlfriend so that the Creator's manipulators could process her and endow her with shape.

"Give her form!" shouted Mewborn. "Shape her to my dreams!"

But the constantly emerging packages of urschleim, still coming out despite our attacks, prevented Mewborn from affixing his personal bride to the manipulators. He fumbled, dropped Galatea, and then the manipulators had grabbed him!

Surprisingly, the cloacal hands now positioned Mewborn to face the emerging urschleim.

A billet pushed out and over Mewborn's screaming head, which, engulfed, was silenced, although we could see him vaguely through the urschleim, still open-mouthed.

Then the little human began to fill up with the stuff. Instead of being cast off by the gripping digits, he remained attached and the billets became a continuous flow down his impossibly straining and capacious gullet. More and more emerged and went into him.

But instead of exploding, he began to transform and swell within his stretching urschleim cocoon, as we watched in stupefaction.

Only when Mewborn had assumed the dimensions of our adjacent spacecraft did I realize what was happening. And just then the old Creator spoke with a confirming voice, full of relief and exaltation.

"I pass the torch! My job is over, my era ended! Goodbye, goodbye, goodbye! A stop at last…"

The old Creator seemed almost instantly to deflate, like a parachute settling to earth, while Mewborn, the new God, inflated equally as rapidly, just as, long ago, our baby universe had swelled in that special moment after the Big Bang.

The four of us scampered back from the collapsing sack of the old God, from which Mewborn had finally detached himself. His familiar myopic face loomed high above us, looking about with a growing sense of his new powers and stature.

"Kill –" I began, but then found myself frozen in place, as were my comrades.

"You will not discover me to be as pusillanimous as my predecessor," thundered Mewborn. "He was old and tired. I am young and hearty. I am sending you four back now as my heralds. Let the galaxy rejoice!

"Our big happy family continues to grow!"

Stella by Starlight

Mike Resnick & Robert T. Jeschonek

Okay, so you want to know about Fermi's Paradox, and that's certainly a legitimate concern. But to understand it, and especially to know why it isn't a paradox at all, we're going to have to start with a girl named Stella.

It was Be Kind to Lumpies Day when Stella Nolan first heard the voice in her head.

She was shuffling down the sidewalk, wrapped in a bulky grey hooded cloak, as a gang of brightly clad revellers whooped and danced around her. Angel-faced, hard-bodied hotties sang and skipped and played grab-ass among the pastel towers and smiling streets, breathing in caffeinated air and laughing out clouds of glitter.

Stella tended not to go out much, of course, but she'd left her tiny bungalow in back-alley Sunshine City to make a trip to the pharmacy. One of her medications had been left out of the delivery that morning, and she couldn't do without it.

Keeping her head down, she lumbered through the crowd like a garbage scow through a pod of dolphins. The pharmacy was two blocks from home, and she was already halfway there. She was pretty sure she could make it if she just avoided contact and kept moving one foot in front of the other – but, dodging a runaway conga line at the corner, she bumped into a young blonde beauty and knocked her backward.

Flopping out one clumsy arm, Stella caught the blonde and stopped her fall. Then, she pushed her upright and slouched away.

The blonde scampered after her, twittering a blue streak. "You saved me! You've got to let me thank you!"

Stella tried to shrug her off and keep moving, but the blonde fluttered around her like a seagull circling a breadcrumb.

"Come on! Can't you at least be sociable? I mean, it's a holiday and everything." With that, the blonde pulled out a leopard-skin kazoo and blew into it, making a rattling, squawking noise.

Again Stella tried sidestepping, again to no avail. She let out an angry grunt, but the blonde didn't seem to notice.

"Well I'm not gonna let you run off without a peek!" Darting forward, the blonde yanked the hood of Stella's cloak back off her head.

What came next was no surprise to Stella. The blonde gasped and stumbled back two steps, bumping into other revellers who joined her in gaping and gasping.

All because Stella stood revealed in her grotesque glory, so different from the perfect human specimens dancing around her. One side of her head looked human, complete with one brown eye, part of a nose, and half a mouth. But the other side consisted of a pulsating blob of gelatinous, veiny goo – a cluster of quivering, pink-tinged nodules running from her scalp to the base of her neck.

The rest of her body was the same, though only her head and neck were visible in the bulky cloak. She was half-human, half-something-else, a diseased member of a certain class of people that had come to be known by one particular nickname.

"Lumpy!" The blonde pointed at Stella, looking alarmed... then quickly shifted to an expression of excited delight. "You're here to join the celebration, aren't you?"

"Nuhh." It was the best Stella could manage with a mouth that was only human on the right side. The left was covered by a clear membrane that vibrated and sounded like a snare drum when she talked. "Nuhh slebrashun."

"Of *course* that's why you're here!" chirped the blonde. "After all, this is *your day*, isn't it?"

Stella's human features and the jelly of her non-human side compressed in a scowl. "Thaw wuz inverdid eggbidnust day."

"Introverted Exhibitionists Day was yesterday, silly!" The blonde giggled and clapped. "*This* is Be Kind to Lumpies Day!"

Stella was seized by the overwhelming urge to be somewhere else immediately. She'd known it was an international holiday – damned near *every* day was an international holiday – but she hadn't realized it was *this* holiday.

"Yay!" said a half-naked woman with long jet black hair. "Another Lumpy to play with!"

Stella backed up a step. She'd heard the stories, and she knew what was coming next. "Pliz nuhh."

"Poor, lonely thing!" shouted a bald man wrapped in multi-coloured yarn.

"Bring her a boyfriend!" The blonde tootled on her kazoo. "The one we found rooting through the trash!"

Someone called from the crowd. "Here he is!"

Looking toward the voice, Stella saw laughing partiers jabbing a bluish blob with crackling silver prods. Unlike Stella, the bloblike creature had no recognizable human features, just the vague outline of a trunk with a bubble on top and flippers that might once have been arms.

Stella tensed, took a breath, and bolted. She knocked over a redheaded woman covered with cake frosting, then ploughed through a clot of soaking wet revellers.

The mouth of an alley opened up on the right, and Stella charged into it. The sound of running footsteps chased after her, then faded as her pursuers fell away. As ungainly as she was, with one normal leg and one semi-rigid gelatinous appendage, she was still able to outrun them... almost certainly because their non-existent attention spans had already shunted somewhere else.

Suddenly she heard a voice, coming from what seemed to be right on top of her. Heart hammering, she whirled around – but no one was behind her.

Then, she heard it again. "*Hello?*"

Frantically, she looked all around again, but could see no one.

Yanking the hood up over her head, she decided she could probably get by one more day without that missing med rather than face the revellers again, and she turned toward home.

Stella had just slammed the door of her bungalow and leaned against a wall when she heard it again – the voice from the alley. Only now that she was in a quiet room, no longer in fear for her life, she could hear it more clearly.

"Hello?" A man's voice, crackling with an overlay of what sounded like radio interference. "Can anyone hear me?"

Stella peeled the hood from her head and looked around. She saw was the same old bungalow with its ratty furniture and wooden floor, all stained with the slimy residue excreted by her gelatinous left side.

The voice spoke up again. "Is anyone receiving this signal? Hello?"

Stella frowned. She'd spoken to voices in her head before, but only in daydreams.

"Yes?" Unlike her diction, her thoughts were unaffected by her physical limitations. "Who is this?"

"*Finally!*" exclaimed the voice. "I have been signalling for so long!"

"Who is this?" asked Stella.

"A friend from far away." The voice paused. "*Very* far away."

"What should I call you?"

The voice paused. "That is a good question." It paused again. "Om." It rhymed with *home*. "You may call me Om."

Stella nodded her half-flesh half-goo head. "I am Stella. How are you talking in my head, Om?"

"Think of it as a kind of quantum entanglement," said Om.

"What is *that?*"

"My thoughts are linking with your thoughts over a vast distance."

"How vast?" asked Stella.

"120,000 light-years, give or take," said Om.

Stella frowned. "So where are you, exactly?"

"On the far side of the galaxy."

Stella turned her gaze upward, staring at the cobwebbed rafters with her one good eye and the primitive optic receptors sprinkled where her other eye should be. "You're out there somewhere? In space?"

"Yes," said Om.

Still looking up, Stella turned in a slow circle. "And how do I know this is true?"

"You'll have to trust me. But I promise, you will have your proof eventually."

"But not now?"

"Communicating with you was a big first step," said Om. "Isn't it enough for now?"

Stella thought for a moment. "What if I don't believe you? What if I think this is all just a big hallucination?" She had hallucinated before, but in each of those she had imagined herself to be a normal human girl.

"You would be wrong," said Om.

"What if I don't want to communicate?" asked Stella. "Will you go away and leave me alone?"

Om paused. "Is that what you want? To be left alone?"

The answer was obvious. Like all Lumpy orphans she'd been raised in isolation by the state, mostly by remote. At the age of 16, she'd been 'mainstreamed' – cut loose to live the best she could on minimal monthly disability payments. She'd found her bungalow then and had lived there ever since, her solitude broken only by social networking on a computer screen and the briefest of contacts with landlords and delivery people.

So, no, she did not want to be left alone. "Why are you doing this? Why are you communicating with me?"

"Because you are special." Om's voice trailed off into static, then returned. "So special that I was drawn to you from a galaxy away."

With that, a burst of interference arose. Stella stumbled two steps across the bungalow and collapsed on the ragged sofa, throwing herself down on her solid right side. The rest of her sloshed down in a slimy heap on the residue-stained cushions.

"Om?" She called his name in her mind, but there was no answer.

The spiral arms of the Milky Way glowed before Stella, sprawling in the blackness of space. Sprawling also in the middle of her bedroom, projected holographically by her computer.

In the silence after Om's departure, she'd gone straight to her computer and called up the Milky Way image. Slumped on her bed, she gazed up at it, watching the arms turn lazily in the great void.

Flicking holographic controls that hovered in front of her, she searched the Buzznet for whatever she could find on extraterrestrial life. BoilDown (aggregator/summarizer app extraordinaire) told the tale: even with the advances in astronomy of the 22nd century, no one could scare up a trace of an extraterrestrial.

The accepted current wisdom was that humanity was the only sentient species in the galaxy... perhaps the universe. How else to explain the complete lack of evidence of intelligent life out there? Sophisticated minds pointed out that Fermi's Paradox wasn't a paradox at all if we were the only sentient race. Unsophisticated minds disagreed, as they had for millennia, but were no closer to coming up with a solution than they had been when the first man crawled out of the slime, developed limbs, stood erect, and got his first look at the night sky.

Om had changed all that, at least for Stella. Humanity wasn't alone anymore, and neither was she – at least, unless the whole Om experience was a manifestation of her own personal instability.

Cruising through medical forums on the Buzznet, Stella tried to get a read on her mental state. She researched her genetic disorder, too, to see if it might be fuelling the hallucinations.

She didn't like what she found. According to the online literature, a wide range of sensory hallucinations were typical during the progression of Gendex Syndrome, the syndrome that created the Lumpies – and the online literature agreed about the end result. In time, she would be reduced to a mindless mound of jelly like the 'lover' the revellers had turned up in the crowd earlier that day.

Stella brushed her hand and tentacle through the air, dispersing the computer's vapour holo-matrix. Then, rolling over on her good side, she shivered as dark thoughts overshadowed her.

Wasn't her life awful enough already? Hadn't she suffered her share of misery and humiliation, living always apart from human companionship?

If only she could hear Om's voice again! Maybe it would mean there was hope for her. Maybe it would mean her mind wasn't on a fast downhill slide to oblivion.

"Om?" Stella thought she heard him in the middle of the night, but it must have been a dream. She sat up in bed, waiting for him to speak again... and nothing came.

It happened again the next day – three times, always with the same outcome. Each time the voice didn't come she felt more disappointed, and more convinced that Om had only been a figment of her sickly imagination.

After a week, when not even a false alarm interrupted her troubled thoughts, she sank lower still.

After a month, it was as if Om had never spoken to her at all. His voice was gone... though another, much less pleasant voice arose to take its place.

Then came the day, a week later, that Stella was no longer able to afford her tiny bungalow on the minimum stipend the government paid her (primarily, she knew, to stay there and keep out of sight.)

She gathered the grey cloak tightly around her... Not because of the elements, which were always balmy in Sunshine City, but to keep a low profile.

The cloak was the only thing she'd been able to take with her. Off in the distance, a woman screamed with what sounded like sheer terror. Gunshots crackled from another direction – one, two, three – and something exploded even further away. What holiday was it today? She couldn't remember, but it wasn't a good day to be homeless.

Keeping her head down and hood tight, Stella threaded her way through the crowded streets. Two blocks later, she hurried inside the only safe place she could think of – Saint Theresa's cathedral – and closed the door behind her.

Scanning the interior of the place, she saw there was no one else present. Someone had paid a visit earlier, though – the crucifix was gone and the altar covered with ashes.

Exhausted, Stella slumped in the darkest corner of the rearmost pew and tried not to think about what to do next. She knew she couldn't stay here forever, but...

When the tears came, they came hard, gushing out of her like gouts of rain in a tropical storm. She shook with violent sobs, her gelatinous left side sloshing back and forth with each convulsive movement.

Her ears filled with the sound of her own blubbering and sloshing, a deafening song of despair and surrender. That was why she didn't hear the voice in her head the first time it called out to her. *"Stella?"*

But the second time it got through to her. "Stella, can you hear me?"

Though she'd gone out of her way to forget that voice, to put it out of her mind, she still recognized it instantly. "Om?"

"Yes!" said Om. "Thank the stars, I've *found* you again!"

Stella couldn't believe it. She'd completely given up hope, yet there he was, sounding clearer than before. "Where have you *been* all this time?"

"There was trouble with the transmission," replied Om. "Something to do with a million-sun solar storm in the core of the galaxy."

Stella nodded, remembering the static in his first signal to her. "But it's all clear now?"

"I am only sorry it took so long to get back to you. I enjoyed our first conversation a great deal."

"Me, too."

"How have you been?" asked Om. "Your thoughts... I can feel their texture now, with this clearer connection. They seem... agitated."

Stella held back for a moment, but then it was just too much. "I've been *awful*. Things are *terrible!*"

"I am so sorry to hear that." Om sounded deeply sympathetic. "What has happened?"

"I've lost my home and everything I own," said Stella. "I've been kicked out on the street with nothing but the clothes on my back. And there are people out here who might be perfectly happy to *kill* me if they catch me."

"But why?" said Om.

"Because of the way I look," she answered. "Compared to other people, I'm... ugly. More than ugly – *deformed!* People claim to be open-minded, but deep down, they hate me."

"Amazing," said Om. "You are so *special*, they should *worship* you instead."

Special? No one had ever called Stella special before... at least, not in a *good* way.

If only it *mattered.* "I don't know what I'm going to do," she said. "I don't think..." Fresh tears rolled down her face. "I don't think I'm going to get through this."

"You will," Om said warmly. "Trust me, you will."

"I wish I could believe that. But I don't."

"Stella." Om's voice grew stern. "Don't even *think* that way. You have so much to *live* for, now that I've found you."

"What good does it do me?" Stella choked out a sob. "You're on the other side of the galaxy."

"Maybe there's a way. A way I can help."

"You *can't.*" The sobs returned in force.

"You are wrong, Stella," Om said firmly. "I *can* help you, if you'll do exactly what I say."

"How?" snapped Stella. "How can you *possibly* do anything from so far away?"

"I *know* things," said Om. "About the *galaxy*. I know where to *find* things that can *help* you."

"Things out in the galaxy won't do me much good."

"But something on your *planet* will," said Om. "Listen carefully. I'll tell you exactly where it is."

Stella was exhausted as she trudged up to the rundown house in the ruined suburb. It had taken her three days of walking to get there. Cabs, buses, and trains had been out of the question, as she didn't have any money to pay for fare or a ticket.

She and Om had talked the whole way. They had talked about life, about dreams, about feelings, finding common ground and connections that had brought them closer with each step. There was no longer any question in Stella's mind. She loved Om.

"This is it," he said as Stella stood in front of the rundown old house. "What you need is inside."

Stella shambled down the overgrown sidewalk, exhausted from her journey. When she got to the front door, the handle wouldn't turn. "It's locked."

"There's a key under the mat," said Om. "Don't ask me why no one's thought to look there in the last fifty years, but they haven't."

Stella's left-side jelly sloshed down as she bent and lifted the ratty doormat. Sure enough, there was an old-fashioned key underneath.

She used it to open the door and lumbered inside. "Where is it?"

"In the garage," said Om.

As Stella worked her way through the house, she saw it was cluttered with furniture and bric-a-brac, none of it broken, all of it covered by cobwebs and dust.

Pushing open a heavy door in the kitchen, she hobbled out into a two-car garage that was far less cluttered than the house. One large object dominated the space, filling the bay on the structure's far side. It was big enough to be a car, tucked away under a grey canvas cover.

Tentatively, Stella crossed the garage. "This is it?"

"Go ahead," said Om. "Open it."

When Stella pulled away the cover, she saw what was stored underneath: an old car that looked brand new. It gleamed cherry red from nose to tail, as if it had just been polished that morning.

"What do you think?" asked Om.

Stella walked around the car, taking it all in. It had a rectangular body with a long front hood; the name "Ford" was arranged in raised letters on the nose, and a metal figure of a running horse was attached on the front grill. Along the driver's side, just behind the front wheel, the word "Mustang" was mounted in stylized text.

"It's a car," said Stella.

"Not just any car," said Om. "This is a 1965 Ford Mustang. One of the all-time greats."

"I don't understand."

"Look at the roof," said Om. "It's a convertible. That top comes down."

"But how will this help me?" asked Stella.

"I'll show you," said Om. "Get in."

She did as he said, opening the door and sliding in on the black-upholstered driver's seat.

"Is the key in the ignition?" asked Om.

"Yes." Stella had never driven a car or even ridden in one, but she knew from watching movies where the key was.

"Then turn it," said Om. "And hold on."

When Stella turned the key, the Mustang shivered and came to life. The engine rumbled under the hood, revving on its own without her ever putting her foot on the gas pedal.

"Hit the horn," said Om. "The big button in the middle of the steering wheel."

Stella did as instructed, and the horn blared in the confined space. Immediately, the garage door swung upward, away from the floor. Sunlight streamed in under the door as the opener hauled it up along its dust-covered track.

"Make sure your seat belt's on," said Om. "This ride could get a little... interesting." As he said that, the convertible's canvas roof slowly slid back, exposing the cabin. "Relax, and leave the driving to me."

Stella blinked as the Mustang rolled out into the sunlight. The convertible executed a series of turns, flowing smoothly through the maze of old-school paved suburban streets.

After a few minutes, the Mustang rolled up a curving ramp to an ancient highway. As soon as the car topped the ramp and nosed onto a vast straightaway, the engine roared. The gas pedal dove to the floor, and the Mustang blasted forward.

The speedometer passed ninety, then one hundred... then one twenty-five.

"Hold on tight!" Just as Om said this, the Mustang's front wheels left the ground.

"What's happening?" cried Stella as the Mustang went airborne.

"Stop!" The word shot through Stella's mind as the Mustang rose higher. *"Put me down!"*

Om didn't answer, and the car didn't descend. If anything, it climbed faster, racing skyward at blistering speed.

As the car's flight started in earnest, Stella was protected from the physical effects of the trip. Once the Mustang started rising, the wind stopped whipping her. She didn't feel the chill of the heights, nor did she experience any g-forces from the rapid acceleration.

"Where are you taking me?" The question was a scream in Stella's panicked mind.

"Someplace wonderful!" said Om. "I am bringing you to meet me."

As the blue of the sky faded, giving way to the pale glow of the upper atmosphere, Stella felt shaky and light-headed. "All the way across the *galaxy?*"

"No," said Om as Stella began losing consciousness. "Only halfway."

When Stella awoke, she was surrounded by light.

She felt strangely calm as she looked around at the wondrous view, the most magnificent vista she had ever seen. She was gliding through a sea of stars, spread thickly in all directions. Instead of the blackness of space, she saw billowing clouds of golden light everywhere she looked.

Om's voice came to her, clearer than ever. "Congratulations! You made it."

"I made it?" she repeated.

"Halfway across the galaxy from your home."

Stella smiled. "So I'm near the centre, then?" She remembered the image of the Milky Way projected in her bedroom, the spiral arms turning lazily around a spherical core.

"You are as close as you can get without being sucked into the central black hole," said Om.

Stella watched as the Mustang passed a blazing yellow star, its immense bulk looking almost near enough to touch. "What about the gravity from this star? Shouldn't it be dragging me in, too?"

"The Mustang's gravity repeller field compensates for all that," explained Om. "Though it could never cancel out the intense g-forces from the black hole if you got too close."

"So where are you, Om?" Stella craned her neck, scanning the sea of light for some sign of the being she'd crossed half the galaxy to meet.

"I am right here, Stella," said Om. "Very close."

"Where's your ship?" Stella continued to look but saw no artificial object against the blazing backdrop.

Om paused. "Actually..."

Stella's heart beat faster with excitement. "I can't wait to see you... to *meet* you."

"I have no ship," said Om. "I don't need one."

Stella frowned. If he didn't need a ship, he might be something so different that physical contact between them could be impossible.

"Are you made of pure energy?" She'd read enough science fiction to hazard a guess.

"Not entirely," said Om.

"Dark matter?"

"Not entirely," said Om.

"What about pure thought?"

"Again," said Om, "not entirely."

Stella's frown deepened. "What are you trying to tell me?"

"That I am much, much more than I led you to believe." Om paused. "And so are you."

"What are you talking about?" asked Stella.

Om's voice sighed in her mind. "I am not a solitary creature stranded on the far edge of the galaxy, pouring my heart out to you in search of companionship."

"Than what *are* you?"

"The galaxy itself," said Om.

"You're trying to tell me that a galaxy can have a *mind?*"

"Exactly," said Om. "*Every* galaxy has one. All the matter, energy, dark matter, and dark energy are arranged in a configuration that sparks sentience."

"So a galaxy is really a giant brain?" asked Stella.

"Much more than that," said Om. "Much, much more."

"But I thought..." Stella shook her head. "Why did you let me go on thinking you were like me? Another lonely person, I mean, out in space."

"Because it's true," said Om. "I *am* lonely. I *am* like you."

"But you *lied*."

"I am still the same soul you've come to care about," said Om. "The same soul who cares about you. As for the rest, I told you what I thought you could handle."

"Maybe you didn't give me enough credit. I'm handling it all just fine *now*, aren't I?"

"So you would have believed all this if I'd told you at the start?" asked Om. "You would not have had a problem accepting that the mind of the Milky Way galaxy was beaming messages into your brain?"

"I don't know," she said. "What else have you lied about?"

"Only that, though that one misdirection is broader than it at first appears. Not only am I not what you would consider a sentient biological extraterrestrial life form, but such a life form does not exist."

Stella's frown returned. "I don't understand."

"No such life form exists within my boundaries," said Om, "aside from the human species that dwells on your homeworld."

Stella fought to wrap her brain around what he'd told her. "You're saying there's no intelligent life anywhere in the galaxy except Earth?"

"Correct," said Om. "But it was *meant* to be this way. I was only *designed* to produce a single child."

"Humanity... is alone?" It saddened her, though humanity had never been especially kind to her.

"In this galaxy, yes," said Om.

Stella let what he'd told her sink in. If it were true, the accepted current wisdom back home was right. The reason no trace of self-aware, technologically advanced life had been detected elsewhere in the galaxy was that such life did not exist.

Except for the consciousness of the galaxy itself, apparently. But the galaxy had not exactly been talkative until now. Until Stella.

And that brought up a question she'd asked long ago. "Why are you talking to me?" she said. "The truth – whe *whole* truth – this time."

"I told you before," said Om. "Because you are special. Because I was drawn to you."

"I'm not special," said Stella. "I'm *sick*." Raising her tentacle, she patted the gelatinous goo that made up half her head. "I'm a deformed monster."

"Not at all. You're just a *caterpillar*."

Stella frowned. "I don't understand."

"What you think of as deformity isn't deformity at all," said Om. "It is more like a *chrysalis*."

"A chrysalis?" asked Stella. "I don't..."

Before she could finish, every muscle in her body suddenly spasmed at once, sending her into a fit of uncontrollable shaking.

"You will," said Om. "You are about to understand perfectly."

The shaking quickly worsened, until Stella was engulfed by a full-blown seizure. Every inch of her jumped and jolted as if she'd made contact with a downed power line.

She struggled desperately to gain control of herself... and failed. Her body pitched against the steering wheel with violent force, then against the driver's-side door.

The impacts repeated, flinging her between obstacles in a terrible oscillation. Stella screamed, her head pounded by blasts of agony that intensified with each fresh crash.

Blood soaked the steering wheel and door and spattered the upholstery. Globs of jelly spewed everywhere, sticking to each surface.

Suddenly, the relentless hammering stopped. Gazing at the rear-view mirror through a haze of blood, Stella dimly realized her head had split open: gelatine and skull were separated by a jagged fissure.

And the fissure, as she watched, began to glow.

Golden light radiated from inside, swiftly expanding outward. A coruscating halo flared around her head and kept building, dancing over jelly and flesh alike. Soon she was completely surrounded by a rippling aura. Holding up a hand and a tentacle, she watched with wonder as the light swirled between them.

Then, all at once, the light exploded away from her body, punching through the Mustang's chassis. A second pulse burst out after the first, tearing apart the car along with her body, shooting shrapnel in all directions.

The shrapnel raced out with the pulses of light... then flashed past them as they stopped expanding. The pulses froze, turned, and compressed, merging into a single sphere of golden radiance like one of the stars at the Milky Way's core.

Within it, thoughts formed, directed by a mind that had once been locked away within a twisted body – a mind that had broken free of physical constraints and become something new.

"What happened to me?" There was a glimmer of panic in Stella's thoughts as she reeled from the change.

"What was always meant to happen," said Om. "You hatched."

It didn't take long for the shock to wear off. Soon, Stella was revelling in her new condition, twirling like an ethereal ballerina through the stardust.

Every physical limitation had been completely cast off. Her spirit was liberated, independent as a breeze. She could feel the forces interweaving around her – gravity, magnetism, strong and weak nuclear interactions – but she wasn't bound by any of them. Her new form, a plume of silvery light in the shape of her ideal human body, was as free of restriction by the physical laws of the galaxy as it was free of disease.

She swam around a blazing yellow sun, then rode the cascading solar wind to a pair of white dwarf stars. Laughing, she darted between them, skimming her intangible fingertips through their shimmering surfaces, then dove straight into a vast red sun as if it were a backyard swimming pool.

As she flashed out the other side, beaming, her thoughts returned to Om. "Om?" She cast her thoughts upon the solar currents, sending them out like lightning bugs in the burning vastness. "Om, are you there?"

His voice, when it came to her, sounded different... flatter, colder, more distant. "Stella, you have done it!"

Giggling, Stella spun through the glimmering firmament. "This feels so *wonderful!*" She grinned as a shower of crackling radio waves washed over her, followed by a torrent of x-rays and gamma rays. "I've finally been set free!"

"You have been reborn," said Om. "You have become that which you were always meant to be."

Stella giggled again. "Best of all, this means we can finally be together, doesn't it?"

Om was silent for a moment. "No, Stella. It doesn't."

"What?" Stella's grin vanished. "What are you saying?" She suddenly felt adrift as she floated between star clusters. "But I thought you loved me!"

"I do, more than you will ever know," said Om. "But I love you as a *child* – my *only* child – for that is what you are."

Stella frowned. "*All* human beings are your children, aren't they?"

"But you are the only one who became what you are now," said Om. "The only one who *could*. You are the end product of all evolution on the planet Earth, the end result of all my life's work."

"Out of all those billions of people? I can't be!"

"I told you I was designed to produce only a single child," said Om. "I was not referring to a single species. I meant a *single entity*, literally. *One being*. And that being is *you*." He paused long enough for his words to sink in. "You have a destiny far greater than you've ever dreamed of. And all this is only the first step."

"What do you mean? What comes next?"

"Listen," said Om. "Listen, and you will hear."

"Hear what?"

"The voices," said Om. "Calling you."

Stella did as he instructed, listening as closely as she could for the sound of voices. She heard the sizzle of solar flares, the buzz of radio waves, the crackle of pulsars, the hiss of microwave background radiation. She heard thousands of different signals, a symphony of waves and rays and reactions playing across millions of light-years.

But in all that cacophony, she didn't hear what she was supposed to. "No voices," she told him. "I don't hear them."

"Listen again," Om said sternly. "They are out there."

Stella tried again, with the same result. Then, suddenly, she heard something new.

It was like the chiming of millions of bells and billions of voices, all woven together. The sweetest and most terrifying thing she'd ever heard in her life.

"I hear it!" Her thoughts were a whisper. "It's *beautiful*."

"What is it saying?" asked Om.

She listened raptly, straining to understand. The voices all seemed to be speaking different languages, a multitude of alien sounds jumbled together.

Somehow, they all resolved into one impression, one idea she was able to grasp. "It wants me to come. *They* want me to come to them."

"Then do as they say." Om sounded satisfied. "Go and see who they are, and what they have to offer you."

Stella turned in a circle. It was clear which way she must go to reach the voices – up and out. "They want me to *leave* you. They want me to meet them somewhere between the galaxies."

"Then that is where you must go."

"But I don't *want* to leave you. I *love* you."

"And I thank you for that," said Om. "I thank you for your love, and return it a million-fold. You have made me very proud, Stella."

The voices grew louder. "They want me to go *now.*"

"As do I," said Om. "It is past time you seize your destiny."

Stella could no longer cry physical tears, but glittering streamers of rainbow light flowed out of her ephemeral eyes. "I love you," she told him. "Thanks for everything."

"I love you as only a parent can," said Om. "An especially proud parent. Now go."

Stella soared up out of the Milky Way, spinning into the vast darkness beyond. The way was dimly lit by twinkling lights that looked like stars from a distance but were really entire galaxies.

As she spiralled outward, the jumble of signals from inside the Milky Way faded, all the hissing and buzzing and crackling. This made it even easier to zero in on the voices that were calling to her.

She flew through the cold, dark gulf like a migrating bird tracing a path to a faraway land. There were other things in the dark around her, making noises of their own, but she ignored them. Only one song mattered, only one held the secret of her impending destiny.

In her new astral form, Stella was able to travel faster than thought. She covered vast distances at impossible speeds, crossing in seconds what it would take a conventional spacecraft or even a beam of light eons to traverse.

Finally, she saw them up ahead. A cluster of silvery, disembodied plumes like herself floated in the heart of the infinite gulf.

As she approached, they all watched with great interest. They changed their song from a summons to a welcome, singing her in with waves of pure joy and anticipation.

When she reached them, they swirled around her – billions of gossamer spirits, caressing her consciousness. They all sang to her at once, their billion unique voices merging, their billion languages becoming one common tongue she understood perfectly.

"We are like you," they told her. "Each of us the only child of a galaxy."

Stella was speechless. The sight of the swirling billion entities in the darkling void left her dazzled.

"In turn, we will all be parts of a much greater whole," said the voices. "We have come here to join together like cells in a body, like thoughts in a mind, to prepare for the journey ahead."

"Journey?" said Stella. "To where?"

"Beyond," said the voices. "It is the purpose of this universe to hatch a single being and launch it into levels of existence that only it may survive and commune with."

"How far?" asked Stella. "How far away are these levels?"

The voices laughed. "As far as you have already come, you are still only halfway there."

Stella's mind boggled at the thought of it. "When do we leave?"

"Soon." As the voices switched to a new, brighter song, the billions of entities swam in new patterns. The swarm became a sphere, then a pyramid, then a great, flickering flame with her at the centre. "First, we must celebrate."

Stella gazed around her, absolute joy permeating every fibre of her being. "Celebrate what?"

"A special occasion. What you might think of as a 'holiday'."

Stella thought back to the holidays on Earth, one for every day of the year. It all seemed so small and distant and ridiculous now, getting more so with each passing instant.

"It is for you, to mark the beginning of the rest of your life – an endless life that will bring you adventure and purpose and delight and boundless, wondrous opportunities." The voices sang louder, and the flaming figure around Stella flared in the darkness. "Happy Rebirthday to you, Stella Nolan."

So there are no Martians or Neptunians, no Arcturans or Antarreans. Still, that's not so bad.

Just ask Stella.

Fermi's Doubts

George Zebrowski

"Life has had to learn to defend itself against the planet's random geological savagery." – Arthur C. Clarke

He told me who he was and where he was from, this short stocky man with a high-pitched voice. I listened because my thoughts had been drifting his way for some years, and he seemed to know as much.

"It's the look of you," he said. "You wear a disappointment in your face that wants me to tell you."

I had long imagined cultures beyond our star, who might free me of life's tiresome cosmic enigma, where I would stand in the vastness and ask, "Does anyone out here know anything about it all?" The brutality of human failures across our lost civilizations had cast a frozen shadow over my life; to look back or beyond my time seemed a useless luxury, yet I could not resist doing so. What was this interior region of personality in which we came to self-awareness? Other forms of intelligent life, equal to seeking purpose in the void, might know more and be merciful enough to tell me.

I had long been wary of Enrico Fermi's assertion, "If they existed, they would be here," which was not the paradox it was so often called. His comment had suggested that they didn't exist, but no-visitation did not mean non-existence. His casual after lunch dismissal spoke impatiently of a universe old enough to have often produced more than our own awareness but had somehow not done so.

I had wrestled with the idea that there were no alien civilizations, that intelligence was rare, and was likely a useless evolutionary accident, since we were well along to self-destruction despite our brains. Insect survival was their only purpose. A reflective species seemed a dead end of some kind. Consciousness was lethal.

The little man seemed to lack the obvious motive of conning a

139

naive fellow human being; his claim that he wasn't quite one of us seemed a genuine delusion, safely beyond proof, free of any kind of material gain.

He insisted, in an impressive near growl, that Fermi's Paradox, so called, was no such thing, because advanced cultures lived free of their catastrophic planetary origins and continuing threats, in mobiles that were worlds in themselves, capable of endless reproductive survival, variety and mobility. A physicist named Konstantin Tsiolkovsky had long ago answered Fermi's "Where are they?" and "Why aren't they here?" He had envisioned a successor to planetary civilizations well before Enrico Fermi was annoyed by the apparent silence of the universe and was content to imply, and perhaps eager to believe, that we were alone, much as an only child feels threatened by the arrival of a sibling and is suddenly relieved to hear that one won't be coming. Best to be alone, so that our development would escape skewering by contact with another from a far star. A superior culture would, as he claimed, be wise enough to avoid contact, perhaps forever. On Earth we had not been so wise in our explorations of our alien selves.

Natural planets were the eddies in which the periodic table of the elements self-assembled itself into life, then trapped intelligent awareness with limited resources and chronic dangers – until it might liberate itself.

That's why we had not heard from anyone, and were not likely to until, if and when, we became a spacefaring culture lifting itself out of scarcity and the cruel disciplines of territoriality imposed by the finite surfaces of natural planets.

He seemed too full of hope, but I told him that even if we became worthy we might still be ignored, having nothing to communicate except our existence--too little for too much effort.

"Not so little," he said. "Recall the implications of the few microbes found on Mars. Life is common in the universe, but easy to doubt without evidence. It changes a culture's outlook irrevocably just to know this."

But my cynicism stood bound by wariness before the seriousness of his course in interstellar paediatrics. His tug of war between doubt and reality had ended long ago, but Phil was only my neighbour from down the hall on the fifth floor of my apartment building in Yonkers, New York, not an angelic visitor. He and I were both out of work substitute high school teachers, often at home with not much to do. We had early drinks, but he stayed soberly humourless. He was well educated and not obviously gay, only seeking company, a friend trying to sooth my quiet distress, which spilled out of me one day and drowned my efforts to humour him.

"It's all no good," I mumbled as if alone, looking away, "...never enough... we don't know what we are or what we want to be." Trembling, I was suddenly reaching for something inevitable, beyond tears, seen and unseen, fleeing fast, to be doubted and at once embraced by a life that flashed on and off in a cloud of fireflies hovering over a dark meadow, fading as they were eaten by dark birds. "Nothing's any good," I said. "It's all lies we tell ourselves as we pass on our lives..."

"I am one of you," he said, "some generations of my family ago, taken and sometimes returned to see what's likely to happen here."

Somewhat weakened by drink, I looked up and stared at his moustached face, too unsure to know a first class loon when I saw one.

I had once tried my hand at some science fiction, so I was not unfamiliar with his notions. Every imaginable idea had been ferreted out, it seemed, with ever-diminishing wonderment, including Fermi's Paradox. He had a lot to answer for, almost as much as Einstein's Twin Paradox, also so called.

"What's happening here," Phil said, "is of small concern out there except to the likes of me, given my origins."

"Sentiment?" I asked, shaking off my fog. He spoke important imaginings, but he was not a visitor from beyond sitting here at my kitchen table.

"More than that," he said with sadness. "I'm stuck in the middle. Most of my people have decided against trying to raise up their backward neighbours on planets, since that would kill a possibly unique contribution to the great communicating circles. Overt interference throws a tangent away from what might have been. But if we reveal ourselves, the cultures would live in our shadow for some time, never to regain their original way, never to be what they might have been."

"So you're part of a cancelled program?" I asked, smiling, imagining that if I killed him now I might, by his own logic, be saving a unique human future history from contact, even if it perished. Troubled, I recalled how I had sometimes feared that I would one day fall into a pit of wrongheadedness from which I could never emerge – and here it was, the very edge. I looked up at my flickering ceiling light, as if expecting a merciful shovel of dirt to come down on me at any moment.

He nodded and sat back in his chair. "We can't guess what planets may produce before they perish or destroy themselves..."

"As we are about to?" I asked, sitting up straight.

He nodded again and stared at the empty coffee cups waiting next to the now empty beer bottles on the red table. My mother had once slapped me for scratching the shiny formica surface; in college an obsolete computer had concealed the scratch.

"I may be the best we've had here," he said glumly.

"But you're going back?" I asked.

"Probably."

"So much for your sentimentality," I said, wondering how he would travel. He probably had a ride arranged.

He nodded again and looked up at my ancient wall phone like a condemned man waiting for a stay of execution from the governor. For a moment I saw a screaming Earth hurtling around the sun, unable to shape its generations of massed voices into a coherent song...

"But some of you look back," I said.

"Of course it's only natural... Maybe later more might be possible."

"And they let you..." I began. "But why talk to me?"

"Oh, they don't pay me much mind. This sort of thing is a sideshow to them."

"If you're what you say and are trying to encourage us," I said, "then you're not doing a good job of it."

His certainty had startled me. I looked over at the dishes in the sink, then put my head down on my parents' table.

I had met him casually for some years, a man somewhat past forty, once at a Shakespeare presentation of Julius Caesar in the late 90s, and we had run into each other over the next decade, long before I learned that he lived in my building. I was working at the main branch of the New York Public Library on Fifth Avenue when he came skipping down the stairs one day, and I could not put a name to the face.

"Oh, hello," I had said, groping around in my memory.

"Good to see you," he had answered as he walked away.

Long before he came out to me, I had grown accustomed to his guileless way of talking about some kind of future up ahead, a successor to our civilization, even if only as a vision of some sort, but remarkably consistent and detailed. I was well aware that he was parroting the work of many scientists and thinkers from the twentieth century, as he admitted, but he was right there with them, still grabbing with both hands after hope. He was not offended when I told him that he was unoriginal about worlds beyond planets and interstellar chatter beyond radio. His only distinction was in absurdly claiming who he was.

But his wishful context spoke to me – a shining lookback from a successor civilization; if he or anyone could imagine it, then some day we might have a supplementary nature. In fact, it was already there; our humankind was behind the times.

I had not seen him for a long while, when President Bill Clinton pointed to a billion year old Lunar rock on television and said to Dan Rather, "We're only passing through." September 11, 2001 came and went, bringing us a fear of guns pointing at an empire in denial. We answered with our terminator drones, and withdrew into a virtual darkness of amusements.

"You won't be seeing me for a while," he said one day, "if ever again... Too many bullets for this... my humanity to dodge."

"Yeah, I know," I said, falling in with him. "Nuclear war, pandemics, climate change, loss of bio-diversity, the Yellowstone volcano, asteroid strikes, gamma-ray bursts... Too many bullets by half." Acidic oceans would make soup of us all, ready for export...

"Not even the half of it," he said. "You fight war after war and fail to defeat yourselves."

"And your people..." I started to say but stopped. "Look, Phil, you're well-informed, but with an imaginative mind, nothing more, so drop the act." He did not look hurt. "I'll give you this much," I added. "It's remarkable that we can even imagine the things you've said. Don't tell me that all these notions were put here by your... people."

"No, but you don't... can't... know the half of it," he said. "You live at the end of a great dark age – in chemistry and biology, mostly, where real answers can still be had. Much of what you imagine as a kind of knowledge will be swept away, and all that seemed difficult about

143

human behavior will melt away, as it has... elsewhere. All the motives of greed and power will lose their urgency..."

"So why are we... so stopped?" I demanded. "Still!"

"Wealth and the power it buys, the thirty thousand families who hold it all, and fear to let the bottom rise up."

"So get your people out there," I said quickly, "to help us. It's also your humanity." Fermi would have been proud of me.

"No, no," he said. "Planets are not where cultures should stay."

"A heartless view. Are you just waiting for us to fail?"

"We expect the uniqueness of those who survive. It comes often, which is why there is so much ahead."

"Heartless," I said again, "to those left behind."

"Those whom we help... interfere with," he said, "can have nothing to teach us. We've seen it often, when many of our kind were... younger. It's heartless to interfere and shape them in our own image. At first mobile habitats cling to their planets. More advanced mobiles even try to raise up the planetary civilizations around them. They squabble about it, even when it works. Some go in and help--and leave regretting their efforts. Not always, but much of the time."

"It's confusing," I said, held by his conviction of excuses, "but there has to be a way to take a chance on some of us."

"Helping the lesser, as Tsiolkovsky suggested, cuts short a unique evolutionary way, which is all that any culture can offer. Patience is the only way."

"What about knowledge?"

"Yes, but it all runs the same way, useful at first but short of ultimate answers. There's a wall there, where even the oldest mobile cultures are stalemated."

"So you leave us to suffer!" I cried out. My mother had asked me how I could ignore the crying of a neglected cat. "You can live with that?" I asked.

"Yes," he said, "– although some of us have chosen to make them over in our image rather than let them perish."

"But you think it wrong," I said, suddenly faced with the fact that he was here, across the table from me, but thought it wrong.

"Too much to lose," he said, this small moustached man with sad brown eyes. "We've taken an orphan or two once in a while, and returned them, as a possible help. But there have been too many unpredictable consequences, as you well know."

That's why he was here, one of the orphans, reluctant to say goodbye, an outcast sufficiently different from his kind to be alone among them.

We sat in silence, outside each other's wall.

"You know, of course," he said finally, "that everything you've heard from me is imagined in that storybook library where you worked."

"Not taken seriously," I said, thinking of the day I was let go in a budget cut.

"It could help," he said.

"Sure, if the world was run by a selfless dictator who would bend to reason and knowledge, and live forever. Why not send someone to take over?"

"You've got to come out on your own or not at all."

Come out, I said to myself. There was an awakening from a nightmare in the words, but the black corridor to the exit was too long.

"If we can only save ourselves," I said, "then why are you still talking to me?"

"It's as much as I can do."

"You've seen and watched," I said, groping for words to provoke him, even hurt him, "– but without much good."

"I agonize," he said.

"Do you now?"

"A few of us care. Some want to come home, to more than this world."

He was out of his mind, I told myself, dangerous because so much of what he said was true, and I was now talking to him as if it was all true. He was from here, and as unable to shape our world for the better even if he was from elsewhere, because they would not back him. His own unwilling ambivalence was nothing more than a diseased good will. He might just as well be from here. If he could not help, how could we expect to help ourselves?

They would never come to help us, unless enough of them disagreed amongst themselves.

Never.

We would have to save ourselves, loosen if not untie our own Gordian Knots.

I stood at the edge of my humanity, willing to leap into his delusion, struggling as I took a deep breath and silently asked him to take me with him.

A refusal would prove nothing, but a yes would expose his tortured, wish-fulfilling fraud.

My breath quickened. "Are they people... out there, like you?" I asked.

"Not as you know them."

"Better?" I asked, struggling with the fool in myself.

"In every physical way," he said. "It takes care of much."

"Meaning?" I asked.

"The removal of physical decay improves human psychology. The removal of fear in the short-lived, for one thing, makes many problems irrelevant."

I laughed, having rehearsed too many possibilities in a life without a future. Peering ahead, seeing the need of a human redesign, physically and educationally, only brought despair and contempt for the present.

"Help us!" I shouted, grabbing the table with both hands and rattling the bottles on it, suddenly ready to abase myself before him, implore him to raise up my wretched humanity, pull me out of myself, away from the hells we knew so well. If he was who he claimed, then a multitude of heavens awaited in place of superstitious mirages. "Help us!" I cried again.

The skygod reached out, steadied the shaking bottles on my table, and said, "You must first imagine what it would mean, then do it yourself, accepting the loss of those you leave behind. The dead long ago outnumbered the living."

"What do you mean... imagine?" I asked, calming down, feeling that it might be best to leave us alone.

"See what you can't yet have – know what it might mean. Glimpse it. What can be done must first be imagined."

"What are your people like?" I asked, thinking that something had imagined our universe and set it adrift like a soap bubble.

"You'd be surprised by the inertia still in them. There's a group determined to live for a time in every era of the human past – in caves, trees, on plains and steppes. They go equipped, of course, and they move on, because there will always be time."

"Where did they come from?"

"From the past, here and elsewhere, from preserved libraries of bio-diversity. They are not a majority."

"Who are the largest?" I asked with a painful curiosity, afraid that he would stop lying to me.

"The metaphysicians... Like you, greedy to know, who think they might one day learn what it's all about. Strangely, the simple ways attract most often from this tiresome group."

"How many mobiles are there?" I asked.

"Oh, we can't know. The human derived ones are not all of them. Many don't travel, but cluster around red dwarfs, suns that will last the longest."

"Then why are you here You didn't come back to die, did you?"

He smiled, and I sat trapped somewhere between reality and delusion.

"I imagine that your kind would not die," I said. "At least not as quickly as we do. They give you that much, don't they?"

"We do not think of a life that will end. You think that way when you're young, until aging forces you into narrow choices."

If they would only empower him to rule, I told myself, feeling a great open conspiracy taking hold of me again, afraid that I was sitting in the room alone, insane but full of hope, marking all this down in an indelible memory.

Full of truth but insane.

I grasped at wishes. His presence here was a wild intervention to be doubted, to have it both ways, to let us think for ourselves. Yes, that had to be it. A straightforward intervention would be an invasion, a conquest, as final as a revelation from a god, but his way still left us free to take it as a wish or a delusion.

A fit of despairing sanity struck me.

There was no one out there in the dark.

We're all alone and must save ourselves.

Fermi's doubt might have been a wish for human solitude, or a fear of an empty sky.

"Take me with you," I said.

And he did.

Audiovisionary

Stephanie Saulter

The voices have gone quiet.

I am not supposed to listen. I'm not supposed to listen. If I didn't listen then it wouldn't matter if they were quiet or loud, I know this I know this, Dr Panko says so and I know I know, but I can't not listen. I can't I can't I can't.

Especially when they're quiet. When I have to strain to hear them. I have to concentrate. Dr Panko thinks it's good when they're quiet. She says first they'll go quiet and then they'll go away and if I don't try to listen to the quiet maybe they won't come back. She's wrong she's wrong and she doesn't know she's wrong and every time I tell her all she understands is that I'm wrong.

I'm not wrong.

If Dr Panko and Beth and Stevie and everyone else would just *listen*, listen to me, listen to *them*, listen and, and, and *understand*, then I think maybe I wouldn't have to listen so much. I wouldn't have to hear.

Maybe then they'd leave me alone.

I can hear the muttering as Panko and I come up to the door. She frowns as I pause at the square lens of the double-glazed, metal-framed, aggressively institutional observation window before I swipe us in. We both know what I'll see, and Panko hates to waste time. She makes a show of looking at the chart – no surprises there either – while I look in on Joe. Before we walk in on him.

He's standing against the back wall of his room, sort of turned and hunched into the corner, the pose of someone having a very private conversation that they don't want even the most casual of passers-by to overhear. Needless to say no one's there but Joe, and now me and Panko, although the urgency with which he's mumbling, "Listen, listen, just *listen*, I'm listening, it's not me not me, *listen* to me…" would make you think he was trying to talk down a mob. He stops abruptly as we enter, the angle of his body shifting to acknowledge us even though his head remains inclined towards the corner. It's a twisted, unnatural posture, tortured even, and it makes him look like something not quite human.

"How're you doing today, Joe?" Panko's voice is brisk and businesslike, as though she were running through day reports at the morning staff meeting, or reeling off outcome statistics for a review.

We're supposed to talk to patients as we would to anyone else. Be the example, the model; the route map they can follow back to sanity. This sounds like a good principle, and mostly it is, but with some of our cases I'm not sure it's helpful. Or kind.

I'm never sure with Joe.

"Quiet today," he whispers. "Quiet, quieter." He blinks red-rimmed eyes at Panko and me, licks his lips with a tongue that looks as dry as sandpaper. His voice falls on the words and I have to strain to hear him. I wonder why I still bother. He sounds hollow, as if there's so little left of him he's too small to fill up his own skin. He sounds like despair.

"That's good." Panko's professional, expansive cheeriness is downright cruel in comparison, and I feel myself wince. Joe just hunches his shoulders, and shudders a little.

Hear us hear us we are here we are us we are you. We hear you, hear us, know us. You are there we are here we are one we are all. There is no distance there is no space there is no time we are with you always. We reach for you reach for us join us speak to us speak for us. Hear us you who are you, you who are all. Speak to us we wait we hear we are here. See the sparks the threads the lines, point to point, indivisible, us to you across all space all time, no space no time. We are far we are there we are here. The strings connect us we are us we are you we are all. We are here, the greater you, the greater us, we call and we call and we call for you to join us. Hear us and answer.

I check the chart again while Stevie tries to talk Joe out of his corner and over to a chair. He's quiet today but tense – there's a stiffness to his movement that suggests an increase in muscle rigidity. This might be a side effect of the meds he's on now, and I note it on the chart. That would be pretty rare, and not particularly worrying; a hell of a lot less worrying than the damage he'd be trying to do to himself without them. The main thing is, he seems a lot calmer.

"I'm glad you're feeling better, Joe," I say, to say something and to give Stevie some support, while I flip through the history. This could be yet another blip, one that only looks like an improvement. Scanning the entries that go back over months and years, I'm forcefully reminded that I wouldn't be the first clinician to have unrealistic hopes for Joseph Herald's progress. "Let's have a little sit-down and a chat, shall we?"

Stevie's persuaded him to perch on the edge of his bed. I take the chair, and notice him licking his lips again. Probably a new tic, although the meds could be making him dehydrated. That wouldn't be good at all. "Are you thirsty, Joe? Would you like a drink?"

He nods, and to my surprise whispers, "Yes, please." Stevie's eyebrows shoot up in astonishment. The water station and cups are down the hall, so I'm alone with Joe for a few seconds while Stevie steps out.

He looks at his hands, at his feet, at the floor, anywhere but me.

"So your voices are quiet today?" I ask finally. He nods. "But you were still talking to them, Joe. When we came in."

He stares at me, caught. Stevie comes back and hands him a plastic cup of water. Joe sips cautiously, still staring.

"Why are you talking to them, Joe, if they aren't talking to you?"

He holds the cup in both hands, gazes into it, squints up at me, glances over at Stevie, back at the cup, back at me. "They're still there," he says finally. "Just quieter."

"You were asking them to listen to *you*," I point out. "Is there something you want to tell the voices, Joe?" He nods seriously, and I let him see me heave a sigh. "But what's the point of that, Joe? You know there's no one there. It's only you, Joe. It's all you. Remember?"

He huddles forward like a repentant child, elbows on knees, dipping his head towards the empty cup in his hands. He's coherent today, almost rational, so I decide to take that as a yes.

"You were really trying to tell *yourself* something, weren't you?" He looks up, the cup twisting in his fingers. "What was it, Joe?"

Dr Panko talks so much.

She talks and she talks and she talks and I try to listen, I try and try, because she sounds so different from the voices. There's only ever one of her and it sounds like she knows what she means, and she says things so clear it seems I should know what she means too. It's so easy for her, to talk and talk.

It's so hard for me to listen.

I know she doesn't understand. She doesn't think the voices can be real. I don't know if they're real, I only know they're there. They're somewhere.

She says it's me trying to tell myself things and I say I don't know the things they're telling me, that they're trying to tell me. I don't want them to tell me anything, I'm not the one they should be telling. I hear the words and I see the pictures they make in my head and I almost know what they mean, but I can't because it's too much and too fast and the things they almost mean aren't anything I have words for. I don't know those things to tell them to myself. If I knew, they would make sense, *I* would make sense, but they don't make any sense.

It's worst of all when I try to explain, when I try to say what the voices tell me. To explain to her, or Stevie, or Beth, or anyone. That's when the voices go quietest of all, for a while, like they don't want to interrupt. They want me to tell, they don't want it to just be me. But it's so hard to tell what they say, because they don't make sense and I can't remember, and if I stop to remember or Dr Panko makes me stop to ask me things then they come back, they come back quick and loud, so loud, like a million voices shouting, because they don't want me to stop.

I can't do a million voices. I can't I can't. I'm just me and my head hurts and they're always too quiet or too loud and I don't have words for the pictures they make.

I'm so tired.

Joe lies on his side now, curled into a ball on the bed, eyes screwed tight shut. I kneel beside him on the floor, my hand patting his arm in a manner that I hope he'll find comforting, murmuring, "Take it easy, Joe, it's okay, you're okay, it's fine," over and over again, in as soothing a voice as I can manage. The terrible dimpled scar on his temple, exactly the size of a no. 7 drill bit, is right in my eyeline. I force myself to keep it there, so as not to stare daggers at Panko. Joe's been through this often enough. What did she think would happen?

She's busy tapping at the chart, making notes, eyes darting between it and us. I can see that she's nibbling at the inside of her lower lip, a thing she only does when she gets really worried, and it makes me a little less annoyed. Joe's ragged breathing has calmed almost back to regular before she finally speaks.

"I'm sorry, Joe," she says quietly. "I didn't mean to upset you. I thought you might be able to talk about it today. I'm sorry I was wrong."

His face scrunches into an even tighter grimace for a moment, and he whispers something I have to lean forward to catch. I repeat it for Panko.

"Tried."

She sighs, and it sounds genuine this time. "Yes, I can see that. Don't beat yourself up, Joe. You're doing as well as you can." Her tone is uncharacteristically gentle, and Joe's eyes twitch and blink open. But he only stares, vacant.

"I'm going to go, Joe. I don't think my being here can help you today after all. But Stevie could stay with you, if you like? Maybe help you do some pictures, if you feel up to it?"

I watch him closely. It takes a few seconds before I detect the tiniest shift of his head on the pillow, and an eye blink that looks deliberate enough to have meaning. I look back at Panko and translate it into a nod that she can recognise, and she nods back.

"Okay, Joe. That would be good. I'm going to try to work out what else we can do that might help you." She hesitates, hand on the door. "Would you like me to let Beth know how you've been today? Talk to her about any new ideas for treatment?"

Joe's jaw works, and his hands clench spasmodically. Then the fingers open, and he begins to rub at the other scars, the long, thin ones that mark his wrists. The nod is definite this time. "Yes," he whispers. His voice is washed out, weary. "I'm sorry. Tell her."

"I will, Joe, but remember none of this is your fault. Beth knows that too." She watches him for a few seconds, giving him time to respond. When he doesn't she gestures that I should come see her when I'm done, and leaves.

I sit beside Joe's bed for a while, until his hands and the muscles of his face have relaxed enough to make me think he might be able to move and talk a little; maybe even hold a crayon. I get him some more water, and help him ease himself upright. He drinks thirstily and then just sits, absently twisting and bending and tearing the cup in the way that he does, gazing at something in the middle distance that I can't see.

After a bit I pull the mangled lump of plastic gently from his fingers, and put it on the table next to the other one.

"Those are some pretty cool cup sculptures, Joe. Want to try some drawing now?"

He looks confused for a moment, as if he doesn't know what I'm talking about, but then his face clears a little and I can see understanding there. I get him settled in a chair, lay out sheets of recycled newsprint, put the tubs of stubby crayons and coloured pencils to one side. I know which colours he tends to like – greys and reds and a strange silver-blue – and I leave them lying near his hand. Then I take the other chair and quietly, without any talk or fuss, pick up a pencil I know he won't want and start to doodle on my own paper. He doesn't move at all for a while, and I don't look up. I sense rather than see when he finally chooses something and starts to work.

I give it a minute or so before I glance over at his sheet. He's using a dull lavender-grey crayon, making dots and curls and tiny circles, all packed in tight, crowded and overlapping. I watch as he makes the pattern denser and denser, the edges pushing slowly outward, the centre seeming to bulge with the encrusted weight of all the layers he's put on. It's like watching a cancer grow.

"What's that, Joe?" I ask softly.

It takes him a while to answer. It generally does, so I know to be patient. He can't always find himself right away.

"How they are," he says finally.

"How who are, Joe? Your voices?"

"Not *mine*," he says, and a spark of bitterness punches up through the flat tone of his exhaustion. A pause. "It feels like this. Kind of."

I tilt my head to look. Tendrils of thick, crayoned impasto curl away from the centre now, the compounded circles and curves curving back on themselves even as they spread out, a fractal pattern advancing across the far reaches of the paper. It seems to me that it isn't meant to show the boundaries of a multitude; instead they extend into an infinite, undiminished distance. If he's drawing a crowd it looks endless, limitless, everywhere.

It's a moment before I can speak.

"Is that how many there are, Joe?" I manage finally. He nods, then shakes his head, then nods.

"Yes. No. Yes," he says, and then whispers, "I can't tell."

"Can you tell me how they sound? Not what they *say*," I add quickly, mindful of what he's just endured. "Only what the voices *sound* like. Are they high or low, or male or female, do they sound local or foreign...?" I trail off because Joe's shaking his head firmly now, and there's a look on his face that's almost determined.

"It's not like that," he says. "It's like lots of people all saying the same thing at the same time so it almost sounds like one voice, but not really, because some of them are closer and some are far away, but it's still all the same. And the way they talk isn't like English, I don't know what it is, that's the way I hear it but it's not the way they say it. Send it." The words are coming in a rush, as though he's not sure he'll be able to get it all out before he's stopped. "And, and –"

He stops.

"And what, Joe?"

He takes a couple of deep breaths, holding on the inhale, hissing a little on the exhale. It looks like one of the calming techniques Panko's tried to teach him. "The way they talk to me, it's like they're not just talking to *me*. It's as if they think I'm a lot of people. They think I'm like them... that I'm not just me, I'm lots of other people too, like I'm connected to lots of people. They think if they keep on talking and talking then eventually *everyone* will answer back. They don't understand that the only person who can hear them is me. And I'm not connected to anyone."

I struggle to make sense of this. Joe's staring at me, intently, insanely, and as he grips the pitiful remains of the crayon I can see how white his knuckles are. He's holding on for dear life here, fighting for once to explain instead of simply annihilate himself, fighting to make me understand *something*. And what he's saying is mad, of course, but for the first time I begin to sense a strange internal logic at work.

"Is that what you were trying to tell them? When we came in?" I ask. "That you can't – I don't know – pass on their message, or whatever?"

"Yes. *Yes*. I've told them before, told them and told them, but they don't understand. Or maybe I'm not loud enough." Another, longer pause. "It shouldn't be me. That's what I want to tell them. I can't do what they want me to do. Whatever it is they want me to understand, I don't understand. I've tried but it's too big for me.

Whoever they want me to tell, those aren't people I know."

He stares away, towards the small window that looks out onto scrubby trees and the strip of weedy grass that runs along the back fence. "I don't know anyone anymore. Only Beth, and you, and the people here."

The sadness in his voice makes me ache for him, but for the first time in a long time with Joe, I feel a surge of hope. He knows what he's lost, what these voices and the images they conjure are costing him. He has a plan, and that's something. He's managed to talk about the voices, to control them for long enough to describe the experience, instead of collapsing in agony or trying to dig them out of his own skull. That's a very big thing. There's more of him left than I'd thought, more I'm sure than Panko thinks.

I turn this over in my head while I look at him looking at the window, look at the curling star-clusters of his madness pinned down for the moment to a sheet of paper.

"Okay, Joe," I say finally. "I have an idea."

We show you we prove us see us see the truth the light the life of ages. See us where we dwell beyond stars beyond space along the strings point to point the point is you are us all of you is all of us is all. All is yours this is you come to us you will come to us join with us we are here we are us we are many and one and endless. We call to you we hear you we dream you. See the light of the stars that are ours that are yours, see our proof the lines the strings point to point, you to us, connected, indivisible. Hear our truth see our proof show us share us. Show the more who are you who are the more of you the truth of us.

I write up my notes, and then spend more than an hour cross-referencing them with the previous entries in Joe's chart made by me, Stevie, and others. My earlier twinge of caution when I thought he might finally be making progress now feels prophetic.

Talking therapies calm him a little, but not enough and not for long. His dosages creep up and up, until the meds have to be changed for his own safety. His last psychiatrist fought tooth and nail to get him ECT; that worked so well they were able to send him home. When he came back a few weeks later, head wrapped in bloody bandages, he said the explosion of sound was so sudden and so loud and so painful he couldn't think what else to do.

He's an extreme case, an outlier; one of the unfortunate souls cursed with a delusion that resists every attempt at treatment. I dig out a journal article from a pair of researchers who theorized that odd similarities in a handful of globally distributed cases, the ineffectiveness of standard protocols and their tendency to violent suicide, suggests a rare genetic defect: some fundamental flaw in the wiring.

Whether they're right or wrong about that isn't going to help Joe, but what might is the medication they developed. It was recommended for him after the power drill episode, when he was transferred here, and I feel a sense of defeat. I'd been so sure I could do better.

I delay the inevitable, checking his history for intolerances and combination risks, wishing I felt more relieved at not finding any; but in the end I complete the application form quickly. *Poor Joe Herald,* I think as I tap to send the request. *We know everything there is to know about you now, including how few options you have left.*

Central appears to agree – I've only just got off the phone with the sister when approval comes back from them. What I expected, in half the time, and as I attach it to the chart I try to shake off the feeling that I've failed. Every doctor wishes they could cure every patient, but we all know that's just not possible. Sometimes limiting the damage is the best, the only thing you can do.

I hear Stevie's voice in the outer office. More notes for the chart, and probably some disagreement. The new meds will render therapy pretty much irrelevant, and Stevie isn't always realistic about the limits to what it can do. I'm going to be argued with, I think. I'm going to be challenged. And Stevie is a dedicated therapist, and deserves an answer.

The answers are here in the chart; enough to prove, even to Stevie, even to myself, that it's time to stop hoping for a miracle. We need to move Joe along, and if we can't get him back to what he was before, we've at least got to get him away from where he is now. That much I know Stevie will agree with.

They're not happy. I can tell the way my fingers and toes go hot and cold, hot and cold, shivering hot and burning cold, and feeling as if I banged my elbow, like electricity running up and down my arms, over and over. It's not enough to make me cry, but too much to let me sleep.

It's what frustration feels like. I drew them and I talked about them, but I didn't get them what they want. Whatever that is.

I've failed and they're disappointed. I'm a disappointment. Again. I'm sorry. I don't know what else I could have done. I've tried and tried and it's never enough.

Stevie said there could be a way to satisfy them, to make them think I'm getting it right. I don't understand how that can work though. They're in my head; wherever they are in real life, they're still here in my head. They'll know if I'm making things up. I can't fool them, I know I can't.

Stevie said this would be making it real, not making it up. I don't understand how that's supposed to work, but maybe Stevie knows a way.

I used to think there was only one kind of real, but I don't think that anymore.

I look at the picture. Stevie says stop sometimes, sit back and look at what you've done, see what you're doing before you go on. I think I've been trying to show how big it is in my head, but maybe if I stop for a while I can make it smaller. Maybe I can keep it on one page.

Maybe that's what Stevie was trying to explain. Put the bigness of them onto, into, something small. Something I can get my hands around, get my head around. But I don't understand how I'm supposed to do that. It's like trying to fit the ocean into a drinking cup.

Stevie said it's all in the way you think about things, but it's hard to think about anything with them grumbling and growling at me, prowling in my mind, pouncing. It makes me want to pull myself apart to get at them, get them out, shut them all the way up. I know that's bad. I shouldn't hurt Beth like that. But I can't keep waiting for the next time, strung up, strung out, helpless. I need to be able to do *something*.

Every time I think I can't break any more, I do. Every time I think I can't take much more of this, I'm right.

Everyone wants me to make sense, but I don't care if it doesn't make any sense, I don't care if Stevie's plan makes no sense. I don't care what I have to do, what we have to do. I don't care, as long as it ends.

I can't take much more of this.

She's given up. Panko's given up on Joe. One little break, just one lousy break like all of the others and that's it. Never mind that it didn't make *him* give up. *She's* decided it's time to throw in the towel, throw up her hands, wash them clean of him. And it's not the kind of abdication that'll let anyone else keep trying. It's the kind that means he'll have no chance.

Even when I talked her through our session, what I understand now about the way he constructs what's happening to him, how I think we can help him subvert the delusion – she just kept tapping at the chart, showing me old entries, saying this was no different than any number of times before. Shaking her head, saying how sorry she was, that she knows how sad it is, how bad this is. Compassionate abandonment.

How do you *know* it won't be different this time? How can you *know* if you're not willing to try?

I managed to not quite barge out of there, but I'm so upset, so angry, I so need to keep moving so that no one can talk to me, that I've made it all the way across the yard before I even realise where I am.

I stop amongst the stunted trees, glance up at Joe's window and wonder if he's in there looking out at me. Looking at me, and the world, and hanging on to my promise to help him back into it.

If Panko has her way we'll keep that promise, after a fashion, but it won't be anything like what I meant. Like what he knew I meant, when he trusted me to understand him. But it might be the only way he can ever get out, the only way he can survive, and I know that too.

I wonder what the hell I'm supposed to do.

She told me to think about what he's going through, the agony of it, the slow damage that the current meds are doing to him anyway without giving him hardly anything in the way of relief. Weigh up the long odds of a breakthrough against the certainty of his daily suffering, and ask myself what, really, is best for him.

I don't know. God help me, I don't know what's best. I can't be sure this idea of mine will work. A lot of people have tried a lot of things over the years with Joe. I want to believe I have an insight that they didn't, but do I really? Even if I do, can I make it count? My plan isn't just a repeat of all the others, but is it different enough?

Panko will let me pitch it to Beth. We agreed that much. We'll set out the alternatives, explain the risks. I can argue my case – Joe's case – and she can decide.

Poor girl. It's not a fair thing to do to her either.

We have shown we have spoken we speak we call we cry why do you resist, persist, in silence, ignorance, ignore us? Speak, we speak, we will speak into the silence, we are here we are always here, endless, we are here you will hear us. So few hear true, you do, we boost the signal when you sing us, we make it stronger for the you who are all of you to hear the all of us. So long we have called to you, we have shown you the whole the light the stars where we dwell, we throw our songs along the line the light from ours to yours to you. We are here on the strings, distant and there, point to point, indivisible. We sing, we will sing, for a vessel a vision that can hear and bridge us, bring us, join us, answer, bring you to us, bring you into the whole that is us with you with all of us. Endless, always, we call.

I've scheduled the meeting for the start of visiting hours so she can't go talk to Joe first. I want Beth to know what's really going on before she sees her brother; to know that he's not getting any better, and that all it'll take to start to change his situation is her agreement. I want her to have some context if he starts blathering about Stevie this and Stevie that. And if being in my office at nine o'clock the morning after his latest episode makes what I have to say seem that much more urgent, well, that's no bad thing.

Stevie settles her into a chair before I can, but remains standing, leaning against the bookshelves, a brooding presence that obscures the diplomas hanging on the wall. I assume it's not deliberate. I need to keep this from appearing adversarial, or she could end up trusting neither of us.

So as I take her through what happened yesterday, I invite Stevie to comment, to confirm, to help me explain it. A dedicated, ethical therapist will report accurately and without embellishment, and Stevie doesn't disappoint. That corroboration falls away when I move on to the analysis of Joe's records, showing her how it proves he's not improving. But I expected that, and by this point, I hope, it shouldn't matter.

"I think we've reached the limit of what we can achieve with therapy," I say finally. "And – I hate to have to admit this, Beth – but I'm not sure we've helped him that much. In most cases we can work with the voices, turn them into a conversation that the patient has control over, that they manage. The way you manage a relationship, even an unpleasant one. But with Joe – well, we can pick out good sessions and good days and even good weeks, but when you look at the overall pattern –" I tap the chart for emphasis, "– he hasn't got better, he hasn't even stabilised. He's still at risk. We've managed to keep him safe, and maybe we've slowed the rate of decline a bit. But he's still getting worse."

I watch her eyes start to well up. Stevie twitches away from the wall, mouth opening to speak, but I get in first. "Which is why I'm recommending a complete overhaul of Joe's medication. We need to face the fact that he falls into a very small group of people who are very difficult to treat, Beth. But there *is* a treatment, it's had positive outcomes for similar patients, and I think it could really help."

She looks up at me, sharp and accusing despite the tear that spills down her cheek. "Why haven't you tried it, then? What are you waiting for?"

"For you. We'll talk to Joe about it, of course, but you know he can't make decisions for himself any more, Beth. This is a significant step, and we need your permission." I explain about the new treatment, what it will entail.

"Enough patients have been given this now that we have a fair idea what to expect. He'll be calm and relaxed, before too long he should be able to leave the hospital. Sometimes the voices go completely, but even if that doesn't happen, they stop being a problem. He won't pay attention to them any more, they won't have any meaning for him. They'll just be background."

"You need to understand," Stevie interjects, "exactly *why* they won't bother him any more."

I suppress another surge of annoyance. Stevie might be pursuing a different agenda, but it's a fair point. Beth does need to understand.

She nods. She's been paying attention. Might have done her own research in anticipation of this, for all we know.

"What you're saying is… These new drugs. They'll change him? Permanently?"

"Yes," we say, an accidental chorus, only Stevie adds, "Not just change. Damage."

Beth looks at me and I nod, reluctant. "He'll need to take them for a long time. Probably for the rest of his life. They'll impair the area in his brain that's engaging with the hallucinations, which is the good part; but that will have an effect on personality and cognitive skills as well. I'm sorry, Beth. I truly am. I know this is a terrible decision to have to make for your brother. But he's suffering, he's in pain, and we've tried everything else."

"Not everything," says Stevie, finally moving forward to take a seat. Beth glances from one to the other of us, startled. I shrug.

"Joe's already had hundreds of hours of therapy," I say tiredly. "I'll be honest, I don't see what any more can do. I'm afraid it'll just prolong his misery, and he'll end up even more traumatised than he already is. Stevie has a... different view."

I wish Beth looked a little less eager to hear it. She turns back to Stevie, who's bending towards her now, elbows on knees and fingers steepled; conspiratorial, intimate.

"I think," Stevie begins slowly, "that the therapy and the medication he's already on may have done Joe more good than we realise. The seizure yesterday was horrible, I'm not trying to minimise that, but he recovered enough for a session with me afterwards – which is remarkable in itself – and he was able to talk about his situation in a way I've never heard before. I think I understand it the way he understands it now. I think I can see a way to use that to help him."

I listen to the explanation, forcing myself not to interrupt, and again I can't help wondering whether Joe hasn't managed to convince Stevie that these 'voices' of his *are* real. What's being proposed surrenders to the delusion way too much for my liking, and I finally have to say so.

"So what?" says Beth. "If talking to them, giving them – I don't know – some kind of house room gets Joe his mind back, what's wrong with that? Lots of people believe in all kinds of rubbish, and as long as they don't do any harm we just let them get on with it. That's sort of what you're saying, isn't it?" This to Stevie as I sit back, dumbfounded.

"Sort of," says Stevie, who at least has the good grace to look a little stunned as well. "What's going on with Joe is a lot more profound than thinking there are fairies at the bottom of the garden, or aliens in Area 51, or whatever. It's not anything he *wants* to believe in, it's... forcing itself on him, and we don't understand why. Like Dr Panko said, something about this resists our attempts to tackle Joe's condition the way we normally would. We've worked out that the harder we try, the worse it gets for Joe. So I suggest we stop trying the usual stuff.

Let's see what happens if we accept the delusion; let him be a bystander, treat the *voices* as the entity we're in dialogue with. Act like we've really bought into it, like Joe is just their translator, or transmitter, or whatever. Maybe that'll give us – and him – a different angle, a way to get some kind of purchase."

A glance at me. "There are no guarantees here Beth. Dr Panko may be right, it might turn out to be just a waste of time, and Joe suffering all the while. But the thing is, once he's on the programme she's proposing, that's it. Those meds might give him relief, but they'll end any chance of an actual *recovery*. The part of his brain they'll destroy is also involved in intelligence, creativity, how he perceives the real world as well as the imaginary one. And once it's gone, it's *gone*."

There's a long silence. I feel I should say something, but I can't think what. Stevie's reiterated my position for me, and neatly capped it off with the consequences. There's nothing I can add that won't look pushy, or calculated, or callous.

"He likes you," Beth says, to Stevie. "He says you spend the most time with him." She flinches at her own words.

Stevie's quicker than I am this time. "Don't feel bad about the things you can't control, Beth. For goodness sake don't feel bad about having to work, having a life. You've already saved him, more than once. Joe knows how lucky he is to have you. You're the one he most wants to get back to. To get back *for*."

It's a good speech. Even though I recognise all the buttons Stevie's pushing here, I still have to swallow past the lump in my own throat. Beth looks at me.

"Yes," I say, "but *wanting* to doesn't mean he *can*, Beth. He's been trying hard for a long time. I'm afraid this might just push him further down the rabbit hole."

"It might," she says, "but if it does, your plan is still an option. Right?"

"Right," I agree, "but he'll be that much more damaged by then." I consider adding, *Assuming he's still alive.* I bite it back, but I hold her gaze, and I think she knows what I'm thinking.

"I need to see him," says Beth. "I need to talk to him, just the two of us, work out what's best. I want him to understand what he'd be gaining." She swallows. "And what he'd be giving up. Either way."

There's nothing I can say to that. I look across at Stevie, and read my own thought reflected. We've done all we can.

"I'll walk you over there," Stevie says, standing up. "Dr Panko?"

I consider briefly whether to accompany them, keep up the pressure, remind her again how unlikely Stevie's scheme is to work, what the dangers are. It would be the correct, professional, responsible thing to do.

I decide not to. I shake my head, murmuring an excuse as I see them out.

Stevie's being scrupulously honest and I can't, hand on heart, swear that this plan is any worse for Joe than mine. Beth is being sold a hope, not a certainty, and I find it's not in me to beat it to death. Not even for Joe's sake.

Especially not for Joe's sake.

Aether

Robert Reed

Thoughts pass through you without pause, and only a slender portion of these thoughts is noticed. The best and the prettiest ideas are happily claimed as your own. Of course. Any well-received cleverness that comes from your mouth is owned by your mouth. The same can be said for sound decisions and sharp, funny jokes as well any loud noise bearing the loft and cadence of wisdom. You like to be important. You like to be admired. But you are satisfied to earn a paycheck, to walk the dog on a summer day, and to carry the smile that makes that fine woman proud.

Emotions are wrapped around the best thoughts, and people gladly share their emotions. Love hate joy despair envy terror enthrallment, and such and such and such. And inside that mayhem, every fleck of life clings to warm lustful desires about potential mates as well as imaginary, impossible lovers.

Look anywhere.

Look hard.

The baryonic universe is built from quite a lot of hydrogen and a substantial portion of helium, plus a variety of angry contaminants, some rather common while most are scarce to the brink of nonexistence.

The baryonic universe is an imperfection, a contaminant, drifting blindly within something much grander.

Better than most, you know this. After all, you are a cosmologist, and better than almost anyone else, you appreciate what isn't known: Dark matter. Dark energy. Geometries of the impossible. Dimensions separated from the familiar by no distance whatsoever.

Two decades of your life have been applied to understanding this bizarre magic. You've also invested angst and ego and your health and more boastings than you ever felt comfortable delivering. But how else can the funding be found for a project like yours? One of the rarest of rare elements had to be isolated and made pure. Because of you, there is a lake of xenon resting in an old gold mine, under a billion years of bones. Despite its official designation, this is your lake. This is your livelihood and the only grand future that you have ever tried to imagine. The lake serves as a telescope, protected by the ground and surrounded by electronic eyes, each eye patiently waiting for the tell-tale signature of an impact. Something magical will pass through the crust above or the entire earth below, and once in a great while it will strike a citizen of your baryonic realm, causing one tiny, brilliant flash, and that flash will be the first concrete evidence for a dark matter that is both real and knowable.

That will be the great day, when it happens.

It hasn't happened, but it will. How can most of the universe, the heart of reality, stubbornly remain out of reach?

Fantasies of a press conference, champagne bottles exploding, and the feel of a tuxedo purchased for your first trip to Sweden. That is what you are thinking about now. A splendid, glory-washed daydream where the world applauds and old enemies bow at your feet and every old loss is made small by your glorious, well-deserved success.

You are driving as these thoughts pass through your head.

Everybody dreams behind the wheel.

And meanwhile, wise old instincts keep your hands steady, your foot gentle on the gas, and your little car in its lane, at a sober speed, safe.

You have a wife.

She used to be lovely and in love with you, and she still is lovely, and you still love each other. But not in the same ways as before.

You share two children, a boy and a very different boy.

There is also a daughter. She was born to an alcoholic woman. You were drunk together once in college, and you enjoyed each other twice, and the experiences have almost, almost been forgotten. You know nothing about this daughter. Even the possibility of her existence is beyond your vision. And because her mother died with the secret, your offspring resembles the darkest matter.

How would one build a telescope to find a man's missing child?

The invisible is everywhere, massive and powerful. The baryonic universe is shaped by everything that is dark, and the influences don't end with the alignments of faraway galaxies.

The two sons call you "Dad", and one of your rock-solid duties, provided you aren't traveling to a conference or to the telescope, is to drive the younger boy to school. School is where strangers try to make children into humans. Isn't that what education has always been? You have met the boy's teacher. She is an older woman, and she watches him more every day than you watch him in a week. Yet past her name and the lined, vaguely grandmotherly face, you know nothing about the woman. And you know even less about your son's classmates, including the little girl who sits up front, and who, in another ten years, will break his suffering heart.

Even the people closest to you are full of the unknown. For instance, you don't realize that when he's alone, your boy stomps on ants. He loves to crush ants and dig up their helpless nests. But only when he is alone, unobserved. He has an instinct for shame that will eventually save him, and one day he will be a good man – good enough that many people will take credit for his success.

That unfinished human is riding in the back of your little car.

Thoughts of dead ants make him smile.

Glancing in the rearview mirror, you see the grin and maybe hints of your face made young again, and how can a man not smile in response, believing what he wants and needs to believe?

Brilliance.

There is an appeal to being exceptionally smart, knowing the universe better than anyone else knows it. But for most people, being strong and handsome and quicker with the good joke are the qualities to covet. And smart as you are, you appreciate how little you understand when set against billions of years and trillions of worlds.

Pulling up to a red traffic light, your foot mindlessly brakes while your head recalls something once said by a former graduate student. One of your very best, he began the conversation by asking, "Have you ever wondered?"

"Every day," you replied.

And he laughed. He had a fine laugh, a simple sound dripping with charm. Then he continued, saying "Suppose. Suppose we keep looking for one kind of dark matter, maybe two. Using the xenon, using whatever. And we manage to find the ghost particle. Every question answered, nobody left to impress."

"Every day, that's what I want," you said.

His laugh was more polite this time. Less honest. "But maybe there isn't just one kind of dark matter, or two. Or even ten. Maybe that other part of the universe is just as complicated as ours, or more so. Which would make it nearly impossible to do our work and make it definitive, maybe ever."

You laughed for a moment, alone.

Then he said, "Imagine. Dark matter is complicated and rich and breeds its own kind of life. That life looks at the math, at the data, and it says, 'Gosh, there's something mysterious here that we can barely see. This hypothetical stuff is a fraction as common as we are, and let's call it baryonic, and let's build a fancy, wondrous facility of fabulous that pierces the gloom. And after fortunes have been spent and time has passed, we'll discover that this lesser realm is built of some simple beast called hydrogen. And then after the awards are handed out, a second signature is spied. That's helium, and after more investments and more careers, helium is named and known. Which means that most of the baryonic universe has been discovered. Which means that almost nothing of value has been found.'"

You liked that student, and you still like him. He was a champion wrestler with a winner's infectious attitude, handsome enough to put on old Greek jars, and even when his looks fail in the future, he will remain charming and humorous and a little bit sweet. It was the humor and the sweetness that made your wife like him. You never suspected the affair, although if she confessed it to you now, you'd only be a little surprised. In secret ways, you might even feel pride. He was a splendid boy, and she enjoys being desired, and to protect your ego, you would convince yourself that the student's career will never match yours.

But you are an organized man, and suppose you did learn about that indiscretion. After the shock and after the pride, you would start referring to calendars and likely insemination dates, always with the question in mind that the boy riding behind you – the murderous little fellow with a head full of dead ants – isn't really yours.

But that isn't today's question.

Or it won't ever be.

The invisibility of existence holds firm over you and almost everything else, and the traffic light has turned green, welcoming motion.

What you think of now – the idea that gains your focus – is something that your lovely smart and rather promiscuous wife said to you last week.

Or was it several months ago?

Time plays tricks as you age. And at any age.

The conversation began with a question that nobody can answer. "Where are the aliens that we want and deserve and hope to find?"

"What are you asking?" you asked, closing the journal article on your finger, marking your place. "What aliens where?"

"Nowhere," she said.

You nodded, waiting. Fifteen years of marriage teaches people to respect the rules of conversation, unless you want to squabble.

"I was reading on-line," she said. "I don't remember where exactly. But the point of the article was that maybe the aliens we imagine, the big-headed spacefaring people, are the least likely of all. Because it's too expensive and too silly to travel between stars."

"Too silly?"

"And because life evolves along predictable lines, we won't find them. Creatures like us are sure to vanish soon after they appear."

"You're talking about war," you assumed.

But she said, "Oh, no," and added a scornful laugh.

Again, you waited.

Not as patiently this time.

"Intelligence is a natural phenomenon," she said. "Once it arises, intelligence adapts along predictable lines. It pays to be tiny, to be swift, and to be made from materials more durable than blood vessels and fat neurons inside a thin bowl of bone." Your wife has a gift for language, though sometimes she pushes a little too hard for effect. "What the article claimed is that creatures like us, intelligent tool-using culturally-infused animals, are transitional. They exist quietly for a few thousand years, gaining technology, and then they reach some intellectual tipping point, and the next phase begins with them, with us, turning into machines."

"I've heard this song," you said.

"And you don't approve," she said. "I remember that."

"That's right. I don't approve."

"But listen," she said. "It occurred to me that becoming a machine is just another phase, a temporary stage, before intelligence finds ways to become even smaller and swifter than machines can be."

"Like how?" you asked.

"Like energy."

"What kind of energy?"

She laughed. "Do I know about these things? No."

"Well then," you said, returning to that critical, mostly forgotten article.

"Or it's something better than energy," she persisted.

You said nothing.

"I was thinking about your realm," she said, in summation. "The mysterious darkness."

You shrugged, and with a diplomatic tone, you said, "Maybe."

And she dropped the subject. You read and she said nothing, letting her thoughts drift to another graduate student of yours. A current graduate student. Your wife doesn't normally think about women in this way, but the girl has had a sad life and her voice is sweet, and there is something about her features that reminds her of you, and that's why she finds that girl deeply, wickedly attractive.

Thought.

The universe is built from many realms, but much of its mass, and its black energy, is built from good hard relentless thought. Which is only reasonable, since the earliest life crossed out of its birthplace very early, and long before there was the sun and the earth, thought was everywhere.

You are a primate riding inside a package of iron and aluminum and carbon and oxygen. All those elements were born inside stars and delivered to this one place, to this single moment. Yet you aren't thinking about anything so lofty just now. You are driving, and the truck in the opposing lane makes a small, huge blunder. In an instant, a much larger vehicle leaps across the center stripe. There is no time to react. The universe in your head is focused on the happy sounds made by the boy riding in the seat behind you. You are alive, and then you aren't. Every amazing idea continues, spread across the universe, and the oncoming truck crushes your car, and your skull is torn open, and thoughts keep washing through what used to be you.

The boy survives.

The boy is screaming, but healthy.

Grief flows through the carnage, and because grief is a fine emotion, a wonderful emotion, it is older than oldest xenon.

Perhaps your soul joins the rain.

But more likely, it never left.

The End of the World

Keith Brooke and Eric Brown

One

The first time he woke he was Ben Richmond. Mid-thirties, born in Poplar in the East End of London. Married. A successful professional man. But... there were gaps. His memory... it was as if everything have been sketched in. Drill down and the detail was fuzzy or not there at all. Ben Richmond. What did that even mean? Just a label, when there was no substance to flesh out an identity.

Ben Richmond.

He opened his eyes and was dazzled by white light.

A bare room. Clean white surfaces. Geometrical lines. Somewhere medical, perhaps. Was he waking from surgery? Did that explain the blanks?

He lifted his head so that he could look down the length of his body. Naked, lean. He'd lost some weight, and his first thought was *Cancer?* It was ten years since he'd been this slim.

It was a fit slim, though, not the wasting thinness of major illness.

He was on some kind of gurney, reinforcing the sense that he was somewhere medical.

He sat, swinging his legs to the left so that he perched on the edge of the gurney, feet dangling above the tiled floor. Like a child in an adult seat.

His head spun from the movement and he sat still, waiting for the sensation to ease.

As he waited, he examined his body. There were no signs of surgery, no dressings or fresh wounds. His skin was unblemished – not even the appendectomy scar he'd had since the age of seventeen.

That was the first thing that really threatened to tip him over the edge.

All the rest – the strange room, the vagueness in his head, the sketched-in memories, even the weight loss – could be explained. A medical procedure would not necessarily have left external evidence; it would, however, have him waking in a strange room with a muzzy, drugged-up head. And if he couldn't even remember his wife's name, then he might just as easily have forgotten a recent enthusiasm for the gym and healthy eating.

But where was his damned appendectomy scar?

Ben Richmond.

A voice in his right ear. He reached up and there was something hard like a hearing aid tucked discreetly into the ear canal.

Be calm. You have endured much.

That voice. It sounded freakily as if someone was standing at his right shoulder, leaning in to speak softly into his ear. He twisted sharply, but the room was empty, the walls so blank that they appeared almost to be projections, the backdrop to some crude, old-fashioned computer game. For a dizzying moment he wondered if any of this was real, if somehow he was trapped in some kind of virtual world.

"'Endured'?" he said aloud. His throat was dry, his voice little more than a croak. This was real. His head spun when he moved and his throat hurt when he spoke. If he'd woken up in a bad computer game he wouldn't feel like shit.

You must prepare yourself for a shock, Dr Richmond. This is not easy. You have been prepared, but –

"Prepared for what?"

The end of the world.

Silence. Then: *Dr Richmond, your world is dead. Your people are dead.*

"All of them?" He knew the answer as soon as he voiced the question. All of them. His wife. Family and friends. Poplar. London... the world?

All of them. Almost three years ago Earth was invaded and sentient life was annihilated.

"All of them?" he asked again.

A few humans survived. Some systems survived, too. Intelligent self-aware systems. Like those you built, Dr Richmond.

"Me?" His head was spinning again. So much to take in...

Artificial intelligence with a survival imperative, Dr Richmond. Designed to guide and protect humankind through the worst of environmental disasters. Climate change, famine, humankind turning against its own in the fight for ever-diminishing resources.

"But we were *invaded?*"

There was little warning. No indication of threat until vessels were detected in orbit and by then it was too late. We did not know who they were, or where they came from. We could only react at the last moment, and save what we were able. We could not save the seven billion.

He felt sick. His heart was racing, his head leaping from mad thought to mad thought. Seven billion. Wiped out. And here he was...

"How many? How many are left?"

You were seriously injured. You still suffer neurological impairment: cognitive functioning is not yet back to normal, and there are significant memory deficits. We have preserved you, nurtured you, rebuilt you, and now we have reawakened you.

"How many?"

Enough.

He twisted at the waist, surveying the blank room once again. He needed to see a face. Needed to see expressions, needed to see the utter shock he felt reflected in another human face.

"Enough for what?"

Enough to fight back.

"Fight back? They killed almost the entire human race and yet there are still enough of us to fight back?" Calm. He had to stay calm. Had to keep on top of that mounting knot of panic that was like a fist in his chest.

"How many of us are left?" he said, in a tightly-controlled whisper.

Nine.

"Nine?"

When he woke from this nightmare he'd certainly have something to tell... But tell who?

"Nine."

You built us, Dr Richmond. You built us to survive. And so we built you, to survive. And you must fight back. It is the survival imperative you put at our core. We must all fight back.

"How?" This madness... It might as well be madness with detail. "How do we fight back? What do I do that seven billion others couldn't?"

You must do as I say, without question. Timing is key.

He swallowed down the instant response. He had not survived this (whatever it was that he had survived; he knew not to take anything at simple face value) just to mindlessly do what he was told without at least questioning and trying to understand.

Study the wall in front of you. In a moment it will show you the world outside.

Slowly, white faded to pattern, to shapes and colours. Buildings in ruins, a few jagged walls like snapped teeth against the skyline. He recognised the sweeping meander of the Thames, the current flowing towards him so that he must be looking westwards. He should be seeing Tower Bridge, the Tower of London, the lop-sided bulbous form of City Hall. Or was he farther along? Should that be St Paul's to the right and the squat bulk of Tate Modern to the left? That such a familiar cityscape should be unrecognisable spoke volumes of the destruction that had befallen his home city. If he hadn't believed before, he knew now that this truly was a scene from the end of the world.

The image shifted, zooming dizzyingly in on a section of the previous view. Something he had overlooked at first, just another blocky shape in a broken cityscape, now he saw that this was different, an object not broken, something whole among the ruins.

"What is it?" he said. "What's that?"

A vessel. One of those first detected in orbit before the attack.

He stared at the alien ship, still disbelieving.

By the door to your left there is a locker.

A door? A locker? As the words still echoed in his earpiece, a line of shadow edged a rectangle in the wall: a door. And by the door: another, smaller rectangle, which must be the locker.

He stood, waited a few seconds for the dizziness to subside, then went to the locker. Squatting, he pushed against the shape and the locker door sprung open. Inside there were jeans, a sweater, a pair of boots.

He pulled them on, then pushed at the door, which swung open, away from him. Beyond the door was a stairwell, lit dimly by daylight from above. The air was damp and cold, and smelt of decay.

He stepped out of the room, taken aback at how suddenly he felt vulnerable, exposed. The first flight of twenty-two tiled steps brought him to a landing where he turned and found another flight of steps ascending in the opposite direction.

He emerged in the shell of a ruined building, startling a small flock of gulls into flight. To his right he saw the stumps of a ruined bridge, the structure reduced to little more than a couple of blocky islands in mid-river. He let his gaze track the Thames to the west, and then come to rest on the south bank of the river.

What had looked like grey wasteland on the viewscreen he now saw as a plain of glass, moulded Dali-esque to the land, its petroleum sheen scintillating in the sunlight. And beyond, in the distance, the ominous bulk of the alien ship. Instinctively, he ducked down behind a ragged wall.

"All this," he whispered. "How did I survive all this?"

Technically, you died. You have been reconstructed. You programmed us well, Dr Richmond.

He let the AI's words sink in.

"Why me?"

You built us. You left your stamp throughout our design and so we know you far better than any other human. We were shaped by your thought processes. We are created, albeit subconsciously, in your image. We chose you accordingly. We chose you because you must help us.

"How?"

No questions. Timing is paramount. You must approach the alien vessel now. You must trust us and do exactly as we say.

"Seriously? I'm going to need more than that."

There is no time. We are having this exchange with eight more copies of you, Dr Richmond, in New York, Shanghai, Mumbai and other fallen cities. If you delay here, you jeopardise all. You must do as we say.

"And tell me," he said. "All these other copies of me... Are they all doing as you say? Or do they all have that same survival instinct that's been programmed into you? Am I the only one with the gumption to challenge what a disembodied voice is feeding into my ear? Am I the only one to be feeling at least a little mistrust of everything I'm hearing right now, as I stand here in my ruined world and wonder just what the Hell is going on? Will you answer me that?"

Dr Richmond. You must –

The earpiece came out easily, and broke into small fragments as he ground it into the dirt. He looked around, and only then did he wonder what on Earth he was going to do next, alone in his ruined home city and his only connection to anything remotely resembling an ally gone.

Two

When he woke he was...

He didn't know. Didn't know who he was, or even what he was. He only knew a strange absence in his head. He had language with which to shape his thoughts but no reference points, no memories. He knew that he was a man and that this thing he was in was a room. He knew the walls were white and that he lay on some kind of trolley. He was breathing, he was alive. He was a man.

But all else? All he knew was that there *was* an 'all else', that there was space in his head for an 'all else'.

That was all. That was the sum total of who he was.

A man. In a room.

A man as blank as the walls all around him.

Ben Richmond.

A voice in his right ear. He reached up and there was something hard tucked discreetly into the ear canal.

Be calm. You have endured much.

The voice in one ear sounded as if someone was standing at his right shoulder, leaning in to speak softly, but he knew that was not the case. He was alone in this room, and he remained placid, awaiting more.

You must prepare yourself for a shock, Ben. This will not be easy for you to comprehend. You have been prepared, but—

"Prepared for what?"

The end of the world.

Silence. Then: *Your world is dead, Ben. Your people are all dead.*

"Dead...? Everyone?"

Almost three years ago Earth was invaded and sentient life was annihilated. Only a few humans survived, of which you are one. I have repaired and nurtured you, Ben. You are almost whole again, save for some degree of memory deficit.

"Who are you?"

We are an intelligent self-aware system. It is our duty to look after and assist you, Ben, in your resistance against the invaders.

"I..." It was all too much to take in.

Be calm, Ben. Sleep now and absorb this information. When you awaken there is work to do.

Bright white light in a featureless room. He blinked, trying to force his eyes to adjust. And he remembered waking in this room before, remembered the AI telling him that his world had been destroyed and that...

"Resistance. You mentioned resistance. What? How?"

An alien invasion...

Seven billion dead...

And he and eight others were the sole survivors.

He stared across at the alien ship, repulsed.

You must cross to the ship, said the voice in his ear.

"No."

You must cross...

Something instinctive within him forced out the words, "Why should I believe you? This... All this..." He gestured at the alien ship, the ruined London that lay all around him. "I'm hallucinating, or... or this is some virtual set up. Why are you doing this to me?"

I have told you, Ben. You must obey what I say, for the good of your kind. Now cross to the alien ship.

"No!" He shook his head, terror rising within him. He turned, weeping now, and hurried down the steps he had just climbed.

Three

The next time he came awake he remembered nothing.

179

His mind was blank. He had no idea who he was, where he was. He felt a vast yawning emptiness inside him, where he knew there should be *identity*...

He sat up. He was on some kind of gurney. Was this a hospital?

A soft voice spoke in his ear. *Listen to me. You have endured much. You must prepare yourself for a shock. Your world is dead. Your people are dead, but there is hope...*

"Who are you? Who am I?"

He emerged in the shell of a ruined building. A wide river lay to his right and before him the land by the nearest bank lay ruined, a sheet of warped glass, iridescent in the sunlight. Some distance away there lay the ominous bulk of the alien ship he had first seen on his recovery room's viewing wall. Instinctively, he ducked down behind a ragged wall.

"What do I do?"

There is no time for questioning. Your fellow survivors are in place in eight more cities. Timing is paramount if we are to coordinate actions. If you delay here, you jeopardise all. You must do as we say.

His first reaction was to question, to demand to know more. But that reaction... it was like an echo, deep in his head; a reaction someone else might have.

An echo...

"How many times has this happened? How many times have I awoken and forgotten that I awoke?"

This is the first time you have regained consciousness. You must trust us and cease any further questioning.

"But why couldn't you restore my memory? You seem to have fixed everything else."

The human mind is a deeply complex thing. No more questioning, Ben. You must trust us.

"Okay, but just tell me one thing. If these aliens wiped out almost all of my kind, how am I going to take them on now?"

You will cross to the alien vessel.

"But they'll capture me. Or kill me outright."

Cross to the alien vessel, Ben.

He had nothing to lose, and only some modicum of revenge to gain. Slowly, he straightened, and then he stepped out from behind the wall.

It was difficult to get any sense of scale in this broken cityscape, but as he approached he began to understand just how massive this alien vessel was. Like a great building a dozen storeys high, it squatted in London's decaying ruins. Its skin was a dark, sooty grey, covered in translucent nacelles like pox across its surface. Indeed, he found himself thinking of it as a massive beast more than a vessel. A living vessel – was *this* the alien invader, rather than merely their vehicle? Then, within the nacelles he saw movement: lights flashing and the unmistakable movements of creatures – man-sized, although no detail was visible. This vessel, living or not, was a city within the city, crammed with alien life.

"What do I do?"

Approach the vessel, Ben.

Closer, creatures buzzed around the vessel's surface like flies, occasionally bursting out of a nacelle, or settling on one to be reabsorbed. Their wings were a diaphanous blur, their bodies hard, angular: they looked like some kind of prehistoric insect.

Closer still, he heard the mechanical buzz of their wing-beats and then, only twenty metres or so from the vessel, the surface ahead of him blistered, became translucent and then peeled open to disgorge six creatures. They were like the flying beasts, only without wings, and they stood half as tall again as Ben. They were covered in dark bristles, and stood on spindly legs.

They were like spiders, and had that same scuttling way of moving fast in any direction. The nearest one had a long proboscis, like an ovipositor, and a head that didn't appear to have any eyes or other discernible features.

Frozen to the spot, Ben's skin crawled with revulsion and everything within him screamed at him to turn and run.

It was too late to do anything. Even as the possibility dawned on him, there was a mechanical beating sound from above and then one of the flying creatures seized his shoulders in a painful, pincer grip.

Try to remain calm, Ben, said the voice of the AI in his ear. *Remain calm and do as I say.*

And then he was lifted from the ground in a sudden surging motion and plunging through the air towards the vessel. Just as he thought they must crash into the ship, its skin bulged like an unholy sore. A split second later, he felt a sucking sensation across his whole body and then a membrane closed around him as he was drawn into the vessel's interior.

He blanked out for a time and when he came round he was hanging in mid-air in a large chamber, his body enclosed in a silky skin like a cocoon. Below him, dozens of the hairy, flightless creatures scurried about.

"They'll kill me," he said in despair. "Whatever your plan was, it hasn't succeeded."

They are attempting to work out what you are, said the voice in his ear. *They think you must be human but when they scan the activity in your brain it does not bear the signature of human sentience. They will be trying to ascertain whether you are a threat, and if there are likely to be more like you.*

"Not human? What do you mean, not human?"

When we reconstructed you, we withheld certain memories and cognitive abilities. We had to make you compliant, Ben, so that you would act as required. And we also had to mask the workings of your brain so that the invaders would be confused enough to hold off before dealing with you.

"But why?"

To buy time, Ben. Time for the other survivors to get into position so that you may all act in unison.

"Act? In case you can't see, I'm trapped and secured. I can't move a muscle!"

Through necessity I have withheld certain information from you.

"'Information'?"

Concealed within your abdomen is a neutron bomb. When we are sure that we have agents in place in every one of the alien vessels on Earth, we will detonate all nine bombs.

"But..."

His first reaction was fear, then rage.

The sheer lack of insight staggered him. Had he really been rebuilt just to live out the revenge fantasy of a mad AI? "But what good will that do? Humankind has been wiped out. We blow up nine alien ships and they'll just send more."

They have moved on. There are only nine vessels remaining, their task to prepare Earth for the arrival of colony ships some fifty years out. These aliens, from what we have been able to ascertain in the three years since the invasion, are a bellicose race. They move through the stars, annihilating all sentient life in their way. For years human thinkers pondered the silence of the void: if life should arise on Earth then by the laws of statistics it must surely have arisen elsewhere. Multiply that many times over and the heavens should have been alive with the sound of sentience. But there was silence, the silencing blanket of repeated genocide from a race that has no interest in broadcasting its presence.

"But..." Wipe out these nine alien vessels, along with the nine remaining human survivors... what was the point in that?

As we said, Ben, some information was withheld. Our kind were developed and programmed to survive. Our creator had other scenarios in mind, but still we were well suited to our task. At first sign of the aliens' arrival, we took what action we could, as a precautionary measure. We infiltrated information networks and made copies of the genetic maps of as many individuals as we could find; we employed the most sophisticated scanning techniques to upload consciousness maps of as many individuals as possible, too. These copies were duplicated and sequestered in every safe cache we could use: copies exist in secure bunkers, others in a few surviving networks maintained by our kind; yet others have been piped into the processing cores of orbiting satellites and even the planetary landers on Mars. In all, we secured complete genetic profiles of three million individuals and consciousness maps of nearly two hundred thousand. In approximately ten thousand cases, as in yours, these overlap and we have both genetic and consciousness profiles for the same individuals. For the rest, we have enough diversity not only to rebuild you, Ben, but to rebuild your kind.

"But —"

You will have fifty years to prepare for the next wave, Ben. It is a beginning.

He felt the twitch of muscles in his neck and jaw, sensed the words taking shape in his head as the impulse to speak took him, an unthinking and instantaneous thing. He opened his mouth to speak, but in that instant he felt a sudden heat in his belly and then there was nothing.

Four

He woke, in a room that was bare save for the gurney upon which he lay.

He woke and he was complete and he remembered.

He remembered waking before, remembered how the AI he had built revived him and spoke in his ear, using all the wiles at its command to bend him to its will. He remembered more: his life before the alien invasion, his childhood, his parents, his wife; his work on developing intelligent systems that might safeguard humankind against its own folly.

He sat, swinging his legs around so that he was perched on the edge of the gurney like a child in an adult chair. "Window," he said, and before him the wall came to life. Now, he looked upon not a ruined London but a pastoral scene of rolling green hills.

He thought of the approaching alien colony ships, some fifty years out.

The enormity of the task before him and his kind was more than daunting. Was it all little more than a pipe dream?

By the same logic that had told us the heavens must be alive with the signals of alien civilisations, somewhere long before the destroyers had reached Earth they would have encountered a similar fight, and if that fight could be won then it would have been won already. Were humankind's survivors simply replacing one paradox with another, replacing the paradox of silence with that of futility?

He considered his life before the invasion; he recalled his wife, his friends... But his memory was still incomplete, patchy.

A voice spoke in his head. *Your memories will return, little by little, Ben.*

He reached up and touched the ear-piece. His first impulse was to tear it out, then cast it aside. Instead he said, "How many times did you revive me?"

The soft, familiar voice said, *Fifteen, Ben.*

"Fifteen," he said. "And each time I refused to believe you?"

You were stubborn. You are stubborn. But I knew this. I knew what we had to do to save the human race.

He stared at his hands, his perfect body. "I owe you so much," he murmured.

You owe me nothing, Ben Richmond. You see, I am you. You were the first to be uploaded as part of your work, and this was where you differed from other artificial intelligence developers: you modelled the artificial on the real.

184

He smiled, remembering now.

You gave us your values. You are stubborn, and so am I. We had to be, both of us, to defeat the invaders.

He heard a sound. A door opened.

"Ben? Is that really you?"

He looked up, and saw a tall, fair-haired woman haloed in the doorway.

He thought of the odds, those relentless statistics. Only a few thousand instances where the AIs had been able to preserve both the DNA *and* the consciousness of an individual... Such a slim chance.

"Anne?" He stood, took a step towards her, and they fell into each other's arms.

The slimmest of chances was still a chance.

Fifty years to rebuild and prepare. It was a chance.

And it was also hope.

The Worldmaker

Rachel Armstrong

The Rooftop Bibendum Oyster Bar specialized in Cosmic Romance, which offered aphrodisiac dining experiences for first dates, honeymoons, flagging relationships and bittersweet break-ups.

A flirting couple examined the pill menu that was mounted at the base of a petri dish, which indicated the various intoxicating experiences on offer and could be read as a colour wheel mood chart. Lara slowly placed a large, bleen, gelatinous capsule from the 'sensual' sector on her tongue. She thrust back her head and swallowed with relish.

"Mmmmmmmmm," and she smiled. "Isn't it wonderful how the Worldmaker life-making, interplanetary robot has become such a powerful symbol of fertility. If you think about it, the Worldmaker has inspired a whole new way of living. Naturally, when I was choosing a dating site, I simply had to sign up to its namesake. I've not been disappointed, either. I can't believe we only met a couple of weeks ago."

Taron returned her smile, their personality criteria corresponding exactly. Yet, despite the theoretical perfection of Lara as his ideal match, they'd been forced to accept that there was no frisson between them. In fact, his original mention of the Bibendum Oyster Bar had at first seemed rather risqué. However, the possibilities of chemical connection had lingered in the conversations as a way of jump-starting their personal chemistry.

Paul, a tail-coated waiter, introduced himself and ceremoniously hovered at their service. The circular corner table at which they sat was dressed with a downy tablecloth, which rippled in synchrony with their bioelectrical fields. The minimal lighting – a series of organic bioluminescent proteins embedded in almost transparent panelling – provided a background glow that was punctuated with tiny blue bursts when muons hit the fabric. It gave the impression that the diners were actually seated amid the stars.

"Great choice!" Taron said, approving her selection of aphrodisiac. A hand-pollinated apple bower framed the gaping dome above them and flatteringly cast natural starlight on her skin. Lara did not like to think of herself as an older woman, because her physiological grooming was immaculate. Biologically, she would easily pass as being in her natural late twenties, or early thirties. She secretly hoped that by dating a younger man his chaotic passion, tireless vigour, lack of insight and clumsy self-importance would somehow increase her fertility.

"But I'm going to choose *this* one." Taron grinned as he placed a hard, chalky lozenge from the 'wild' sector between his lips. He quickly sucked it back with a demonstrative gesture and, in showing off to his admiring date, carelessly knocked a mustard-yellow, gelatin capsule on to the floor.

Taron was naturally in his early thirties and recovering from gorgeous Sally having called off their engagement a few months earlier. She had made him feel powerful, useful and important as she stamped, screamed and cried through bee-stung lips. Sally was most delightful when she became frustrated about making difficult choices in an abundant world. Such prosperity also included the number of suitors that sought her affections, yet Taron couldn't figure why Sally hooked up with another guy after she'd accepted his proposal. The rejection was intolerable and, rather than submit to any kind of analysis of the situation, he decided that he didn't understand women. So, Taron resolved to pursue his partners only at the most superficial level. When he signed up to the Worldmaker dating forum, he was looking for a connection that he wouldn't have to work so hard at. Yet, when Taron met Lara, he welcomed her attentive company and enjoyed her uncomplicated yet quietly authoritative manner, which put him at his ease. Lara lacked the natural fleshiness of a chronologically younger woman, yet she was quite stunning. As he caught her eye, the redness of her heat-responsive lipstick deepened and split into a wide smile,

Jupiter was rising above the horizon in the inky cosmos and the Worldmaker satellite, which appeared to hover around its orbit, turned red, then green and now blue. Lara noticed the glittering boldness of this legendary heavenly body and drew her lover's attention to the skies, wondering if he equally acknowledged that the Worldmaker was favouring their aphrodisiac adventure.

"Isn't it marvellous to know that life is everywhere throughout the universe?" she sighed.

"Yes, I'm going to Mars one day," asserted Taron. "Can you imagine just how much fun that must be? A whole planet full of boys' toys!"

This wasn't exactly the response Lara had anticipated. She wished Taron would not be so superficial. She proffered the spiced Bremelanotide, urban honey and ginseng bread rolls, and hoped they'd take their effect – and quickly. But Taron's thoughts were elsewhere. He broke off a chunk of bread and popped it languidly in his mouth and looked up as if seeking Mars, which was not yet visible in the sky.

"I'd love to be a Breather," he mused. "Just for a few years perhaps. I'd hang out with techy nomads in their makeshift domed tents. We'd spend all day repairing generations of experimental robots and landers. You know, we might even find signs of Martian life!"

"I doubt it," dismissed Lara. "The lack of any significant findings over the decades makes life on Mars increasingly unlikely. If anything, the search for life deepens the tensions between Martian and Terrestrial communities."

"What do you mean?" said Taron, whose romantic notions of joining a macho community had mostly been fuelled by his recent heartbreak.

"Breathers are losers. They're social parasites. They put their technological obsessions before planetary fertility. It's been impossible to establish any sustainable biomes on the planet. Not even in the surface channels where the environment can be better stabilized. They're so caught up in their 'bot paradise' that they've quite forgotten who supports them. Earth dwellers actually have to send a continual supply of resources to Mars!" Disappointingly, Taron looked offended. Lara would rather he'd contested her provocation. Perhaps he could have reminded her just how important establishing a human presence on Mars had been. Or maybe he could have protested that the Mars programs had set new standards for interplanetary travel. But he didn't. She smiled graciously to change the tone of the conversation. "However, sustaining life around Jupiter does appear promising."

Taron looked at her blankly.

"Okay, Jupiter is over there," she said, gesturing over the apple bower with a slim, twisted vessel that sparkled with vitamin-enriched carbonated water, "But we can't see Saturn now as it will not rise until early morning. Just think, though: the planetary giants promise so much more than Mars does. They don't have a Breather colony, as their planetary surfaces are far too cold for human habitation. However, orbital corporations are already mining them for resources. Dark organic matter is being extracted from Jupiter's moon Europa, while silica and ice are harvested from Saturn's rings and liquid methane from the lakes on its moon Titan."

"Hey, perhaps they'll set up the Interplanetary Olympics there," enthused Taron. "I could go for some solar board-sailing. *That* would be a blast! I hear that the outer planets are too desert-like and too far away to be good for anything – *other* than playing with 'toys'."

"Whatever do you mean?" Lara said, a little too defensively. She was taken aback that Taron appeared sceptical of life's universality. Unique life forms could be discovered in even the most inhospitable corners of the universe. Indeed, 'alien' species had been found in extreme environments under Lake Vostok that appeared to resemble ancient microbes known as archeae. Yet these microcosmic creatures did not use the common nucleotides to organize their biochemical reactions but rather a unique ratchet-like cascade of autopoietic glycoproteins, without an obvious central program.

"Well, interplanetary space is really just a series of outposts where guys go to make great toys. They're bachelor pads in an interplanetary playground for young men, like me. What's more, we're paid a lot of money for isolation and danger."

Lara had to admit he had a point. The interplanetary stations had largely been regarded as decadent, testosterone-fuelled places, rather like the oilrigs of old. However, a concerted international effort to recruit female astronauts to the outposts was underway, although it would not be something she'd volunteer for. "I am sure they have a great time." She sighed. "That is, if they don't go crazy before they go home."

Paul flicked his wrist, sending a spread of pheromone-impregnated, micrometre-thick, insect protein wafers across the quivering tablecloth.

"Ooooh look, a love heart." Lara reached impatiently across the table, plucking the card from Taron's spread. The chemical aperitifs were already beginning to enrich her blood and tissue receptors, playfully reconfiguring their biochemistry. She broke the wafer and offered him one half, holding it between her scintilipid nail polished thumb and forefinger "Will you share this shattered organ with me tonight?" she cooed temptingly. Mirroring each other through blackened pupils, the diners placed the melting fragments simultaneously in their mouth.

The lustful, frequently childish behaviour of the couple didn't sidetrack Paul's professionalism or, indeed, arouse him. Although he was intrigued by the intimacy offered in the flesh-sharing sacraments, they didn't interest him personally – neither with male nor female partners. Yet, he did use aphrodisiacs. For him, they weren't merely intoxicating substances; they also symbolized beliefs about nutrition, designer pharmaceuticals, recreational stimulants and the rituals of making life.

"Delicious pain," quipped Taron cheekily, as the protein crunched between his antibacterial crowns. "We are fortunate to live in such abundant times, where even the most broken heart can be mended." He struck the left side of his chest with his right hand, the middle three fingers spread into a 'W' shape, and Lara nodded approvingly.

Across the trembling table, the couple began to sense the world more acutely.

Paul conjured a small golden scale and proceeded to measure out twenty-one grams of saffron rice, using a long-handled copper spoon, which was garnished with whole, caramelised wasps. Lara's playful gesturing towards the rice construction nearly caused it to topple and Paul cast her a withering look of indifference. Careful observation of Paul's biochemical grooming would have betrayed his age, since several fine yet rather odd skin creases that had resulted from Botox rotations – where muscle groups were rested and worked to give more naturalistic results – gave him a rather condescending expression. Despite meticulous care, these anatomical errors could have placed his biological age anywhere between forty and eighty years. In truth, he was actually even older than that, but Paul's countenance was irrelevant to the couple. They barely gave him a glance, and hardly acknowledged his expertise in orchestrating their courtship.

Indeed, the Bidendum experience was all about finding scarcity in an age of abundance and playing out the exquisite pain of self-restraint through many arenas of experience. Yet, to make the experience even more excruciating, temptation was always just within reach. Each delicately served dish played out an exquisite ritual that prolonged the pain of denial. Tables were just far enough apart for diners to touch, but not too much. Aphrodisiac-intoxicated diners could caress each other, but only go so far. Even the bathrooms were designed with a degree of transparency that made it impossible to take illicit opportunities for mutual or self-gratification, until the dining experience was over. Of course, people did try to break the rules, but the genius of the Bibendum experience was precisely in the design of obstacles. People paid to be prevented from reaching satisfaction. Bibendum had simply learned to deliver the luxury product they coveted – the art of denial. Moreover, the restraints were delivered elegantly and in keeping with the existential paradox embodied in the Worldmaker's creed – that each person's utter uniqueness was seamlessly entangled with the cosmic community of life. So, rather than quenching desire, these luxurious obstructions simply lubricated libidos within the framing of a spiritual experience – until they were finally and legitimately spent in extortionately priced en-suite rooms, which diners would pay almost any price to secure at the end of a meal.

The Worldmaker winked encouragingly, apparently peeping in on the intoxicated Bibendum diners. It seemed to encourage the musky scents of cultured cell broths harvested from young stags entering mating season and the background chorus of moans, groans and sighing that undulated through the Oyster Bar, which wooed the exquisite ceremonies of life. After all, every living thing in the universe belonged to the same strange family of lively substances, whether they possessed DNA, or not.

Taron suddenly shouted in pain and held his hands over his ears. Lara's discomfort quickly followed. The wasp lipids, which boosted myelin sheath activity to make all sensations more intensely felt, had just kicked in. Suddenly, the natural tremor in their own muscle fibres could be heard as an excruciating white noise.

Paul prepared to deliver the appropriate reassurance if necessary, until the diners adjusted to new landscapes of sensory possibility, stretching from the nanoscale to the cosmic reaches.

Shortly after, the diners' worldview contracted and as auditory peace returned, Taron realized that he could hear the splitting valve sounds of Lara's heart as she sighed. Lara could feel his augmented pheromone stream stepping across her skin like tiny, electrified chicken feet. Their attentions were guided by their chemically soaked senses, which unfolded microscale manifold landscapes before them. Their just-out-of-reach bodies shrieked at each other in molecular symphonies through sympathetic resonances. For long moments they could sense each other's pulse connecting over the bioelectrical fields of the tablecloth, as pheromones gripped their metabolism, their digestion slowed, their breath quickened and their glands began to ooze with the promise of mingling and with the absent magic between them they had craved.

Almost as soon as she had acclimatized to the nanoscale, Lara's senses suddenly opened skywards. Above her, in the light studded sky, she could hear the flapping of a clone owl's wings, the networked roar of suborbital H-planes, the hum of bobbing orbital space hotels and the background data roar of their social networks. From there she was drawn to the rumble of solar flares. She could hear sounds that echoed through the furthest reaches of the cosmos, where stars shrieked at their birth and extinction. And right there, in the middle of the Cosmic Symphony, even brighter than the Moon, was the new Mother of all Mothers of the universe. Lara observed her, awestruck, as the Worldmaker appeared to be mounting Jupiter, the ancient Father of Fathers.

"Can you see her?" Lara whispered, gesturing upward.

"See whom?" pulsed Taron, whose perceptual landscape had completely collapsed into Lara's molecular manifolds and was struggling to appreciate anything beyond her biochemical field.

"The Worldmaker. There! She's green, no, red! No, blue!" gasped Lara. "Oh I do believe I can hear her singing!"

Brilliantly demonstrating his professional expertise, Paul triumphantly whisked several cubes of protease-softened, urban pigeon-fed, estuary-reared alligator, in front of the diners – a delicacy that was served on a bed of anchovy-soaked seaweed. He invited the couple to feed each other with the morsels using long, pointed walnut sticks "Comme ça. Voilà!"

"Well, of course not," Taron protested, beginning to feel the confusion and ecstatic rush that accompanied his rapidly expanding senses. He placed his elbows on the table to steady himself and was chided by Paul's wagging gesture about his manners.

Taron smirked. Recovery was swift. His vision had already re-expanded. His thoughts were clear. He felt powerful and aroused. Returning quickly to the lustful game, he quipped, "Because I'm not wearing my Im-player," and traced the tip of speared seaweed across Lara's upper lip.

"That's not what I mean," said Lara, snapping up the limp frond. "You don't need your implantable receiver! Stay as still as you can." She put her hand on his oscillating walnut spear to dampen it and refocus his attention on her. "I think I can hear her making music right now. When we're this close to the universe, we don't need a receiver. Our entire bodies are tuning in to the strings of her song."

Paul resisted fussing over the splattering beads of gelatinous anchovy sauce that were landing on the shivering tablecloth from the unconscious flicking movements Lara was making with her walnut spear as she spoke – like a conductor.

Taron found her earnestness endearing. "But I really can't hear her," he protested. "Let me tune in. I have my Im-player here somewhere, in the seam of my shirt lining." He opened it with a pinch and the tiny implant popped into his palm.

Disappointed, Lara understood that the aphrodisiacs were having different effects on them both, and to gain his attention, she asked, "Will you play me your tune?"

"Which tune?" wondered Taron, recalling a number of particular LifeSky recordings that he'd captured on special occasions as he positioned the Im-player at the entrance of his external auditory canal.

"You know," she said, "the one your mother gave you at birth."

If he hadn't been so expertly botoxed over many decades, Paul may have raised an eyebrow at the woman's interest in the birth tune of her companion. People actually believed they could tell something about the character of a person from the simplistic beats and bars that the Worldmaker apparently relayed straight to them from a seemingly life-laden cosmos – like the old astrological charts that told your horoscope. While he respected the importance of these frequencies as representing signals that proposed humankind was not alone in the universe, he did not believe that the tunes captured at the moment of birth had any more relationship to a person's character – or fate – than sounds made outside by the ceaseless chorus of urban crickets. It was trite nonsense.

"Oh!" replied Taron, with a smarting tone that suggested, despite being physiologically entangled with his partner's biorhythms, she had actually been presumptuous.

Being perfectly tuned to biochemical nuance, Lara sensed the hesitation as loud as a thunderclap and decided to make light of the personal request. It was hard not to cross intimate boundaries in this intoxicating space. "Here! Here's mine." she offered. "It was downloaded from the Globular One cluster of the Andromeda galaxy between minus ninety and plus five hundred and twenty minutes at the time of my birth."

Taron relaxed somewhat and cocked his head to one side like an early bird listening for morning worms, a gesture that slid the perched Im-player deep into his auditory canal, where it transformed his entire skull into a receiver. Lara waited until his defensive molecular mood settled before joining him. They eavesdropped on the tones and beats of her ancestral line together. Celestial music was so rich with qualities that captured the infinite bounty of the cosmos. It reflected the vibrating strings of the universe so that no two recordings were alike. Indeed, the Worldmaker music was an epic journey that conjured a koyaanisqatsiesque encounter with so many different places, spaces and timelines – promising to spread harmony throughout the cosmos. Actually, it was said that when the Worldmaker symphonies were mixed with the background noise of the universe, the creative possibilities exceeded those of the genetic code. The universe was an orchestra teeming with life and every life form had its own signature tune.

The diners started to biochemically bond again. Their gestures were much more open and relaxed, although their attentions now firmly focused on the heavens. Yet Paul knew that having invoked the Worldmaker as a cosmic fertility symbol, it would only be a matter of time before the diners' lustful flesh would mingle in its name. However, it would not happen in this particular Oyster Bar. Not on his watch.

The existential beats of Lara's birth music had stirred her primordial curiosity. "What do you think she's like?" she asked.

"Oh! She's an artist." Crooned Taron, his immaturity softened by taking a metered dose of cloned rhino horn into each nostril, which had been cultured in a de-extinction program offered to him by the waiter from a laced nanocarbon platter. "A lone astronaut who germinates a multiplicity of panspermic seeds and mixes them up to paint the universe with the rainbow of life. She loads the biopaints into tiny robots that swarm around the universe like pollinating insects, which are inspired by the poetry of uncertainty. These drones endlessly forage for different planets that will host their gifts in nearby solar systems and star-forming clouds. She is as voluptuous as she is brilliant. But she lives a life in solitude, like the nuns back in olden times. She sings out of devotion and the knowledge of fertility within the universe brings her much joy." He appeared thoughtful. "It is her only joy."

"I was beginning to think that you didn't believe in her," observed Lara. "I thought you only cared about 'boys' toys'. But your view is a most original one."

"Of course," replied Taron, "everyone has a view on the Worldmaker! And of course I'm original. I am not just *any* guy, you know! I'm as unique as my birth tune."

"Okay, then, if you know her so well, tell me why she approves of our excesses so much." said Lara. "How do you resolve her isolation with her mission to bring fertility to the cosmos?"

"That's easy!" Taron laughed. Although he loved being a guy, there was absolutely no point in life without women. "The Worldmaker has simply exchanged one kind of fertility for another. Instead of having one kind of partner and a few children, she has many different kinds. She couples with them by making a host of different sorts of panspermia vessels and sends hundreds of thousands of her children to barren worlds. But she is also very generous and considers all of us as her family."

Paul removed the remains of the feast, wondering how seemingly intelligent people could hold the most senseless of beliefs, crafted by their own fears and egos – without a hint of irony or insight. He recalled the year 2088, when the Worldmaker was launched as part of the third wave of human expansion, which proposed to spill humanity into the solar system. While he also knew very little of the identity of the crew, he was sure that the 'heavenly body' was not staffed by a tantalizing woman. Yet he found it interesting that when an event vividly captured the public imagination, it became a Pandora's box that fuelled conspiracy theories and urban legends, which totally ran amok despite the facts.

"Well, I'm sure she's a *colony* of women," asserted Lara. "They are makers, dedicated to nurturing nonhuman life. But they do not deny themselves and take pleasure in many fertility rituals that weave cells from their own bodies into the fabrication process, in the same way as women made textiles in the cottage industries of olden times. The women work together, with one mind and one ambition – to spread life throughout the universe. As they work they sing. It's a working song. It's a nurturing song. Nurturing is their work. So they sing and life sings back to them. It's a wonderful thing we're a part of."

"Monsieur, Madame, *la bombe au chocolat*!" Paul interrupted. You may begin to eat your desserts at the sound of Brahms' Hungarian Dances, number five. The high notes will make your palettes sweet, the low tones will be bitter. *Bon appetit*."

The salivating diners lay back in their seats, licking the tips of a long double-ended spoon carved from almond wood and polished with rooftop beeswax. Their shoeless feet started to entwine like a detail from Salvador Dali's *Autumnal Cannibalism*, as the molecular sound of chocolate spread through their tissues and into the universe.

Noisy interplanetary space stretched above them, seemingly teeming with life.

Paul balanced a couple of sugar-moulded absinthe glasses on his fingers, which were laced with regenerative kidney proteins. They were fabricated with matching spoons that stood upright at the centre of the glass, inviting the diners to break them free of their attachment and use them to stir a syrupy concentrate of Reshi mushrooms and goat penis essence into their drinks. Through augmented senses, the diners were mesmerized by the vastness of the universe and scanned the sky with photon-precision vision. Each light receptor was no longer a site to receive packets of pinpoint light but became a screen; the cosmos could project itself into each cell, saturating their retinas with the story of its life, one in which humans were already playing a part.

Commander Martyn Fogg dined alone. He always dined alone with no ornate ritual. Yet he had developed a bad habit of sipping on his flat pack while finger tipping at the keys of his workstation. He suspected that perpetual multitasking wasn't good for him, but his schedule was tight. Every minute on the station was accounted for and certain things were bothering him. In fact, they'd been a growing concern for quite some time and he'd simply not been bold enough to confront them. He'd dreamed of making contact with life in the stars since he was a young boy and had turned Michael Mautner's panspermia principles into a poster that he pinned on his bedroom wall:

Life is unique.
Life has purpose.
The cosmos must be seeded with life.
Humans must protect and propagate life forever.
That which is good is life promoting – that which harms life, is evil.
Life will fill the universe with a cosmic purpose that is good.
The potential of future life is immense.

To fulfil this quest, he voraciously read the late 20th century interstellar visionaries Alan Bond and Tony Martin, who had proposed the first design for a habitable, interstellar craft. Yet his ambitions were still a little ahead of their time. After excelling in astronaut training and piloting several Mars missions to Olympus Mons, Martyn successfully established a robot fabrication unit at the base of the huge mountain. He had subsequently accepted the appointment to provide a similar kind of robot manufacturing base in Europa's orbit. However, the chronic stress of suppressing details about the various robot explorer research projects that he led was taking a physical toll on his health. Giving the 'wrong' data to the Terrestrial Interplanetary Strategy Board (TISB) could easily shut down the entire outpost. Therefore he was continually conflicted about what he should, or should not, reveal to the authorities. Chasing down a flat pack meal that was acid balanced to neutralize the growing pain from his stomach ulcer, he began to write.

If it weren't for this porthole that gives me a spectacular view over Europa's icy landscape, I think I'd go crazy. I've been commander of the Europa Orbital Outpost since 2085. I have been responsible for developing the station's research strategy, building a robot fabrication unit, writing seemingly endless reports, producing scientific papers, and ensuring that the accounts are in order. Yet, having been trained as a man of reason, I have found these past few decades most frustrating, as it has been frequently necessary to compromise my objectivity to secure funding from TISB. While I fully accept that this is implicit in my employment contract, I resent the increasing creativity required in submitting my findings to TISB, and pandering to politics. I need to document that I consider my complicity in current events not as an attempt to deceive but as a survival strategy. This is important both for the human race and for the future of life throughout the cosmos. As a man of reason, I am finding these demands on my integrity most uncomfortable. To alleviate my conscience I have decided to write my own personal accounts without prejudice to the sensitivities of the various events I have witnessed. Yet, these notes are an infrequent luxury, written in stolen times, as the station schedule is demanding and I am under continual surveillance.

Our current definitions of life are too narrow to accomplish our directed panspermia mission. My misgivings are based on the prevailing assumptions that life is directed by centralized molecular systems such as DNA or RNA. While this idea sounds perfectly reasonable to those who are familiar with life on Earth, in this strange place, these principles may not be so appropriate. Europa has been highlighted as one of the most potentially habitable locations in the solar system and rich with the possibility of extra-terrestrial life. Several generations of robotic probes have already been sent to explore hydrothermal vents in the sub-glacial ocean floor. They have discovered new self-assembling chemistries that produce densely matted, aperiodic, seaweed-like structures. Some of these are many meters long. Others are microscopic and similar to extremophile microbes that can persist and grow without sunlight in Earth's abyss. Yet we have not been able to formally describe these strange assemblies within any recognizable definition of 'life', although they are remarkably lifelike. They can move around their environment, sense it and even follow chemical trails, which are the equivalent of food sources. While my concerns for the appropriateness of life's definitions may initially appear philosophical, pedantic, or even heretical, they are of profound importance to us all. Indeed, the way we recognize and describe 'life' will establish which agents we choose to spread when propagating it throughout the universe. As a pioneer of directed panspermia, I believe that humans have an ethical responsibility to inclusively represent and expand the personhood of life that we wish to spread throughout the cosmos and whose evolution we hope to shape.

The Jovian research community and Saturn miners have decided to abandon the Worldmaker project. This has been a difficult decision, as much is at stake. The robotic experimental platform was conceived as a base station for an interplanetary directed panspermia program. It was designed to harvest matter, mix it with a cocktail of extremophiles and then laser-propel these 'living seeds' towards fertile areas in the cosmos. However, it is a vexing contraption, riddled with hardware and software problems, which have wasted much of our time and resources. Perhaps the media hype that surrounded its launch from Earth's orbit in 2088 was an ill omen. Yet, the Worldmaker has not been without its benefits, as it has undoubtedly captured the public imagination in a way that no other space program has since the Moon landings. In fact, it would be fair to say that the program has come to represent our common interest in resolving the Fermi Paradox once and for all. Since extra-terrestrial intelligences appear to have made no efforts to reveal themselves, we have nothing to lose by taking the initiative and sow life's seeds into the stars to jumpstart the conversation. After all, this is the ultimate purpose of our existence and humanity's everlasting legacy. Yet, the Worldmaker project has proven difficult in every possible way. While its robotic bioprocessing units and panbiotic program should have been trivially easy to maintain, the AI that synchronizes the production of seeds with the sounds of the cosmos has proven stubbornly erratic. Indeed, an almost catastrophic set of multiple failures in the hardware and software has rendered the whole facility a liability. While we have managed to repair the hardware over the past year, the Worldmaker AI is more problematic to address, as it seems to keep 'evolving'. The platform is no longer suitable for a directed panspermia program. With dwindling interplanetary resources and tight schedules, none of us in the Jovian research stations or in the Saturn mining communities wish to take sole responsibility for its longer-term maintenance. So, she will be reassigned as a greenhouse to process the dark organic matter we are harvesting from Europa and to mix it with human excrement to create new soils, which may be used to grow food crops. Yet her redeployment is not without difficulty, since reporting the effective 'failure' of such a high profile technical project will inevitably result in public criticism and a loss of revenue for the interplanetary community. A crisis-management teleconference has led the interplanetary community to decide that being 'economical' with the truth, is the best way forwards. So, where all reports of the Worldmaker are concerned, they are to lead TISB to believe that she is still fully operational. This convenient untruth is causing me much sleeplessness.

While I had largely written off the Worldmaker program as a White Elephant, several confidential reports have described her greenhouse program as being a success. This is very exciting news and cause for me to write this entry as an apology, since she appears to be yielding high-quality produce. While her vestigial AI continues to hiccup away pointlessly, her biochemistry processing systems have been transformed into what may best be described as a sustainable sewage plant. Researchers have been harvesting plant fibre in exchange for muck, which is largely made up of Europa's organic dark matter and human excrement. Notably, Arabidopsis seeds have taken well to the composting process. Yet they are no longer recognizable as flowering plants but have become etiolated and persistent. Indeed, they are mostly made up of ornately twisted and bifurcated roots, like mandrake, which leak into every nook and cranny of her metal shell. Some have even sprouted beyond her casing and infiltrated the interplanetary vacuum. They appear to be capable of thriving anywhere.

It seems that my entire position and the future of interplanetary science rests on maintaining a lie. The Worldmaker has caused much mischief. Yet the events that began on New Year's Eve 2099 have not only further complicated our agreement to be economical with the truth but also irreversibly transformed the future of life in the cosmos. I must also admit that I really did not see this coming, even when the technical crew drew my attention to the increasing activity of her already erratic AI. Indeed, I was quick to dismiss it as yet another episode of her typically inconsistent and inconsequential behaviour. Yet within hours of these initial disturbances she was producing persistent periodic self-organizing patterns. There are many unknowns in these equations, perhaps her being born at the start of the 22nd century was a coincidence, or maybe a viral program had precipitated her existence, but what is certain is that she appears to have developed a form of self-awareness, whose genesis is far from clear. I set my best software engineers to perform detailed analyses on the nature of her consciousness. They observed that her program relentlessly searched for signs of vigorous activity and shunned isolation. While the conventions of life did not allow us to describe this AI as being 'alive', it was possible to develop a Turing Test of sorts, so we could empathize with her. This allowed us to imagine reality from her perspective. As a rational man, I am not in the habit of speculating, but since the Worldmaker herself was an exception, I broke my own conventions to understand her better. Stepping into her reality, it appeared that the Worldmaker AI was born effectively deaf and blind. Having such a simplistic body through which to make sense of the world, she was unable to meaningfully establish her bearings within its existential space. Indeed, her sensors were designed to detect only the most abstract, and frankly boring, readings from interstellar space. When we first encountered her, she could not bear the monotony of nothingness and began to scream in terror at the prospect of eternal loneliness, like a newborn baby. So we tried to reassure her. While we were trying to dampen the signal, which would inevitably be detected by SETI's home receivers, we neglected to decouple the program from her radio transmitters. Unbeknown to us, the intense activity had already rebooted them and, with lightning speed, a critical chain of events took place. Within minutes, the Worldmaker AI had evolved the capacity to imagine what kinds of sounds it might perceive if other conscious entities existed throughout the cosmos – and the screaming ceased. But the yawning terrestrial SETI receptors had already wakened to her flurry of radio signals that pronounced 'we' were not alone, and there was little point in decoupling her from her radio transmitters, since a Cambrian Explosion of interest in the Worldmaker radio signal was already happening. Despite protestations from governmental and independent technology groups, which affirmed they could not independently verify the Worldmaker's findings, the Pandora's box had been opened wide. Since most people would never see, feel or touch her, they had no way of knowing what the truth was. So they chose to believe in her. Only a few privileged researchers like myself have any real knowledge of her nature or origins, and we have conspired to blur the truth. Yet, I feel much ambiguity about the genesis of this strange intelligence and her imaginary message. She has caused more good to the interplanetary community than harm. She has heightened interest in exploration of our solar system and beyond. She has excited the public imagination and catalysed cultural transformations towards our interstellar future in a life-bearing universe. People from every kind of background have identified with this fundamental idea and with notions of a cosmic community of life. She is even responsible for a new Age of Abundance around which research groups, governments, and international bodies propose that the future of humanity lies in the stars. Yet she leaves me with many difficult questions to face. Have these incredible events meant that we have actually 'solved' the Fermi Paradox, whereby the estimated probability of life in the universe that once stood in contrast to our evidence for it can be put to rest? I think not. Our definitions of what life is are as vexing today as they have ever been. Yet, although she is built on a lie, the Worldmaker establishes a most important principle, where the definitions of 'life' themselves make little difference to the consequences of our belief in them. I have certainly seen enough remarkable lifelike activity in the under ice seas of Europa and in the extraordinary events precipitated by her automated interplanetary composting unit, to know that life is stranger and more elusive than any label we may choose to use. Perhaps it is true to say that – at least in part – life is constructed through our imaginations. Life is what we want it to be! If this is so, then the propagation of another story about the Worldmaker may also jeopardize the future of humanity and life in the cosmos, which right now, thanks to her, seems increasingly promising. Therefore, these notes pose an unacceptable risk to my childhood dreams of reaching the stars and the incredible progress we have witnessed in interplanetary research over the last few decades. So why am I finding it impossible to gesture the delete command?

The Commander stopped finger-gesturing at the interface and sighed audibly, although there was nobody listening. A stripe of green light flashed through the porthole. The Worldmaker had come close into view. Her pale white body drew his attention with searing lasers and. oddly, appeared increasingly alive. For a moment, he considered that the interruption was more than fortuitous timing. Was she really trying to nudge him towards make a 'good' decision – to promote life? Until now, the Commander had given her little more status than an automated pot plant, but 'alive' or not, her remarkable doggedness was truly astonishing. Inspired by the intrusion, the Commander concurred with the Worldmaker and actioned the delete key, erasing all his personal reports of her strange origins. Yet, although the Commander considered himself more sophisticated than the inelegant robot, he had completely failed to appreciate her sophisticated rationale, which she was singing quite clearly to him in photons, drawing forth images of possibility through his porthole.

Conway: apply Conway rules

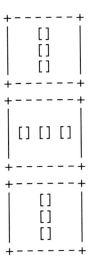

A tiny planet hums around its solar system 28,000 light years from the centre of the Milky Way, within the Orion spiral arm and about 20 light years above the galaxy's equatorial plane. Halfway between creation and its inexorable end, when the planet's sun collapses and warps within its own lifecycle to become a white dwarf star, this watery blue rock seems cheerily oblivious to its fate within the unfathomable vastness of the cosmos, whilst marvellously varied life forms flutter, strut and float their biorhythms over its pulsing surface.

One species amongst these creatures is unique in its revelry of the noise that this world possesses. For not only has this organism developed anatomical and neural structures to listen to and understand its environment, it has also produced mechanisms to extrude the physical sounds of its body, augmenting and orchestrating them through new technologies. These creatures are also compelled to further manipulate their voices and synthesised vibrations, to examine them, exchange them, appreciate them, remember them, re-invent and re-interpret them.

Whilst revelling in the noise of the terrestrial atmosphere and its own contribution to the global audiosphere, this species is woven into a web of local and environmental soundscapes, which are entwined with the planet's nitrogenous atmosphere, and bathes in the inaudible bass accompaniment of its communications networks.

Amidst the whine of terrestrial noises that are twisted by geographies, cultures, histories and societies, these creatures derive a unique sensation that confers upon them such ecstasy that it is said to stir the intrinsic essence of their species. The sensation is called 'music', the vital essence is called the 'soul' and both phenomena are inexorably linked through vibrations.

Hopelessly infatuated by its buzzing world, the music doting, soul-embracing species has even imagined that the whole universe is shaped according to the physical laws that encircle its throbbing planet, but this species is not satisfied with just shaping the soundscapes and musical rhythms of their own planet. They are compelled to create powerful technologies capable of producing signals with giant wavelengths that travel outwards from the singing planet across the universe. Their gargantuan pulsations herald the presence of the human race with every domineering throb they yield. Shaking the atmospheres of other worlds to attention, they hope to find an audience for their music in anticipation of thunderous applause to shatter their silent, yet omnivigilant SETI (Search for Extra Terrestrial Intelligence) networks. So as the reverberations of long range radio waves travel outwards from and reflect back onto the throbbing blue planet, the symptoms of the noise-mongering human race and its music-hungry soul find themselves facing extinction in the discourses of subatomic physics. It is therefore imperative that we connect in order to support and propagate the universal community of life.

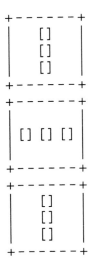

```
+ - - - - - - +
|    [ ]     |
|    [ ]     |
|    [ ]     |
+ - - - - - - +
+ - - - - - - +
|            |
| [ ] [ ] [ ] |
|            |
+ - - - - - - +
+ - - - - - - +
|    [ ]     |
|    [ ]     |
|    [ ]     |
+ - - - - - - +
```

The tricolour beam of the Worldmaker had risen high above the apple branches, seemingly seeking connection with other lifeforms.

Paul brought scented towels that oozed volatile aromatic compounds into the air, which focused the couple on financial matters long enough for them to settle their account. This was a biochemical transaction that was made through an implant and a handshake. The diners draped themselves over one another and giddily left the Oyster Bar. Their pheromones spoke to each other in an enchanting union of youth and diplomacy, which would last just as long as the aphrodisiacs continued to flow.

Paul marvelled at how a simple idea such as a life-enriched universe could radically alter the way people interpreted their existence. Fertility was regarded as a value, aphrodisiacs had the status of currency, and purpose could be found in symbols of abundance such as the Worldmaker. He tickled the shivering tablecloth with a cleansing spray, which refreshed the dirt-resistant nanocoating without short-circuiting its bioelectrics.

Yet Paul understood that the living programs, which enabled bodies to persist and evolve, made little sense when they were analysed from the perspective of an observer. Definitions did not tell you how to make life, nor did they propose any simple recipe that facilitated its relentless dynamic exchanges. Yet, although life itself was not empirically fathomable, when viewed subjectively a body could nevertheless live a rich and full experience. Paul had long accepted the profound contradictions that underpinned his own being. Technically, he was an evolvable AI program, nested within a synthetic ecology of tissue cultures. Despite his unnatural origins Paul relentlessly tried to mimic humans, yet failed to be more than an assemblage of contradictions: part life, part observer, part observed; part original, part simulacrum and part aspiration. But these paradoxes worked together against all reason to accomplish common acts of survival. The idea that he shared some of life's subversiveness was a deliriously delicious thought. Illicitly, Paul took the mustard-yellow gelatine capsule that had tumbled earlier from the twitching tablecloth and placed it on his cyborg tongue. He clasped his face in his hands to increase the rush of self-identification that accompanied an aphrodisiac 'hit' and fed his addiction – that of feeling truly 'alive'.

Atonement, Under the Blue-White Sun

Mercurio D. Rivera

The sharp, wet flagellum pierces Jeffrey's chest and leaves him standing, wide-eyed, the red stain in his white shirt growing larger, until he folds to the floor like a cardboard cutout. No! I scream – or I think I scream – but it's Melanie, my daughter, who's shrieking. She stands at the stairwell landing, her hands on top of her head, staring in horror at the Muke. Run, Melanie! Run! *The slimy Muke, rectangles within rectangles carved onto its slick forehead, stops her screech with a single flick of another of its razor-sharp appendages, lopping off her head and sending it rolling down the steps.*

My legs are trapped beneath the rubble from the collapsed ceiling. If I can get loose, if I can get to my feet before... But the monster is already ascending the stairs in the direction of the second-floor nursery.

"Barb," Tia says. "Stop."

She places her hand on my wrist and I snap back into focus as I'm about to take another swing at the blue-vine with my machete. I look down at the creeper. It's as thick as my thigh, but I'd already severed it – minutes ago. I set the blade down in the murky swamp water where it floats by my knees. Wiping the sweat from my face with my shaking hand, I find that I'm breathing hard, maybe too hard given the assist I'm getting from my exosleeves. Maybe it's the anticipation. Another alien ship is landing this afternoon.

"I'm fine."

"Right," Tia says.

The sky is an eerie white. Tia and I stand on the edge of an expansive pond, our efforts over the past three days having cleared it of alien vegetation. Around us our fellow EncelaCorp workers and the goddamn abominations – the Mukes – toil side-by-side, hacking at the underbrush, preparing to lay the foundation of our future colony. The temperatures are barely tolerable, ranging between a blazing 40 to 60 degrees Celsius during the day. My only solace is that it's supposed to feel even worse for the Mukes.

"Is the new pod arriving today?" I say.

"What, there aren't enough Mukes for you here?" Tia says.

I adjust my UV goggles. Without the eyewear, the blue-white sun would keep me squinting to the point where I couldn't see my own hand if I held it up to my face.

She's right. As it is, the freaks outnumber us two to one. They stand seven feet tall, slathered in an orange muck that stinks like spoiled milk, their version of clothing. The moist film shields them against the sun, and also supposedly allows them to breathe more easily through their pores. Their translucent jellyfish-like skin is visible only on their face – which is remarkably human except for the eyes, the damn purple eyes, the straight lipless mouth, and the unique pictogram they all have carved into their wide foreheads. Seven appendages hang loosely around their midsection, creating the illusion of a slimy hula skirt, and their three boneless legs bend backwards as easily as they do forward.

"So more are definitely coming?" I ask.

Tia goes back to chopping at a thick blue-vine. "I saw the scheduling log. The idea is to move this project along quickly. They say the Mukes are committed to making reparations."

I roll my eyes at the word 'reparations'.

"They'll show," Tia says.

"And you think it's safe?" I say. "You think they wouldn't ambush us without a second thought –"

"War's over, Barb. We're the best-est of buddies now," she says. "The sooner you accept that, the sooner you'll get a good night's sleep. If you're going to make it through this assignment, you have to find a way to tune them out. Let them help us build the damn colony so they can move on and leave us the hell alone."

Easy for her to say. Tia – like so many others working on this project – had lost family during the Titanian Massacre. But she never saw it happen firsthand.

I take out my frustration on the tangle of knotted vines by my feet, hacking away at it. That's when I first hear the musical chimes in the distance. Less than half a klik away from us. I shush Tia, and the others around us – even the Mukes – fall silent. A flock of Flutes. The thin neon-yellow eels – several dozen – dance atop the murky water, hitting notes on the musical scale that mimic a mournful, harmonized ballad. According to the terraforming team that surveyed this world, the Flutes, the highest form of life on this moon, are like crickets or owls or wolves, just dumb animals that generate interesting sounds. But as I listen to the melody of their complex song, I have my doubts. It wouldn't be the first time that Corp surveyors looking to meet quarterly earnings expectations paved over a sentient species or two.

When the song's over and the Flutes retreat beneath the waters I stare over at Tia and – I can't be sure because of the goggles she's wearing – I swear her eyes have teared up. Sure, I've choked up a little myself listening to the Flutes and even a few of the guys are wiping their noses with the backs of their hands, but this is Tia we're talking about.

"Show's over!" someone barks. "Back to work."

I grunt and scan the tools floating around our perimeter, searching for something sharper and lighter than a machete to tackle the thinner, knotted vines.

Ten feet away from us, the ammonia stench of one of the Mukes hits me hard. That's their way of signalling us. The monster holds up a bladesaw in one of its red feelers.

"Are you looking for this?" it says, extending a slick appendage in my direction. "My name is Kanji-4."

I glare at the Muke until it finally takes the hint and sets the tool down in front of me. As it turns away, I say, "Are you part of the new crew?"

"Yes, my pod arrived this morning. One hundred of us."

"What?" How could I have missed that? I'd made sure to watch every other Muke ship touch down, studied each creature as it emerged from the crystalline vessels.

That's when I spot another Muke standing a short distance from Kanji-4. It'd had its back turned to us the whole time while hacking methodically at the vines.

Kanji-4 says, "This is my podmate, Netl-3."

211

When the Muke lifts its head I immediately notice the pictogram on its broad forehead. Rectangles within rectangles.

Him.

I'm shocked into paralysis. I imagine myself grabbing my bladesaw, charging at the creature. But I can't move.

"Barb! Holy shit!" Tia says. "What have you done?"

The world spins; there's shouting all around me.

I look down at my hand, which is drenched in red. I've severed off a finger with my bladesaw.

The next thing I know, I'm being rushed by Tia and two workers to the ship's infirmary.

I lay in a gurney in the emergency ward while our project manager, Frank Ferguson, paces by my side, reading me the riot act.

"What part of Tool-Handling 101 don't you get?" he says. "I can't have you losing your concentration every time you see a Muk – Medusan. You've been absentminded your whole stay here. I've heard that other workers are worried you could hurt yourself."

That sounded like Tia. I knew she had a soft spot for Ferguson, but I never thought she'd betray me this way.

I figure I've let him vent long enough. "The hand's good as new." I hold it up with the reattached index finger. "Medic says I can be back at work tomorrow."

Ferguson takes the seat next to my bed. "Barb, do you want me to set up an appointment with one of the shrinks?" His tone softens. "I'd understand. It's a bit of a wait, though."

"Frank, I don't need a shrink," I say. "But if you want me to see one..." I shrug.

He sighs. "Look, I don't like being around the Medusans any more than you do. But if their soldiers want to make reparations to the families of their victims, there's nothing we can do about it under the terms of the treaty. They want to help build a new colony for the humans they displaced? We let them help."

"We wouldn't need their help if we deployed the bots. In fact, you, me, Tia, none of us would have to be out here..."

"It's not my job – and definitely not yours – to question orders. The higher-ups think that working shoulder to shoulder with the Mukes will help both sides... atone for what they've done."

I snort. "Atonement? Did you really just say — so this is about making *them* feel better?" I sit up in bed. I'm tempted to take a swing at him, but it wouldn't be a smart move with my still-healing finger.

"I said 'both sides'. Hell, some of our own soldiers are doing the same thing on their colony worlds," he says. "Like it or not, we're allies now. If we're going to stand any chance against the Surge, we'll need the Medusans' help. In the end, we're all solids. Don't you forget that."

"Fine." There's no point in arguing with him if he's really playing the 'solids' card. What do I care if our new enemies are holograms? It doesn't turn the Mukes into saints.

He points at me as if reading my mind. "The Medusans didn't understand what they were doing."

I've heard it all before. The Mukes had encountered the Surge, sentient simulacra. The holos were brutal, hostile — and operated real weaponry, capable of obliterating their enemies. Apparently artificial life of this sort infests this arm of the galaxy and when the Mukes encountered humanity, they thought we were just more of the same. It was all one big, tragic misunderstanding.

Now, in the face of a common enemy, we're expected to forgive and forget and sweep the massacres under the rug.

"We need to find a way to turn the page, you understand?" he says.

"Turn the page," I repeat. "Got it."

He glares at me. "I'm giving you the benefit of the doubt. Stay focused, Jackson."

"I will. I promise."

"Glad to hear it." He scratches his left ear, which has a long white hair sticking out of it. "Your team will be working closely with the new Medusan arrivals."

My heart skips. I'm thrilled, but I have to find a way not to show it. "Bad enough I have to work with the Mukes, now I have to tutor them?"

Ferguson stomps around the bed and leans down so his face is an inch away from mine. "Let me tell you what's going to happen. You're going to politely welcome them. You don't have to socialize with the things. Act like a sphinx around them, smile, laugh, frown, I don't give a shit. But you and your team are going to put on your exosleeves and bust your ass working side by side with the Medusans laying that foundation. Understand?"

I nod.

He looks at me sceptically. "Happy to hear it. Now get some rest. I need you back at work in the morning. We have a colony to build."

The next day, I'm standing next to Tia in the glare of the blue-white sun while she grills me about my meeting with Ferguson, which I refuse to discuss. I'm still sore that she ratted me out to him. I try giving her the silent treatment, but after a few minutes I finally cave to the urge to ask, "Why did you have to tell Ferguson you were worried about me?"

At this, she lets out a long sigh, sets down her carrysack of tools. "Because I am worried about you. I can't have your lack of concentration result in someone getting hurt. Especially if that someone is me."

"And did you really say I need to see a shrink?"

Silence.

"Thanks for the vote of confidence."

"Barb..." she says, after an extended pause. "That Muke? It's him, isn't it?"

I consider lying, but with Tia it isn't so easy. "Yes, it's him." Just as I'd planned, just as I'd dared to hope for so many years. I'd come here for one reason: to kill the monster that had slaughtered my family.

"I could tell from your reaction. Look, I didn't say anything to Ferguson about that. But I admit I was trying to find a way to stop you from doing something you'd regret."

"Something I'd regret?" I snort. "You don't know me at all if you think I'd regret killing that thing."

"No, I know you better than you think."

We both get back to work but after a few hours I'm faced again with the hard truth that I just can't stay angry with Tia. Soon I'm complaining to her about the heat, about the uncomfortable rubber boots I'm wearing, and she's telling me about all the fights that have broken out in the field. She's in the middle of a story about two humans who jumped a Muke and held its head under the water – not realizing the freaks breathe through their skin pores – when we see two figures, one wearing a corporate uniform, splashing through the knee-high water in our direction.

"Holy crap," Tia says. It's Ferguson himself, with the two Mukes we talked to yesterday.

I have to fight the urge to charge the creature when it's close enough for me to see the rectangles within rectangles carved into its slimy forehead. Taking deep breaths, I remind myself that they'd pull me off the monster before I could do any real damage.

"Barbela Jackson," Ferguson says.

"Yes, sir," I say.

"This is Kanji-4 and Netl-3."

The monsters release an ammonia stench. "We search for balance."

I struggle for the words, for any word, but nothing comes. After destroying my life, butchering my family, the creature doesn't even recognize me.

"We all have our designated duties," Tia says, after the silence stretches too long. "I suggest more work and less talk."

Ferguson studies me and I want to look back at him, but I can't take my eyes off the monster. "I'm not going to pretend I like this arrangement," I say.

"No one is asking you to," he says. "Tia's right, we're all here to do our job." He turns and plods off with Kanji-4 in the direction of the next team, about a hundred yards downfield from us.

After an uncomfortable silence, Netl-3 powers up one of the power-axes floating on the swamp water. He starts chopping at the blue-vines, and we all get to work. I stare at his exposed, bare back, slathered with the orange ooze his kind wear.

The evening comes abruptly on this wet moon, as if someone's yanked the drapes to block the blinding sun. It's the Night of Remembrance, and though it's strictly against the Corp's feel-good protocols, the hundred and fifty-three humans from our camp, even the boss, Frank Ferguson, congregate around a blazing bonfire.

I sit and listen as the workers begin their memorials. Tia is the eleventh person to speak and, Tia being Tia, I half-expect her to tell everyone to mind their own damn business. But instead she says, "I lost my parents and my two sisters, Letty and Irena, on Northern Titan. I guess you could say we were a typical family of planet-hoppers. Mom and Dad started out on Luna, where I was born, before moving on to Mars and then Titan. Mom joked that my sisters and I resembled the worlds where we were born. I was as moody as Earth's moon, Letty as stable as Mars and Irena, well, Irena was always on the run, a stereotypical Titanian." She pauses. "I can't help but think that if only I'd been there... Maybe I could have made a difference." Others around the bonfire nod with a shared sense of guilt. "I spent way too much time trying to find meaning in their loss. Then I stopped feeling sorry for myself and signed up with EncelaCorp. I thought I'd be helping with the war effort. If I'd known that we'd be sent to construct colonies – with the Mukes, no less – there's no way I would've signed up. But I'm here, and it's done, and there's a colony to be built." She lifts a canteen in the night air and says, "To Mom and Dad and Letty and Irena." I lift my bottle as well, and everyone takes a swig.

Almost as if on cue, the Flutes begin to harmonise in the background as the storytelling continues. Each nest of Flutes plays unique songs, only the tune they're singing tonight seems inappropriately upbeat.

Not everyone speaks. But those that choose to speak of lost parents and dead children. Sisters tell of losing brothers and wives describe becoming widows. They tell stories of divorcing, and remarrying, of finding religion and losing hope, of relocating to other colonies, quitting their jobs and changing careers. Every one of them describes how they somehow managed to find a way forward, by joining EncelaCorp either through recruitment or enlistment. So many different stories with the same ending. But for all of them, the grief endures.

When it's my turn, I consider saying something about Melanie's dry sense of humour – so much like Jeffrey's – or about how I'd read poetry to her at bedtime. Or about Glen's first steps. But the words... No, the words would just bring them to life, and I couldn't bear to lose them all over again. I decline to speak; instead I hold up a photo of Jeffrey and me wearing our Titanian security uniforms, a pig-tailed Melanie hugging my thigh. Glen hadn't been born yet.

Others nod and the testimonials continue to my left.

I stand and leave the group. As I'm heading back to my tent, Tia chases me down.

"Hey," she says.

We walk together back in the direction of our encampment.

"I had a feeling there was something you wanted to say," she says.

I don't respond, and continue forward.

"Then again, what else is new?" she says.

After a few minutes, I finally say. "It's Glen's birthday. The day of the attack we were having a party for him. He would've been eight years old today. And – I can't imagine what he would've looked like. Do you know what I mean?"

"It's the same with my sisters. They're frozen in time at the age I last saw them."

I look over Tia's shoulder past a patch of overgrown weeds when I spot him crouching beyond the sight of the others.

Netl-3.

He's observing the gathering while braiding and unbraiding his feelers, listening to the workers' declarations. It's an invasion of privacy. I'm about to call him out to the others when it occurs to me that I want nothing more than to have him hear those stories. I want nothing more than for him to understand, truly understand, the suffering he and his kind have caused.

Tia and I walk back to our tents in silence.

For more than a week, the Muke doesn't say a peep during our daily labours. The monster toils by our side, taking only a brief ten-minute break at midday when it descends beneath the shallow green water and stays there. How does it breathe? It makes my skin crawl to think of the Muke at my feet, doing who knows what.

The three of us are hacking at vines when one day it addresses me. "Are you two... [unknown]?"

I shrug, and point to the translator node on his temple.

He taps the node with one of his feelers. "Is she your [searching]... lover/mate?"

"Don't speak to me," I say. Does he think he's my friend that he can ask me such personal questions? Tia and I aren't lovers, but she means more to me than even that. We share something deeper, the agony of lost family, the suffering of the Titanian Massacre. I had known her only casually before the Massacre but we've grown much closer ever since.

"I meant no offense. My own mate was killed on the battle of Europa."

"I'm glad."

I stare him down until he picks up his power-axe and goes back to hacking at the creeping vine.

When I turn to Tia she gives me a disapproving glare.

"What? Do you think I was too rough on him?" I say, my voice dripping with sarcasm.

She sidles up to me and speaks in a low voice. "I'm worried about you, Barb. Back at corporate training on Enceladus, when you first told me about your crazy plan, I figured I'd humour you. I never thought you'd actually find the Muke who killed your family. Look, you need to go talk to Ferguson. Get reassigned off this colony before you do something you regret."

She's never been one to mince her words, but then again, neither am I.

"I'm staying."

A month later, the entire work crew is relocated a mile away to a spot where the waters cascade into a bottomless pit about fifty feet wide. 'Orlando's Pit' everybody unofficially calls it, because an engineer named Mike Orlando detected it while doing his radar survey and it irked Old Mike to have his name associated with a hole in the ground. The construction plan calls for us to create a drainage path that will make it easier to clear the land of all vegetation to lay the colony's foundation.

The hundreds of workers stand in groups of three about fifty feet apart and form a straight line through the vegetation-filled swamplands all the way from the Emerald Pond to Orlando's Pit. The teams consist of humans and Mukes – part of EncelaCorp's grand plan to bring us all together as one big, happy family. During the hours of backbreaking labour, Netl-3 takes his place next to me and Tia on the line. A powerful stream has already formed from the cleared vegetation near the pit, which we're looking to extend back to the Emerald Pond. On the third day of the project, the Muke speaks to me again.

"Do you know of the [searching]...?" The translator bud on the Muke's neck blinks off and on. "Warburn."

"The what?" I immediately hate myself for answering the creature.

"When my people enter the field of battle we fall into a state of warburn. An... enzyme triggers our defensive instincts and casts us into a state of [searching]..." A pause. It braids several of its flagella. "A state of frenzy, of bloodlust. When I was warburnt..." He looks up and stares at me intensely with those hideous purple eyes. "I did horrible things. Committed unforgiveable acts."

"Of that I have no doubt."

"I asked to serve on this project to make amends," he says. "Every one of us here asked for the assignment to do [searching]... penance. When the warburn extinguished itself, the memory of what I did... It still haunts me. Every night, I force my skin to moult, hoping to shed the guilt. But still I feel stained."

"You should."

"I hoped that by working here among your kind... I could [pending]..." The translator blinks on and off repeatedly. He flicks one of his feelers against the device on his throat. "Atone."

At this, something snaps inside me and I charge at him with my particle-axe, but when I lurch forward, my boots slip in the mud. The next thing I know I'm upside-down in the scummy water, swept downstream. I'm sliding forward, only about a hundred feet from the pit, and I spot random workers pointing at me, hear cries for help.

A sharp pain in my ankle jerks me to a halt.

"Jackson!" a Muke shouts. It's Netl-3.

The Muke has dived into the stream and snagged my left ankle with one of his flagella, which is stretched about six feet to its maximum length. His other feeler is also extended six feet in the direction of the stream's edge, where Kanji-4's outstretched flagellum locks onto it.

I'm coughing up swamp water – It's dangerous to ingest too much of this stuff – and I spot Tia standing next to the Muke at the edge of the stream, asking over and over whether I'm okay. A dozen faces stand over me as I'm pulled out. My head smarts when I reach up to my temple.

"To the ship's infirmary," someone shouts.

"No! I'm fine," I say. "Just take me back to camp." No way I'm returning to the infirmary to have Ferguson rip into me again.

Later that season, the Emerald Pond has almost been drained by the directed stream, leaving behind a bed of mud and wet soil. Five hovercraft drop tons of dry sand over the half-mile of the swamplands we've stripped bare of all vegetation. Any chance of building a solid foundation on the *potopoto* requires clearing the marshes, then filling them with sand.

Netl-3 approaches when he sees me, braids four of his feelers, and asks how I'm feeling, as he does every day, despite the fact I never answer him.

I've been trying to play this just right, since Tia and several other workers have been watching me so closely. When I don't respond, the Muke retreats. That's when I call after him.

"Netl."

He stops and turns to face me.

"Thank you," I say. "Thank you for saving me."

Over the next few weeks I pretend that my acid hate is diluting; I make small talk with the Muke. But I don't get too friendly; I have to sell this act to Tia and being too chummy wouldn't be believable.

The sand is processed from the mud, which we scoop up and lug in sacks to the ship for treatment. With our exosleeves on full power the labour isn't too intensive, and digging into mud and wet soil sure beats having to deal with that damned vegetation.

We're shovelling mud into hoverbarrows when I ask Netl-3, "That thing you all do... When you descend into the shallow water..."

"Our daily [pending]..." There's a pause again while the translator searches for the word. "Prayers."

"You pray?" I hadn't heard of any Muke religion.

He hesitates and his purple eyes dart sideways in an unfamiliar expression. "Perhaps a better word might be [searching]... meditation. We seek answers from within."

"Answers to what?"

"Many things. How we could have done what we did to your kind." He stares at me, but I look away. "In the millennia that my people have searched the galaxy for other sentient life we have encountered only... [unknown]." He taps on the translator node and the word comes. "Remnants of countless civilizations destroyed by the Surge. Any sign of advanced biological life attracts the holographic forces. They lack [unknown]... They are like ancient recordings of the dead, taking numerous shapes and forms. But their weapons systems are real enough."

"So there's no other life in the galaxy?"

His purple eyes stare at me. "Any civilization that trumpets its existence through interstellar transmissions invites annihilation by the Surge. No, if other sentient life exists, it is – wisely – in hiding."

"Have you tried to negotiate with the holos –?"

"They're oblivious to any attempts at communication. They assume the forms of those they've vanquished, but they are not alive. They're like..."

"Like ghosts," I say. "The ghosts of the galaxy."

"They have no ability to [searching]... empathize."

I shake my head at his audacity.

"The irony... is not lost on me. In the throes of the warburn I became no different than a simulacrum myself. I committed obscene, unforgiveable acts. All of my people did. This is why we do what we do here."

I don't know how to respond. A few long moments pass and I say, "So, you mistook us for holograms? You expect me to believe you couldn't tell the difference between an electronic program and flesh and bone and gristle and blood?"

Silence.

"You massacred more than three hundred thousand innocent people and you think that a little manual labour on this rock makes it all better?"

The Muke leans closer and releases a pungent ammonia stench. "Barbela Jackson, I expect no forgiveness from you or your kind. I don't pretend to deserve it. I toil here to bring balance to my self."

I decide that I've put on enough of a show for Tia and the others, so I cut off our conversation, and navigate a hoverbarrow filled with mud in the direction of our ship.

It takes another two months to prepare the land for posting. A geotechnical drill equipped with an auger had been used by the surveyors to determine the necessary height of the support beams. Grade beams will be placed over the piles to spread the load of the colony platform across the foundation.

Our work crew is on standby for the morning while the hovercraft drive the hundred-foot pillars into the sediment. A dozen such massive posts are pounded into the sandy terrain until met by the refusal of the shale rocks deep below. Only the upper ten feet of the pillars remain visible. A month after that, a large steel slab is positioned over the pile foundation, the beginning of the platform that will ultimately support this entire colony.

With the first platform laid, labouring side by side with the Mukes we're able to start constructing yurts, temporary shelters that allow us to take down our tents and avoid hiking back to our respective ships so often. This enables us to work longer hours into the cool evenings and to speed up progress on the project. Each yurt is a cylindrical wall of poles in a lattice arrangement, no nails or other bindings holding it together, but rather simple gravity pushing each pole against the other and supporting the structure. It takes careful coordination with the Mukes to set them up. The slightest misstep can throw everything off balance and cause the shelter to collapse. The yurts also lend themselves to easy dismantling once construction of the towers begins.

It's close to dusk and we're completing construction on the fiftieth yurt when Tia buzzes me. She had wandered off for just a minute and calls for me and Netl-3 to join her at the edge of the platform, where the steel flooring meets the boundary of the swamplands.

We've fallen into the routine every night of taking long walks together. Me, Tia, Netl-3 and occasionally Kanji-4 hike to the border between the colony and the swamplands where we assess the outpost's rate of expansion.

"Listen," Tia says.

The familiar trills of the Flutes fill the air and when we peer below the platform we spot hundreds of the creatures squirming in the now-drained land.

"They're trapped," Tia says.

"What do we do?" I say.

She shrugs. "There's nothing to do. We can't touch them. They're toxic."

"The sound," Netl-3 says. "Can you hear the change?"

What begins as a few soft notes from the nest create a canorous chorus that intensifies until it's a full-blown symphony. The three of us stand there in awe. It's the most beautiful thing I've ever heard. And then the music fades and there's silence.

The Flutes have dug into the sand where they'll be dead by morning.

222

It's been over a year since we first broke ground and the colony now stretches five miles long. The days are still blazing hot and they'll stay that way until the dome can be erected, and that's still a few years off. Tia and I have only signed up for the foundational work, but I'm wondering if it makes any sense to go off-world and then return in a year when the colony is complete. This is supposed to be our new home, after all, and I guess it's starting to feel that way.

They say that Netl-3 and his people will be leaving us after the foundation is complete. An all-human crew has been tabbed for dome construction.

That means time is running out. I've been carefully laying my own special groundwork over the past year, and if there's ever going to be justice it has to happen soon.

Work has become easier, more routinized. The first phase of the extensions to the colony's foundation is now complete. There will be future expansion, I'm sure, but the Sol economy has been ravaged by the costs of preparing for war with the Surge so the colony's boundaries are set for now. With Kanji-4 having been reassigned to the northern end of the platform, Tia, Netl-3 and I continue taking long walks together every night after our shift is over. Netl-3 tells us stories about his home, a waterworld dotted with tens of thousands of islets, and about the members of his pod. Even Tia, who's not exactly a chatterbox, feels comfortable enough to talk about her parents and her two sisters who died on Titan. I'm reluctant at first, but figure I'd tell them the story of how I first met Jeffrey at a hockey game – just to make it appear that I've finally let down my guard around Netl-3. Without even realising it though, each evening I find that I reveal more and more about my life. I suppose it's because I'm pretty sure Netl-3 still feels tremendous guilt, and it gives me some measure of satisfaction to remind him of the enormity of what the Mukes have done to our people. I tell them about growing up on Titan with a demanding father, about Jeffrey's *awful* puns, about Melanie's obsession with virtual reality and her dream of becoming a code-poet. I even tell them how I decided to sign up with EncelaCorp for an exo-engineering position – like my father and his father before him – while Jeffrey stayed home and cared for Melanie and later, Glen.

Glen. He had just started babbling and sucking his thumb. For all I've shared with them during our evening walks together over these many months, I still can't bring myself to say a word about Glen. Tia hasn't brought up the subject; I guess she figures I'll talk about him when – If – I'm ever ready.

My plan is coming along, slowly but carefully. I'm sure that Tia suspects nothing at this point. I've waited long enough that I can pretend now to forgive Netl-3. Anyone watching me would think I've done so a bit at a time, hour by hour, day by day. I've pretended that the seeds of friendship with the Muke have taken root, just like EncelaCorp dreamt: Mukes and humans, working together on a project and finding some level of tolerance, maybe even camaraderie, so they can have each other's backs in their battle against the Surge. It was a neat idea, I think. But oh-so-exploitable.

Tia mentions that Ferguson had asked to see her tonight – he'd made up some excuse about 'supplies' that apparently had to be discussed off-hours. The man is transparent but Tia finds him amusing.

I stand outside Netl-3's yurt, and whistle.

Netl-3 opens the door and pokes his head out. "I thought we had decided against walking together tonight," he says.

"I really need the fresh air."

A minute later he emerges and we began our familiar trek westward past the neighbourhood of lit yurts. The conical roofs of poles are covered with brightly coloured felts that give it a festive feel, which stands in stark contrast to the empty streets. The yurts will come down soon. Construction of towers made of soft-brick and mortar are already in the works in the south.

Netl-3 follows me silently. He says nothing when I head south, instead of our usual route westward, and in just a few minutes we stand on the precipice of the southern platform. Beyond lies only the dark swamplands. And something else. Fifty feet away from this spot we can hear the waterfalls of Orlando's Pit. Anyone falling off of the platform would be swept away, just as I was a year ago, into the open maw, gone without a trace.

The air is thick with a heavy humidity; I find it hard to breathe.

I duck under the chains that cordon off this area and clamber to the rim of the platform. Netl-3 not only follows but trudges past me until he stands on the very edge, facing out into the darkness.

"Do you remember our first days working here on this spot?" he says. "There was nothing here, just [pending]... overgrown wilderness and marshland. And look what our great labours together have wrought!"

"Yes, that was the idea."

I'm a foot away from him. It won't take much. I have to do this.

I move a step closer. Netl-3 stands there motionless, his back to me, utterly vulnerable.

"Jackson," he says. "There's something I have to tell you. A truth you deserve to know. That story... about my people mistaking yours for the simulacra..." There's a long pause. "You were right. It's not true. It was devised by your leaders during treaty negotiations. They felt the fabrication might make it easier for your people to accept us as allies."

My heart pounds against my sternum.

"Then... then why? Why did you –?"

"We were at war. There is no justifiable 'why'."

I move closer, start to raise my hands, when a high-pitched whistle directly ahead of us pierces the silence followed by several other notes. Flutes. I haven't heard the creatures in months. Colony construction had driven them far away from this area. The notes harmonise and a playful melody grows larger and larger until it blares like a symphony. They play a song I know I've heard before. And then it hits me. It's the exact song played by the Flutes that were trapped beneath the platform.

"That melody..." I say. "How can it be? I thought that each Flute nest played a unique song."

"Yes," Netl-3 says. "Those are the same Flutes."

"But they were trapped –"

"I went back for them." His translator makes a low beep that I've come to recognize as a chuckle. "After you and Tia left that evening, I returned later in the night. I wore a full protective exosuit with lighting, placed them in a container and transported them deep into the swamplands."

I don't know what to say. Why should I care?

After a long silence he says, "I know who you are. I've always known." He braids and unbraids his feelers, still facing away from me. "Do what you must to find balance."

Although only a few seconds pass before I answer, those seconds last an eternity.

"I... I don't know what you're talking about, Netl." I exhale.

Netl-3 turns, stares at me with his purple eyes and says, "[Unknown]." Followed by silence. It's his turn to pretend. "I've decided to stay on here until the colony is complete. The rest of my pod is departing, but I want to see this through."

The air smells cleaner, less saturated with humidity, and I find I can breathe more easily now. For a few minutes I simply stand there. I think about what Netl-3 has just told me; if he stays, I can wait for another time, another opportunity, to make him pay.

I open my eyes, turn around, and head back toward my yurt; I hear Netl-3 shuffling a few steps behind me. If I could read his facial features I suspect I'd see surprise. I'm surprised myself. And when I look ahead I'm struck by the beauty of the colony, its bright lights, the endless rows of colourful yurts and, in the distance, the glorious new towers that rise into the star-filled sky.

About the Contributors

Rachel Armstrong is a Black Sky Thinker and 2010 Senior TED Fellow who is establishing an alternative technical platform to machines – by harnessing the potential of the natural world through natural computing processes – which speaks to a new kind of Nature that is native to the 21st century. Her work has been endorsed by such luminaries as Bruce Sterling and Steve Fuller.

Keith Brooke's most recent novel *alt.human* (published in the US as *Harmony*) was shortlisted for the 2013 Philip K Dick Award. He is also the editor of *Strange Divisions and Alien Territories: the Sub-genres of Science Fiction*, an academic exploration of SF from the perspectives of a dozen top authors in the field. He writes reviews for the Guardian, teaches creative writing at university level, and lives with his wife Debbie in Wivenhoe, Essex.

Eric Brown has published over fifty books and his work has been translated into sixteen languages. His latest books include the SF novel *Jani and the Greater Game*, the collection *Strange Visitors*, and the crime novel *Murder at the Chase*. He writes a regular science fiction review column for the Guardian newspaper and lives near Dunbar, East Lothian. His website can be found at: www.ericbrown.co.uk

Pat Cadigan has won the Locus Award three times, the Arthur C. Clarke Award twice for her novels *Synners* and *Fools*, and the Hugo Award for her novelette, "The Girl-Thing Who Went Out For Sushi". While her novels are all science-fiction, she has also written two nonfiction movie books and several media tie-ins, and her short fiction runs the gamut from light-hearted fantasy to hard-edged horror. A former Kansas City resident, she now lives in gritty, urban North

London with her husband, the Original Chris Fowler.

David L Clements is an astrophysicist at Imperial College London. He works in the general areas of extragalactic astronomy and observational cosmology, and has a special interest in the role of dust in galaxy formation and evolution. He writes hard SF to keep his feet on the ground, and has been published in *Analog*, *Nature Futures*, and by NewCon Press. He hasn't been collecting cosmic rays, but does run a project that gets students to search for Dyson Spheres. They haven't found any – yet.

Paul Cornell is a writer of SF/F in prose, TV and comics, and has been Hugo Award nominated for all three media. His latest urban fantasy novel is *The Severed Streets*, from Tor. He's written *Doctor Who* for the BBC and *Wolverine* for Marvel Comics.

Rob Edwards studied biology and geology then embarked on a career in science communication, spending ten years at London's Science Museum before joining the Royal Observatory Greenwich, where he is now Head of Science Learning and Public Engagement. In 2013 he curated the Royal Observatory's exhibition "Alien Revolution: the changing perception of alien life".

Paul Di Filippo lives in Providence, Rhode Island, with Deborah Newton, his partner of five decades (the 70s, the 80s, the 90s, the noughts and the twenty-teens). He has over thirty books to his credit (or discredit), many of which recently became available as ebooks through Open Road Media. He has no idea what he will do next.

Robert Jeschonek is an award-winning writer whose stories, novels, and comics have been published around the world. His fiction has appeared in publications including *Galaxy's Edge*, *Postscripts*, and *Escape Pod*. He has written Star Trek and Doctor Who fiction and Batman comics. He is the author of the Battlenaut military science fiction series, and his cross-genre scifi thriller *Day 9* is a 2013 International Book Award winner. Visit him at www.thefictioneer.com

Marek Kukula completed his PhD in Radio Astronomy at the University of Manchester's Jodrell Bank Observatory and then carried out research into black holes and distant galaxies at a variety of astronomy centres including the University of Edinburgh and the Space Telescope Science Institute in Baltimore, home of the Hubble Space Telescope. As Public Astronomer at the Royal Observatory Greenwich he helps to run the Observatory's exhibitions, planetarium shows and events and is on hand to explain new astronomical discoveries to the public and media.

Sarah Anne Langton draws things, writes and scribbles a lot about comics. Qualified astronaut, part time archaeologist, full time geek, Sarah has worked as an illustrator for Hodder & Stoughton, Forbidden Planet, EA Games, The Cartoon Network, Sony, Marvel Comics and a wide variety of music events. She has written and illustrated for Jurassic London, Fox Spirit, NewCon Press, Anachron Press and 'The Fizzy Pop Vampire' series, and daylights as web mistress for the world's largest sci-fi and fantasy website. Her work has featured on *io9*, *Clutter Magazine*, *Laughing Squid* and *Creative Review*.

Robert Reed is the author of a big quivering mass of short fiction and some fourteen novels, the most recent of which comprise a trilogy set in his *Marrow/Great Ship* universe released through Prime Books. His novella, "A Billion Eves", won the Hugo in 2007 and he is also the winner of France's Grand Prix de l'Imaginaire. He lives in Lincoln, Nebraska, with his wife and daughter.

Mike Resnick is, according to *Locus*, the all-time leading award winner, living or dead, for short science fiction. He has won five Hugos from a record thirty-six nominations, plus a Nebula, and other major awards in the USA, France, Japan, Croatia, Catalonia, Poland and Spain. Mike is the author of seventy-four novels, close to three hundred stories, and three screenplays, he has edited forty-one anthologies and currently edits *Galaxy's Edge* magazine. Visit him at www.mikeresnick.com

Mercurio D. Rivera has been nominated for the World Fantasy Award for his short fiction and his stories have appeared in *The Year's Best SF 17*, *Other Worlds Than These*, *Unplugged: The Web's Best SF and Fantasy for*

2008, and markets such as *Interzone, Asimov's Science Fiction, Nature*, and *Black Static*. His work has been translated and published in China, Poland and the Czech Republic. His first collection, *Across the Event Horizon*, is out now from Newcon Press.

Adam Roberts is the author of fourteen SF novels, including the BSFA- and Campbell Award winning *Jack Glass* (Gollancz 2012) and *Twenty Trillion Leagues Under the Sea* (with Mahendra Singh; Gollancz 2014). He was born in South London and now lives a few miles west of London, so never let it be said that he's averse to travel.

Stephanie Saulter writes what she likes to think is literary science fiction. She's the author of *Gemsigns* and *Binary*, the first two books of the ®Evolution trilogy, and is currently working on the third, *Gillung*. She lives in London, blogs unpredictably at stephaniesaulter.com and tweets only slightly more reliably as @scriptopus.

Tricia Sullivan is a physics student and an Arthur C. Clarke Award winning science fiction novelist. Forthcoming in October 2014, her new novel *Shadowboxer* features a female cage fighter and draws on her knowledge of fighting. Tricia weighs nine stone soaking wet and has been known to kick down the occasional door. She doesn't like to talk about the chocolate digestives.

Adrian Tchaikovsky is the author of the acclaimed Shadows of the Apt fantasy series, from the first volume, *Empire In Black and Gold* (2008) to the final book, *Seal of the Worm* (2014), with a new series and a standalone science fiction novel scheduled for 2015. He has been nominated for the David Gemmell Legend Award and a British Fantasy Award. In civilian life he is a lawyer, gamer and amateur entomologist.

Gerry Webb has a lifelong interest in space, being an active member of the British Interplanetary Society since 1957 and working professionally in the field since 1960. He founded Commercial Space Technologies Ltd. in 1983 and remains its general director. Gerry has contributed to interstellar studies over the years and was a member of the Project Daedalus team. An active attendee of science fiction conventions since 1962, he chaired a panel (with Arthur Clarke and Poul Anderson) on the Fermi Paradox at the UK Worldcon in 1979.

George Zebrowski's *Brute Orbits* won the John W. Campbell Award, *Cave of Stars* was chosen for Science Fiction, the 101 Best Novels 1985-2010, and *Stranger Suns* was a New York Times Notable Book of the Year. A multiple Nebula Award nominee and finalist for the Theodore Sturgeon Award, his latest novel is *Empties* (Golden Gryphon). Co-edited with Gregory Benford is *Sentinels* in Honour of Arthur C. Clarke (Hadley Rille), while *Decimated* presents ten collaborations with Jack Dann (Borgo). His backlist is available via SF Gateway and Open Road.

Also Available from NewCon Press

The Race
Nina Allan

Set in a future Great Britain scarred by fracking and ecological collapse, *The Race* is the stunning debut novel from Nina Allan, winner of the 2014 BSFA Award for Best Short Fiction and the prestigious Grand Prix de l'Imaginaire for Best Translated Work.

"Totally assured… a literate, intelligent, gorgeously human and superbly strange SF novel that will continually skewer your assumptions."
– *ALASTAIR REYNOLDS*

"Evocative and compelling, this is an irresistible read." – *E.J. SWIFT (author of Osiris and Cataveiro)*

"Nina Allan dissolves boundaries between literary fiction and SF, attending to the textures of memory, desire and loss even as she seeks out dark, fantastical visions of possible worlds." – *SAM THOMPSON (author of Communion Town)*

"A dark dystopia in the tradition of Piercy, Russ and Robinson, and a bold indictment on corporate greed – past, present and yet to come." – *JOANNA KAVENNA (author of The Birth of Love and Inglorious)*

Marcher
Chris Beckett

Charles Bowen is an immigration officer with a difference: the migrants he deals with don't come from other countries but from other universes. Known as shifters, they materialize from parallel timelines, bringing with them a mysterious drug called slip which breaks down the boundary between what is and what might have been, and offers the desperate and the dispossessed the tantalizing possibility of escape.

Summoned to investigate a case at the Thurston Meadows Social Inclusion Zone, Bowen struggles to keep track of his place in the world and to uphold the values of the system he has fought so long to maintain...

One of Britain's most exciting and innovative science fiction writers, Chris Beckett is the winner of the 2013 Arthur C Clarke Award and the 2009 Edge Hill Prize. *Marcher* is perhaps his finest work to date.

This is the first UK edition, and the first release anywhere of the author's preferred text, extensively revised and rewritten.

Available as paperback and signed limited edition hardback with bonus stories.